I LOVED YOU
FOR YOUR VOICE

Sélim Nassib

I LOVED YOU
FOR YOUR
VOICE

*Translated from the French
by Alison Anderson*

Europa
editions

Europa Editions
116 East 16th Street
12th floor
New York, N.Y. 10003
www.europaeditions.com
info@europaeditions.com

Translation by Alison Anderson
Original Title: *Oum*
Translation copyright © 2006 by Europa Editions

This work has been published thanks to support from
the French Ministry of Culture – Centre National du Livre
Ouvrage publié avec le concours du Ministère
Français chargé de la Culture – Centre National du Livre

Library of Congress Cataloging in Publication Data is available
ISBN 1-933372-07-9

Nassib, Sélim
I Loved You for Your Voice

Book design by Emanuele Ragnisco
www.mekkanografici.com

I LOVED YOU
FOR YOUR VOICE

PART ONE

1924-1928

I RECOGNIZED THE CHILDREN TIMIDLY murmuring their names; I had opened my arms to those who were born while my back was turned. My mother continually put more food on my plate, watching me as if she thought I might swallow up my native country in one meal. She did not take her eyes off me: I was her flesh. The expansive body of my family took me in, pressing around me, squeezing—the same blood, the same organs. In the end it was slightly repugnant. But why am I telling myself stories, I had been missing all that; and I was aware of that, in the midst of manly embraces, of laughter, and in the midst of the Arabic, above all, once again, both near and far, the background music of that magnificent language, my true country.

There was ululating, there were questions. I'd known Paris, I'd tasted of the fruit: but how was I to tell the story? My mother and my sister Salwa exchanged expectant silences; they alone could measure my three years of absence. My five other brothers and sisters couldn't count. I had returned, with my degree from the Sorbonne, and I was head of the family at the age of twenty-three. I would think back on my room in Paris with regret. There, I had been no one.

Muhammad got me out of there, Muhammad Abd al-Wahab, my only friend. With his western-style suit and his tarboosh. He'd whisked me away, and we were walking down the middle of the street, carefree, adolescent, together. We were almost the same age, but for him everything had already opened up. He was a singer, composer, and musician; his talent was dazzling. I could never understand why he chose me for his friend. He'd come to spend a week in Paris; he'd pushed open the door of my room, he'd slept on the floor, we never left one another.

And now he was taking me with him, he wanted to impress me. I'd missed Independence Day, the crowds in the street, the overwhelming joy. I didn't know what I'd missed; even the air must have had a different smell to it. I was looking, breathing: nothing had changed, fortunately. The shops, the loud nocturnal sounds, the rattle of the trams and their smell of electricity: this was the real Cairo. I was dazed by how different everything was from Paris. The warm air surrounded us. Streets disappeared along the tram rails, small shops gleamed in the gaslight, the Orient lay hiding behind the feminine calligraphy of shop signs. Displays of spices, fruit, and coffee; men waiting for friends as always, none of those things had changed. As if the first breath of cooler air was a signal: the nocturnal life was now underway.

We paid and went through the gates into the garden of Ezbekia, and I was suddenly fully immersed in the knowledge that I had arrived. Trees and lanes formed a familiar geography, but it was above all the music and the noise: an oasis of sound that I could have recognized with my eyes closed. I had never left.

A crowd was waiting outside the little theatre. There were, as always, fewer women than men, but there were more tarbooshes than turbans, and more hats than tarbooshes. I was wearing my Basque beret; Muhammad was bare-headed. People recognized him and stood aside to let him pass. With the part in his disheveled hair, he looked a bit like Jean Cocteau. The hall could contain only about one hundred people, and we got the last seats. People spilled into the aisles and sat cross-legged on the floor.

The group was already on the stage, two peasants wearing the long brown jubbah, with turbans on their heads, two sheiks who had come straight from their village; in front of them, in the middle, a boy sat motionless, terrified, his hands held together over his stomach, severe in the way adolescents can be. Only his hands and face were visible: he had a round, slightly fleshy face, which might have been ugly without his huge black eyes. In spite of the heat and the projectors, a Bedouin cape covered his body and a headpiece held in place by two rings was tied under his chin.

Nothing was happening, people were talking, the young man didn't know how to proceed. He sang out a note above the crowd. It was the *Fatiha,* the first chapter of the Koran. His voice was childish and unsure, but unusual, driven by a rare force, an endless expiration. The boy started the second phrase on a deep note, and his voice rose gradually, holding the note and causing it to vibrate. People responded with a murmur of approval. The holy text unwound on his voice; he was careful to preserve between each phrase an intake of breath that nothing could disturb. The voice rose again in the middle of the pause, to climb into the trebles, then trill for a long time on the highest note. The final call lingered suspended in the air.

Calls of "God is Great!" could be heard. But from the boy, nothing. His eyes still downcast, without the slightest acknowledgment of the audience, until he started up again, and a wave of heat rose to my face, the verses he was uttering were mine, I had written them just before my departure: *Passion is betrayed through the eyes.* My poem, on those Bedouin lips. I turned to Muhammad: so that was it. I smiled at him but felt like hiding. There was something disagreeable to me about the adolescent's singing. The power, timbre, and mastery of breath were remarkable, it wasn't that, but his voice crept into me despite myself, filled me with something so natural it was obscene, unconscious of itself. Sometimes when a note dropped, a slight hoarseness gave off a whiff of sensuality, something unveiled. I was very ill at ease.

He trembled in his devotion and my words were transformed into what they meant to say; even I believed they were real. They were no longer my words but the thing itself, the feeling, my intimate secret laid bare before everyone. The song was not emerging from his throat alone; his entire body seemed to be quivering, almost wringing itself to project the song. A motionless trance. This smooth-cheeked boy was able to incarnate the pain and the sweetness which I heard myself expressing for the first time, through him. It was inside him.

I knew the melody: Sheik Abu al-Ela had composed it and sung it, he'd had it recorded on an old seventy-eight record. The young man followed the tune through its tiniest nuances; he was utterly faithful to it. His voice made the difference. I'd shaped the letters, but he breathed life into them, there was no end to it. I recognized the final verse: "*My secret, and yours, who will protect them?*"

I was not returning as a stranger: this was Muhammad's gift. He had not anticipated this almost painful emotion, and I did not want to reveal it to him, so I stood up for the ovation. The young Bedouin was also on his feet. He was trying to return from the absence which had seized hold of him; no one could understand that as well as I. He bowed, his arms flung back. As he moved, the sides of his black cape opened; he closed them again with an abrupt gesture. It didn't take more than a second, but as the garment slipped open, I had time to glimpse the curve of a breast beneath the rough peasant's clothing.

It was with an almost immodest gesture that she flung off her headpiece and released her thick black hair. This evening, I sang for you: those were her first words. No pallor lingered on her face, there was no reason for it any more. She was a Bedouin, not even a Bedouin, a simple peasant girl from a tiny

village, Tammay al-Zahayrah, in the delta. The two other people with her were her father, sheik of the local mosque, and her
brother, who was also a sheik; it was a family business, in a way.
There was something indecent about a girl on stage, but she
could earn in one evening what her father earned in a month.
Hence the disguise.

"I was afraid; it was your poem, and you were there."

I couldn't fathom it, she was still a boy-girl in my eyes, it was
not something you could obliterate just like that: that hint of
the hermaphrodite and the beauty of her voice seemed mysteriously linked. It was fascinating and rather monstrous. I was
troubled; in that moment and the one which followed, no
words came to me. Muhammad stood next to me, the two
sheiks stood near their protégée, smiling: it was ridiculous. I
took her hand and raised it to my lips, a silent homage, that
should suffice, but her fingers relaxed at once, her arm opened
and followed my movement. I could feel the slight physical
urgency, her invisible acceptance. She gave a little laugh of
contentment. A spark lit her eyes, the fraction of a second: I
could see it distinctly, her sharp gaze, of pure power, pure
delight.

"We are very flattered . . . it's a great honor . . . a man like
yourself . . ."

Sheik Ibrahim came to my rescue, that's what social niceties
are for, without a certain ritual one is torn apart.

"She sang my poem, the honor was all mine."

I was saying this to the father, but his daughter's eyes never
left mine. There was something Asian about the way she
screwed up her eyes, and she was reading my lips, even into my
mind, openly, as if she were at home.

"Why don't you write for me?" she asked in a low voice.

"I will write for you."

"Only . . ."

"Only what?"

"Write things that I can sing."

"I'm not sure I understand,"

"How many people understand your words? I mean ordinary people, peasants . . . To sing *Passion Is Betrayed,* I had to
ask for help from Sheik Abu al-Ela."

"Poetry is written in classical Arabic."

"Give it up for me, keep it for others. Why can't there be
poetry in a language which everyone understands, why not?"

Muhammad was looking at me, dumbfounded. He sang my
texts, he was my friend, he would never have dared to ask me
such a thing. This young girl whom I had just met: he heard
me, and I heard myself, reply:

"I don't know if I can manage it . . . I can try."

"I'm leaving tomorrow for the seaside with my parents, to
Ras-el-Bar, we'll be spending the summer there. When I get
back, come and see me. I live on Kola Street, in Abdine—
Sheik Abu al-Ela will tell you where."

She gave a slight laugh. She turned to her father, her palms
open; she was restoring the power to him.

IPUSHED OPEN THE SHUTTERS and the sun offered up a vibrant, spontaneous city, formidably real. Drawn by the heat and a physical desire to mingle with people, I went downstairs, to rub up against their voices, their smell, their sweat. The newspaper vendor handed me my change without looking at me; I was one of them. I was the only one whose eyes were open, at random, still a stranger, the streets leaping up at me, I was crazy. I couldn't see any English soldiers. Independence was an optical illusion, the soldiers were camped out by the canal, but had disappeared from the streets. I felt like kissing passers-by. Now I could read on people's faces what Muhammad had wanted me to discover yesterday. As if the air were in love. I was laughing to myself, people were staring at me and I didn't care. The town, that girl, music, everything was welcoming me. All I had to do was let myself be borne away on the current and swim with the flow. Everyone needed poets. Theater troupes came together and fell apart, the nights were thick with shooting stars, anyone could set themselves up as a stage director. There was a place for everyone, and if there wasn't, you could make your own. What was important was to launch a maximum number of mad ventures before the wheel turned—and it turned quickly. Cairo was full of allure, and I was lucky to be there.

Sheik Abu al-Ela. I found him sitting in his garden, at a loose end, looking somewhat melancholy. Old age had grazed his shoulders. His cheeks were sunken, his hair white, and he had the lost gaze of people who think they are alone. I kissed him and gave him the bottle of whisky I'd brought back from Paris; he made an effort and thanked me. He hadn't come to greet me, and he almost never went out anymore. He'd been a friend of my late father's and had helped me to publish my first collection of poetry; I liked him a great deal. We raised our glasses. I told him about my homecoming, the evening with Muhammad, the Ezbekia gardens.

"So you saw her."

"Yes."

"And you heard her sing."

"Yes."

"What did you think?"

I didn't know what to say.

"Did you notice . . . she sings . . . but it's nothing yet. I know what she's capable of. It's still inside her, only a tiny bit has come out . . . She used to sit by my side here, every evening. Here, in the garden, every evening. If she wanted . . . But she's only a kid."

He was full of emotion, burning inside. All signs of age had vanished. We were like two dumbfounded twins. He could not stop drinking, straight from the bottle.

"And naturally, afterwards, you went to see her back-stage . . ."

I didn't reply.

"Did she say anything to you about me?"

"She said you were her master, that she owes you everything. That you taught her to sing my poem, *Passion Is Betrayed.*"

"—that I'm her master, and she owes me everything?"

"Yes, that's what she said."

He wiped his mouth.

"It was a few years ago . . . I'd sung at a wedding in the delta and was waiting for my train on the platform of the station at al-Sinbillawayn, and someone came up to greet me. It was her father, Sheik Ibrahim, and I knew him slightly, he sings and chants the Koran. She was there, he'd taken her with him on tour, she wasn't even fifteen years old yet, a little fury, she was kissing my hand and saying, Sheik Abu al-Ela, it's you, it's you, I thought you were dead! I didn't understand. Sheik Ibrahim was trying to pull her away from me, but she wouldn't let go. I was the greatest singer in Egypt, the greatest, that's what she was saying. She'd listened to my records on the mayor's daughter's phonograph. She swore she'd kill herself if I didn't go with them right then and there, with her father and her to their house in Tammay al-Zahayrah. There was nothing very exciting waiting for me back in Cairo, and that young girl . . . she seemed to really want me to come. In the village she brought everyone together. She asked me to sing, and I sang. She began to sing with me. All it took was for her to open her mouth. I missed every single train. I took Sheik Ibrahim to one side and said, It's a sin, this girl is so gifted, she must come to Cairo. He said no. No is no. I took my leave. It was only last year that the idea came to me: if the head of a great family would vouch for them, perhaps Sheik Ibrahim could be persuaded. I spoke to Abdel-Razzak bey, and he agreed. They arrived at the central station, the father, the brother, the maid Saadiya, with supplies of food for six months, and there she was disguised as a boy. I found them an apartment and introduced them to people, did the best I could, she has nothing to reproach me with."

"But what could she reproach you with?"

"Not a thing, as I said. Every evening, at six o'clock sharp, she was there, it's incredible how she was there. The word work means nothing to her, we went into the music, we went . . . very deep. I gave her what I had and what I didn't have. Singing was in her blood, and I taught her to sing with her heart. But nothing could calm her appetite, her lust for singing. Poets, musicians—she wants them all. She is in such a hurry, as if there wasn't enough time, as if she were going to die, and she's not even twenty-two yet. Maybe she believes I have nothing more to teach her, I don't know. I was a student of Hamuli's, and I'm the one who has carried on his musical revolution. This little peasant girl, you see, will be his daughter, the heir to an entire art form. You'll see. Mounira al-Mahdia won't cut it. The only one who is at that level is Muhammad, your friend. Women and the honors of the court fascinate him, he dreams of the West but there's nothing he can do, he has the gift and he'll be the heir despite himself. But believe me, she is the legitimate offspring . . . Our daily sessions are over. She still comes to see me from time to time . . . Sometimes she comes to hear me at the al-Riche café, how am I supposed to react . . ."

I'd gone to France to learn Persian for the purpose of translating one single poem, the Rubaiyat of Omar Khayyam, the Quatrains. There were no existing translations from Persian into Arabic. The only version available had been translated from English. We were condemned to making a detour through the West.

In Paris I had also learned about library organization; I had seven mouths to feed, so I had no choice. I got myself hired at the National Library of Egypt. I worked a great deal, and didn't go out much. In any case, Cairo slowed down during the summer months; it gave me the impression of a long interlude before real life would start up again.

In the autumn, it would be our turn. Taha Hussein was already giving impromptu talks at the al-Fishawi café, demonstrating that Arabs and the West had shared roots and a shared inspiration, and he'd traced them back to the Greeks. The Eastern branch of the trunk had been allowed to lapse. The revolution that Sheik Abu al-Ela had been talking about, the famous *Nahda*, had affected not only music but also poetry, novels, philosophy, politics, even Islam. My translation of

Omar Khayyam was part of that same inexorable tide. There were those who wanted to forge closer ties with the West, and those who wanted to find the basis for an Eastern modernism within our own culture. We were in the midst of an extraordinary flourishing, or perhaps an extraordinary confusion; how could we know? With the British gone, the country was as young as we were. I was eager to see the end of the summer.

In the evening I would shut myself away in my room to translate Khayyam, to write that other language in my own. It was more than just a poem. In my country fatalism is woven into words, *Inshallah*, God willing, there's nothing we can do, we can find our own warmth within, our destinies are predetermined and unfold beneath our steps, paradise awaits. We are all familiar with this burden, it has been accepted for centuries. As for Khayyam, he stands contemplating the void, the nothingness of the beyond. The certainty of absence is exhaled with every verse; he is a mystic on his lonely path toward God. He wants nothing to do with consolation, community, renunciation. There is only the wine and Sufi intoxication, it is the same. If our destiny is to end up as dust, may that dust become baked earth, an amphora of wine, and lovers will drink from it and lick our skulls with their lips. Nothing will come to appease us, nor should anything, so let us drink, fascinated, until we reach a lucid drunkenness, too lucid, let us drink some more, until we no longer forget.

"Enjoy, in this world of nothingness / That part of pleasure which is yours." I could sense that invitation behind every verse and took it personally, as a reproach. Khayyam was driving me into my desire, however vague it might be. I resisted, and found pleasure in resisting. Every night I would slip a bit deeper into the skin of the poet, into his love of sensuality. Arabic and Persian are different, but both are languages of the East, of a same world. This physical proximity plunged me into an exaltation which kept me from sleep. The passage was within

reach. And when the meaning was revealed, when the music of the poem found its equivalent in Arabic, I felt the liberation of an emotion that was nine centuries old.

In the darkness I grew drunk on the verses. There were times I came up against a rough passage. I would pull myself up, then get back to work. And in spite of that, I found no peace. Something was still beyond my grasp. I could feel something lacking . . . not in the flow of the language, or in the words, or in the rhythm. It was not even something inherent in the text. A resolution was missing, an element which would bring my work to its conclusion and give it all its significance. Suddenly, I knew. It was for her that I was doing this translation. I wanted that girl to sing the Rubaiyat of Omar Khayyam, that was all I wanted. That is what I had to have. The Quatrains, in her throat, would become Arabic, that was it. Everything I had been searching for, three years in Paris, my trips to Germany and Great Britain on the trail of the great Persian poet's manuscripts, and not just that, the ferment I could feel in myself, in my country, Muhammad, Sheik Abu al-Ela and his garden: I had the impression that it could all come together, mysteriously, in her voice. She could be the way; my way.

We'll work together, of course, every day perhaps. And I'll compose verses for her: why not, I had promised to. A poem began to form in my mind, flowing out word after word, a poem in a simple and obvious language, exactly what she had asked of me, like a letter I might be sending to her. I lit my lamp again. And there, in the night, I wrote my first song for her. *I'm Afraid That Your Love.*

I T WAS AN OLD HOUSE, one of those buildings in freestone pet-
rified by the rain of invisible sand which falls continually
upon the city. The house was on a corner, and I could recognize it from a distance by the circular balcony Sheik Abu al-Ela
had described. Seated on stools directly on the pavement were
peasants in long galabias with skullcaps on their heads, and
between their legs were huge straw baskets, horns of plenty offering guava, limes, spices and spotted bananas in the form of a
crescent that you cannot find in France. Strong odors were the
very air you breathed, the very Orient, saturated, a bit nauseating, a viscous layer that would cling to your soles. I wove my way
through it all. The market vendors turned to look at me, or so it
seemed. A peasant stopped me in the alley. "You're the poet!" he
said, in a sincerely enthusiastic voice.

It was Sheik Ibrahim. He grasped me with his hands, as if to
ascertain I was real. He was right. I looked at him, too. He was
real. He blended into the crowd of squatting peasants, into the
colors of galabias and dark weathered skin, into the carrots and
potatoes still heavy with earth; that is where she came from.

"I don't know how to read, I have the greatest respect for
poetry, our house is yours, my daughter is expecting you. I'll
join you."

He did not know how to read, and insisted on the fact. I listened, strangely distracted, everything seemed slightly distort-
ed to me. I saw he was carrying a large empty basket, and
understood that it was hard for him to buy, hard for him to pay

money for tomatoes, for lemons. As for me, I had poems in my pockets. The same astonishment lit his eyes and mine. We reached the door to the building, the laughter and remarks had quieted down, perhaps there had never been any.

I also found the father's puzzled, vaguely admiring expression reflected on the face of the round woman who opened the door to me. Barefoot on her spotless tiles, she emanated a blissful opulence; everything about her seemed to breathe with abundance, and her white veil barely covered her hair.

"A thousand welcomes. The young lady will soon be ready. If you'll step this way."

She bade me enter and stood for a moment gazing pointedly at me as if to assure herself that I was indeed made of the same flesh.

"Are you by any chance her mother?"

She struck her breast with the palm of her hand.

"Of course I might have been her mother, may God protect her, but I'm only Saadiya; the little girl grew up on my lap as much as on her own mother's, that's who I am, my fine fellow, a second mother to her and even a first since the day we came to Cairo, I have to keep my eyes open ten at a time, may God grant her long life, Sitt Fatmeh had to stay behind in the village to look after the animals, she entrusted her daughter to me and sent me here in her place, to this cursed city where all people think about is stealing your money and leading you down the road to ruin, may God protect us from the Evil One, poor old me, in Tammay al-Zahayrah we used to sleep with our doors open. Cairo's no place for us, he's stubborn, is Sheik Ibrahim, he resisted for years but finally the other one managed to convince him, the other evening at the Ramses the four of us weren't enough to accompany the little girl, her Bedouin outfit doesn't protect her anymore, they'll even go after little boys, may God bring about their perdition."

I would have liked to tell her that she needn't be afraid, Cairo was like her, inhabited by peasants who had brought their village with them. I was standing in the living room, or what served as the living room, a room which was almost empty. Worn mats had been thrown on the floor, straw mattresses lined the walls. On my right was a row of burlap bags, baskets, and a pile of blankets.

I went out onto the balcony which ran along the entire outside facade, and leaned against the stone balustrade. Why did I feel so nervous? From above, the market seemed tiny, everything cooking peacefully in the sun. I had reconquered Cairo, my nostalgia had loosened its grip. I looked at the roofs and the open windows . . . then there was a rustling of cloth behind me.

It was Saadiya, bringing tea. I came back inside, and sat cross-legged on the mat. So close to the floor, in the spartan, almost mosque-like room. There was hardly any furniture to speak of, a table, a chair, a sort of platform made of reeds, scattered here and there with nothing to link them together. The only element of decoration was a framed calligraphy of a verse from the Koran, placed against the wall. It was a family of peasants who were camping out here: they didn't live here, between these foreign walls, so far from their solid earth.

The distance was immediately apparent. "*I would renounce God before I would renounce wine,*" that verse alone . . . no matter how cleverly I worked the language on Sufi inebriation it would change nothing, Khayyam was the devil, she would run away. I mustn't speak to her about him right away. First my own poems, and then we'd see. I stared at the door through which Saadiya had left.

She came in from the balcony, like a Chinese shadow-puppet, and my emotion told me it was her. She held out her hand and I could feel the same movement of abandon in her fingers.

"It's hot, come, let's sit outside."

A round wooden table had been placed against the balustrade, but there was only one chair. She sat on the mattress, which was on the floor, and I sat next to her, I could see her at last. She was wearing an orange-colored galabia, one of those brightly-hued robes which draw your eyes to the little girls in the cotton fields. The veil and concealed hair were for the city, where men's gazes wander. Here, we were in the village. She'd braided her hair. She lifted her braids with her fingers, distractedly, smoothing them interminably while observing me through her eyelashes.

"People have told me to watch out for poets."

"Why?"

"They look like dreamers, innocent . . ."

Saadiya came back and sat on the mat in the living room so she could see and hear us. I could feel the weight of her gaze upon my nape, but it did little to restrain me, all my attention was focused on the girl sitting opposite me. She was telling me about her stay in Ras-el-Bar.

"I love the sea, my whole family was there, it felt like being at home. Free and protected. Aziza was there too, my friend from Alexandria. We've always gotten along in the strangest way, we tell each other everything. I'm much more relaxed around girls. With boys or men, I don't know, I think that if they didn't exist I'd be perfectly happy . . ."

She laughed as if at a joke, then blushed.

"Poets aren't the same, there's something feminine about them. Maybe not in their body, but in their soul. I'm sure of that. With you, I am at peace."

I could not have said as much. I was fumbling through the pocket of my jacket to find the poems I'd written for her. She reached out her hand, and I stopped her.

"Yes, read them out loud, that's better," she said.

She sat back and half-closed her eyes. I unfolded the papers. The last poem was worthless, the one before that was no better; as for the third one, it was downright bad. I went back through time to find the poem I'd written the very first night.

"*I fear that your love / Is only pity,*" I read in the most neutral tone possible. It was a very simple poem but it pained me to read it to her. She kept her eyes closed and seemed not to hear, and by the third verse her head began to nod up and down slightly, and her mouth was half open. I had only ever observed that sort of bewitched state among the dervishes of upper Egypt, when the trance of the *zikr* is about to begin. The papers fell from my hands, I knew the poem by heart, and I was watching her with a sort of intensity I had not known myself capable of. Her lips were moving slightly, repeating each verse as I uttered it. It was like a prayer. At the same time, something purely physical seemed to animate her, as if the words were going into her through her pores, and she no longer had complete control over her body. I was afraid of this intensity, it seemed to be without limits. I had the impression I had forced my way into a realm of women, a terrifying place where their instinct is stronger than they are. I alone was conscious of the intimacy which had been forged; perhaps she had not wanted it. Only a few feet away from me, on the same mattress. I should have turned aside, and yet I could not. I could hear her breathing.

I murmured the words in a trembling voice, not realizing that I had changed the tone, and was speaking to her in earnest. It was utterly natural, the poem was something I had written for her. From the way she was shivering everything, mysteriously, was becoming true in advance.

I was silent, and she let a long moment pass. Her body shuddered slightly and she opened her eyes. She was looking at me without moving, staring, not recognizing me. She was totally unaware, or had forgotten everything. In a voice that betrayed no emotion she asked me the meaning of four or five words which she had not understood. I explained, a knot in my throat.

"And now, can you read me your poem again, more slowly this time?"

I plunged back in without thinking, she closed her eyes again. But suddenly this second recital seemed to be an insurmountable ordeal. I'd never manage: the state of solitary, sensual dreaming in which the poem immersed her would be unbearable for me. Fortunately, it was not as I feared. From the very first verse, she accompanied me. The words came to her lips, she remembered it all. Her voice, low and hesitant in the first couplet, gradually grew stronger. By the third couplet I recited more quietly so that she could expand. She opened her eyes and their darkness entered me. Her lips, as they spoke my verses, formed a smile so meaningful that I suddenly had the impression of being a lover caught in a trap, her eyes telling me, in the most intense moment of love, look at what you are doing to me, and what I am letting you see. I held her gaze. This time, we were together.

As we reached the end of the last verse, our gazes locked, I felt we were asking the same question, yes or no? Perhaps I was entirely mistaken. She laughed slightly, a tiny laugh, yet I believe it was sincere, the first utterly sincere laughter. Full of emotion, to be sure, but also pleasure. And there was something else as well, something like respect, or perhaps the triumph of a child who understands that he has just found someone to play with, at last.

And her laughter broke the ice, released us. She turned toward Saadiya, whom I'd completely forgotten. I was surprised to see her there, still in the same place, on the mat behind my back, still quite motionless. But her body, with its peasant's heaviness, a peasant of the time of the Pharaohs, was leaning forward with such tension it seemed she was about to fall.

"So, what did you think?"

Saadiya got up and came over to us. She looked at me and nodded, several times. Her lips pouted approvingly, then broke into a smile which emphasized her round cheeks and made her eyes seem deeper. A tenderness coursed beneath her skin, reached her face and opened it. I sensed that she was much more than a nanny, a counselor, a guide, a sure barometer. She took my peasant girl in her arms and squeezed her, and they laughed together. They held out their hands to me and I grabbed them and rose to my feet, and I was laughing too, like them, a laugh which may have been the finest in our lives. In mine, at any rate.

S HE WANTED TO SING MY POEM at the theater of the Bosphorus, for the season première. There were only five days left. Sheik Abu al-Ela set only classical Arabic texts to music, so someone else had to be found. I had the feeling of having committed an unwitting betrayal. She asked me what was the matter, and I did not know what to say.

"I know what's wrong," she said very quietly. "You take everything to heart. Don't think I don't understand. You must have felt—I think so, yes—the effect your poetry has on me. I'll be alone in a few days, in front of the audience, with the poem and nothing between us. The music must be one with the breath of the poem; Sabri al-Najridi will compose it, he will come. From tomorrow the three of us will rehearse, day and night if need be. It must all be inside me, even whatever you might have missed. I know no other way. Say yes."

I said yes. I wanted to leave. We heard a key in the door: her father. She went to greet him in the entryway. I could hear only his voice, shouting.

"I don't care if he is still here! What have you done to your hair?"

He came into the living room, alone. I felt the same awkwardness in him as earlier, but this time he would not meet my gaze. Saadiya retreated to the door of the hallway, I stayed where I was. Sheik Ibrahim himself could not understand why he was so angry; there was nothing he liked about this city.

She came back in, her eyes down. Over her braids, pulled up

into a chignon, she had thrown a fine black veil which hid her shoulders and her entire body. She was a peasant behind her father, a covered silhouette, mute. There was no one left, we were paralyzed.

"Well," said Sheik Ibrahim without looking at me, "it seems you have written a poem."

I didn't reply.

He turned toward her.

"What are you waiting for, read it to me!"

She went to the table where the sheet had been left. She looked at me with a gaze which said she would die of shame. She began to read. In an inaudible, monotonous voice, without the slightest intonation, she declared my love for her. Pale, as mortified as I was, even more mortified. Her father was nodding his head, as if it were some sort of examination for promotion. One verse followed another, flat, in a line, voluntarily killed, I hated them in succession. And when she finally fell silent the poem was there, a shameful corpse among the three of us.

"That's a very good poem," said Saadiya gaily, "there's nothing indecent about it."

She ran from the room, her naked footstep on the tiles.

"I'll take the poem, but not for more than two guineas."

"But—"

"That is my final offer."

"I wanted to offer it to your daughter. It is the first one I've composed for her."

"You don't want any money."

"No."

His eyes went from her to me.

"If you give it to me, I'll do what I can with it."

"I'll give it to her, with your permission."

"And you'll sign the papers?"

"I'll sign."

His face remained closed, there was something he could not grasp, no one was playing by the rules, even the logic of money was upside-down. From the pocket of his galabia he pulled out a paper, already prepared, which he unfolded onto the table. I turned to her.

"First of all you must accept."

She did not move.

"I'll request payment for the next ones, I promise you, but this one: take it as it came."

She gave a faint nod.

Everything happened as she had said. Five days, every day with her. I would go there upon leaving the library. We rehearsed on the balcony, in the living room, nowhere in fact, on an imaginary set. Sabri al-Najridi was a dentist in Tanta, and he had left his practice in order to join us. He was a little man with fine hands, and he had no modesty in disclosing his adoration for her, his fingers sliding against each other as if the melody were a silken cloth still to be spun. I hardly looked at them, all I could see was her. It was not gentle, but violent.

She rehearsed ad nauseum, the imminence of performance in her eyes. As for me, used to working in solitude, I felt trapped in a shared, obsessive adventure, and she was the guide.

She spoke harshly to Sabri, correcting him, and he would smile, it was of no importance. It was not for herself that she was exacting, but for the tyrannical force that was within her. She was trying whatever it took to attain a certain level, but it was never enough. Her aim was something abstract, the intuition of a possible perfection. Her joy when she attained it, when she was satisfied with a verse, or nearly satisfied! She would laugh with a child-like contentment, both proud and humble. She became truly herself again, a twenty-two-year-old peasant girl; she recognized us, showed us her pleasure, so strong and brief. We too were coming back, we too were real again, included in the aura, happy. But the god she served would not let her go for long, and the trance would come over her again, she had to close her eyes and let herself be led away. In the middle of the night each of us would head home, feverish and eager to begin again.

"You're not looking at me anymore! You're still dreaming."

She was talking to me in that tone.

"It's the last day! I want every minute. If your eyes leave me, I'm not singing for anyone, I can't."

Our breathless race ended there, on the stage of the Bosphorus. The empty hall was watching us, everything was whirling, faster and faster, that detail again, that difficult passage, and that one, again. Sabri was muttering, confusing two melodies, his voice faltering. I saw she was exasperated, strung like a bow, and she burst out laughing. She laid her hand on his shoulder, leaned against him, still laughing. Terrified, he dared not move. She was laughing, did not take her hand away, allowed her shaking body to lean toward him. It was unbearable. Seated at the back of the stage, the two family sheiks had not moved, Sphinxes.

She grew more reserved toward the end. We were all watching through the gap in the red curtain. The theater was absolutely full. No one spoke.

Two seats were ready for Sabri and me in the row of the "Listeners," the faithful, the connoisseurs. The lights were dimmed, I could feel the weight of the theater in my back. Sheik Abu al-Ela was next to me. Despite his illness, he had come. He squeezed my arm.

"Everything all right?"

I reassured him. In her row, Saadiya was chanting prayers between her teeth; I recognized al-Qsabji, one of the greatest lute players; my friend Muhammad was there too, with a journalist from the *Al-Masrah*.

She came on stage, greeted by applause. Her Bedouin gar-
ments were a shock, she'd put her headpiece back on, I hadn't
seen her dressed as a boy since the previous concert. She was
going to start with *I'm Afraid That Your Love.* We should never
have let her, she had just learned the poem and her voice was
not warmed up. She was already concentrating, little Bedouin
boy, long-distance runner before the start. Her eyes locked
onto me, and only me, where I was sitting in the first row; her
voice, too long restrained, suddenly soared, strung tight as a
wire. She sang the first two verses without letting go of me,
then she took a turn and sang them again in the same breath.
*"Your eyes told me, and your hands / My heart too, but it can
deceive me / Your love may be only pity . . ."* The audience
reacted immediately with a long ovation. She lowered her face
and her body absorbed the blow, I caught the smile she was
hiding against her breast. She raised her eyes, plunged headlong. I knew she was following the melody very closely.
Slowness, modulations, hesitations, even the slight hoarseness
on certain syllables. But the structure had disappeared, the
song emerged as if dictated by an utterly free inspiration, the
words became transparent. She had spent all those hours, she
had stolen the secret, she possessed it, transforming it into
sounds, in the trembling of her vocal chords. A little peasant
girl, nothing more, but a medium.

There was only one verse remaining: at the end of her exha-
lation she struck a scarcely perceptible false note. The moment
she weakened, the crowd immediately understood and
applauded. She tried to keep the tempo, there was no end to
the ovation. She bowed her head, defeated by her youth,
defenseless against the wave. Then it ebbed and she continued
the last three verses. But this time, she diverged; she had
already won, she was nearly there, and the promise of relief
carried her. The note she was holding, on one single syllable,
was one she could vary at will. Sheik Abu al-Ela reached over

to grasp me with his hand once again. Her voice was now following an invisible line, she was working without a net. At one point, she had opened a door and gone out, and I no longer recognized Sabri's melody. She'd set herself free from it, and yet she hadn't; she picked it up again further along the way, was greeted with an ovation, and set off stronger than ever. She struck up a dialogue with the crowd, ventured down one path, adopted it after a faint murmur from the crowd showed they had accepted it, and then she pushed it as far as she dared go. The audience played back, the game grew ever livelier. She felt confident enough to risk the most improbable variations, and let herself be carried as far as her voice would go. During each pause there were brief explosions of acclaim, which fell silent again all at once. The silence spoke for the spectators, it was an invisible wave, and she fed off of it to regain strength and produce and release her voice, over and over.

She no longer improvised alone, but with the audience: a two-headed monster, a joint creation. Sheik Abu al-Ela was on the verge of tears. The *tarab*, a shared artistic and physical emotion, a rare instant of fusion, was what his master, Abduh al-Hamuli, had sought (and found) all his life. Oh, night!

She was no longer the same. She was succumbing to the state of trance which had so fascinated me on the balcony. I saw her. And Sheik Abu al-Ela, and Sabri, Muhammad, the entire first row. A violent feeling overwhelmed me. Everyone could see the uncontrolled trembling of her body, wrapping itself around her voice. More and more, she was letting go. The rest of the audience were too far away, but they could feel intuitively how she was giving herself to them, and they responded in like manner, their bodies forgotten. I felt like standing up, like jumping onto the stage, to wrap her in a veil which would hide her from the gaze of men.

Sheik Ibrahim, her father, was sitting behind her. On his face I identified the same emotion which was strangling me, that was all I saw. His jaw dropped, his eyes shone, a burning heat seemed to throb within him, a boundless shame. At the same time he was overcome, filled with admiration, borne away and drowning in pleasure, in an endless emotion.

I looked at her over their heads. She wore an air of abandon I had never seen before. Only women were there around her. She moved from one embrace to the next, using their hands to come back to earth. The most elegant were the Abdel-Razzaks, the mother and her three young girls, her adopted family.

Another woman came in, accompanied. People moved aside to let her pass. She took the young diva in her arms and embraced her. I could tell from the trembling of her lips that she was intimidated. The visitor was dressed in Western clothing, her face looked familiar, gray hair pulled up, her gaze sparkling and moist: I liked her. It was Safia Zaghlul, the wife of the president of the council, the Father of Independence. You can't imagine what independence meant to us. There had been the English, there had been the Turks, the Mamluks, centuries of it. Sa'd Zaghlul had triumphed over the curse. His wife was holding my peasant girl in her arms, acknowledging her voice, giving her life. She held our hands together, like a pact. The new Egypt, her artists. Everyone applauded. This was the same gesture we had made the other day on the balcony. To escape the emotion, I raised my eyes to the rows in the back. And there I saw, forgotten, clinging to the curtains, the solitary form of Saadiya, crying warm tears, ravaged.

5

THE ARTICLE IN *AL-MASRAH* SEEMED PETTY, full of false praise. She did not belong to their world, she was too much of a peasant for their taste, too traditional, they didn't even dare to write it openly. But her photograph with Safia Zaghlul took up half a page. It was less her talent than the changing times which granted her a place.

She recorded her first 78-r.p.m. record. On the jacket a small photograph was set in, a sad picture with her Bedouin headpiece: it looked like a religious recording. Fortunately, there was the title: *I'm Afraid That Your Love.* Beneath the title were my name and Sabri's, in small letters. I was pleased with the record, as an object to touch and look at. Other than that it was merely a poor echo of the concert. Improvisation, variations, silences had all been tossed out, everything that had made the magic of the concert. The length of the seventy-eight was too small a bed for Arabic music. But still, it was her first recording, and it linked me to her.

I had become a familiar presence. Monday was closing day at the National Library, so I went to see her at around eleven o'clock, and we stayed together until evening. It was not something we'd decided, it just happened that way. I brought with me a collection of ancient poetry by Jalal al-Din ar-Rumi, I'd read a few verses to her, on the mattress out on the balcony, the words, the hidden meaning. I could see from her eyes how she marveled at this discovery, an entire continent she had not been aware of. She asked for another, right away, then yet another, as if she were famished. She was brutally demanding, trying to take everything from me at once, everything I knew. I laughed. I could introduce other poets to her.

That's how it began. A virgin territory. In my briefcase I carried all the poetry in the world: Ibn al-Fared, Omar ben Abi Rabi'a, Abu al-'Atahia, Hafez Ibrahim, Ahmad Shawqi, Racine, Shelley, Byron. And a bit of Omar Khayyam, of course, just a tiny bit. I read for her, and she looked at me as if I were offering her the forbidden gate to heaven, right then and there.

As for Sheik Ibrahim, it wasn't costing him a thing. He couldn't figure it out, and he gave up. He left me with my secrets, I left him with his. Saadiya still sat on the mat, keeping watch. When she was preparing meals, one of the other of the sheiks would stay in the living room. Bit by bit the household became used to my presence, and my hosts went back to their normal everyday life, perfectly idle, playing cards or dominoes. The balcony was ours. As long as we left the doors open, we could spend hours out there on our own. I surrendered so eagerly to poetry, moving in another world, that the two sheiks and the nanny came to consider me a relatively harmless fellow. Nor did I care; I preferred it that way, they no longer saw me.

We recited the poems together, and she would learn them by heart from one week to the next. Every line spoke of love, and we had the right to follow the poets, provided a modest veil was in place. She veiled herself in Rumi: "The most beautiful cry of love is that of impossible love . . ."; I quoted Khayyam to her: "For the riddle of true love is solved in a language apart . . ."

Someone knocked on the door, and Saadiya went to open. The police. She murmured the word in a near whisper, with the ancestral wariness peasants have for anything remotely resembling authority. Sheik Ibrahim and Sheik Khaled went to answer, and they didn't seem to be any more at ease. A young man in uniform handed them an envelope. They didn't move.

My Bedouin girl stepped forward, took the pencil, and signed. The envelope bore the letterhead of the president of the council; it was an invitation. She was invited for dinner at the home of Sa'd and Safia Zaghlul. The very next day.

"If you don't go, they'll be angry," murmured her father.

I understood. She didn't know how to behave at table, how to act among people, how to speak in public; she knew nothing. The fear of being an uneducated peasant was tying her stomach in knots. I told her not to be ashamed, it's nothing, it's perfectly normal to eat with your fingers. She burst into tears and ran off to her room. The city was a jungle of impenetrable codes. I didn't know what to do. I turned to Sheik Ibrahim.

"It's nothing but a few idiotic rules. I'm prepared to teach her. You should go and fetch her."

The matter was dealt with among men. In the kitchen was a table which was the right height, and we took a chair from the living room. Sheik Ibrahim came back in, dragging his daughter by the arm. She sat down opposite the carefully laid-out place setting: a flat plate, a soup plate, a carafe of water, salt and pepper. Saadiya looked at me as if I were a doctor about to undress the child in her charge. I stood behind her and slowly lowered my arms above her shoulders, closed my hands over hers holding the fork and knife. Her body offered no resistance. Speaking gently to her I made her cut the meat, grazed her chin to remind her to chew with her mouth closed, took her napkin and showed her how to wipe her lips, made her drink her soup without slurping. She obeyed me with docile immobility, ready for everything. Her brother and father, erect in their jubbahs, which made them seem taller, held back and did not interfere. They watched with burning eyes. I had entered the first circle of intimacy, unaware of myself, dazzled, and beneath their gaze I was making all the forbidden gestures.

We repeated these sessions every Monday. They were somewhat humiliating for her, like an infirmity, some part of her family revealed to the eyes of a stranger. As if to counter their effect, she applied herself to the poetry with an even greater exaltation, letting her body relax.

We shook hands at the beginning and at the end of each visit, nothing more. The family had completely accepted me. The only one who seemed ill at ease was her brother, Sheik Khaled. We were roughly the same age, he was twenty-four, and wore a perpetually touchy, outraged expression. We had not exchanged more than three sentences since we first met.

At the end of the afternoon, the call of the muezzin rang out and Saadiya and the two sheiks would leave the living room. We would continue to work, nothing had changed, and yet. Something relaxed in our gestures, our intonation, the nearness of our bodies. On the balcony we lived in an imaginary country all our own, where everything was allowed. The poets, with veiled words, evoked physical pleasures; she would read each verse in a clear, pitiless voice. The innocence in her eyes was almost perfect. And it was that *almost* which was killing me.

I took out the poems I had written for her during the week, I always waited until the end to bring them out. Up to that point I had only dared to show her those verses where the allusions remained vague, but she refused to understand even the most transparent.

She relaxed against the cushions, her eyes half-closed, her lips slightly parted, her palms turned toward me. Without looking at her, I began to read. I recited the poem I'd composed during her absence in Ras-el-Bar ("*You who are leaving / Keep my love in your wake . . .*"), the one that came to me upon her return ("*Love has grown more tender / And has beckoned to me . . .*"), then another one inspired by the concert at the Bosphorus ("*Your voice runs through my body and my soul / My verses are written with tears . . .*").

Sheik Khaled came back into the living room; I should have carried on, and nothing would have happened. But I fell silent. My silence caught me in *flagrante delicto*. He rushed out onto the balcony like a madman, but found nothing, nothing he could latch onto. It was impossible to reproach us for something he had merely sensed. That made him even angrier: because he was sure, absolutely sure—of what, he couldn't say, but there was no doubt. You should be ashamed, he shouted, you should be ashamed—those were the only words which came to him. His pallor seemed to paralyze his jaw. We were sitting on the mattress on the floor, and he loomed over us with his anger. She wanted to protest; I thought he was going to strike her, he was capable of it.

"Don't try to make fun of me, I'll kill you, you know that very well, I'll kill you! Don't pretend there's nothing going on, that it's just me. Lower your eyes, that's better for you, lower your eyes, don't play with me, go straight to your room!"

She went out. I sat where I was, stunned. My poems were spread all over the mattress and I began to pick them up, stuffing them into my briefcase. I got up to leave, and every gesture seemed like a new confession. He'd withdrawn as far as the door, and was leaning against the doorframe, his hands trembling, a nasty smile on his face. As I went by him he came out with these puzzling words:

"The hairdressers' salons are closed on Mondays, my fine poet friend, you won't find any hair for cutting here."

6

I UNDERSTOOD SHEIK KHALED ONLY TOO WELL, and that made me resent him all the more. He'd pulled back the sheet and revealed to the light something that could survive only in shadow. That relation of closed eyes had been lost, and now I realized how precious it was to me. Without it, the space between the bed and the wardrobe became a desert, my entire life.

There was a knock at the door. Saadiya stood on the landing, her head covered; she refused to come in. I pulled her inside.

"The young lady's sent me. I came to tell you . . ."

Her eyes aghast, looking at the furniture, the paintings, the carpets.

"Khaled sees evil where there is nothing, absolutely nothing, may it please God, you know yourself that there's nothing, already when he was little, you mustn't take Khaled seriously, his father got very angry, he threatened to send him back to Tammay al-Zahayrah, the young lady will be waiting for you on Monday as usual, she's counting on you, don't be too angry, it's so unfair, of all those people you're the one I like the most . . . and the young lady too, I think."

"What people?"

"You mean you don't know?"

"What people?"

I had thought our sessions were unique, but they were repeated every day with different men, and they too might have thought they were unique. She had said nothing about it, not a word: she'd managed to mobilize the entire city. Not just anyone, Qsabji, Sheik Zakariya, the best—each and every one of them held magic between his fingers. In secret. Was there nothing for me? The question kept me awake, night after night. I could not understand the importance that this girl had acquired in my life. It unnerved me, but that changed nothing. And with the others . . . She was so young, her body let go so easily, she didn't even realize. I pictured her with the others. On the last night I was awake until dawn, and finally switched on the light to write about that which was making me ill: *"You share your charms with others than me and you smile."*

In spite of myself, I went back. I had scarcely touched the door and she opened it.

Her hair was down. A black line emphasized the brilliance of her eyes, her cheeks were tinted with rouge. I stood trans-fixed. She'd put on make-up. I felt like rubbing her eyes, her face, until she bled, to erase it all.

She took my hand and led me to the balcony. She motioned for me to sit down on the mattress and sat next to me, without a word. Everyone was gone, even Saadiya. We were alone, it was terrible. It wasn't even that, we had to reinvent a language. Silence actually suited her. She would breathe deeply, let the time go by. Her docile manner aroused a troubling temptation within me. She spoke without looking at me.

"I'm two years younger than my brother. I was born the same night that the angel Gabriel whispered the Koran to the Prophet, the night of Destiny. My father spent the night in the mosque, praying, and he fell asleep. In his dream he saw a woman covered in a white veil, reaching out to give him some-thing, and it was a green-colored jewel, a light wrapped in a cloth. The time it took him to look at it and raise his eyes again, the woman had nearly disappeared. He called out to her and asked her name. She replied that she was the daughter of the Prophet, Om Kalthoum.

"My parents would have preferred another boy, but I was a gift from the heavens, and that's how my mother raised me. Khaled didn't pay much attention, I was his little sister, and that was that. He watched over me, took me to play along the one little path that ran alongside the tributary of the Nile. At night during Ramadan we'd run through the narrow streets banging on pots and pans to wake up the village and call them out to the pre-dawn meal. I wore my red and gold galabia, we were together, we walked barefoot through the dust; Khaled treated me like a boy.

"But we were separated soon enough. My father wanted to teach him religious songs, marriage songs as well so that he could go with him to the ceremonies and help him. Every evening they would shut themselves away and it was unbearable, I would sit with my ear against the door. Maybe it was because of that, the *muwachahat*, the *tawachich*, and the *adwar* that Khaled would stumble over, I learned them so much faster than he did, it was like swallowing water. I didn't dare sing them in front of my father, I'd go up on the roof of the house and shout them out to the sky. One evening my mother heard me. To my eternal woe. She told on me, and my father hit me. I was a girl, I didn't have the right to sing.

"But I couldn't give up. Khaled was sent to the *kuttab*, the Koranic school in the village. I cried, I refused to eat, it didn't change a thing. I learned the Koran over his shoulder, I made him repeat to me everything he'd learned. I was miserable, and tyrannical. He had to give me whatever I asked for.

"My mother is a strange woman, she doesn't even know how to write her own name, but she understood. She saw that I wasn't getting over my misery, and she sold one of her rare jewels. She enrolled me in the *kuttab*, it was thanks to her. When my father found out, she reminded him of the dream he'd had. I was born under a sign, the hand of destiny was on my head, ordinary laws didn't apply to me.

"Every morning I went with my brother to school. I knew the Koran by heart, or almost. God is above everyone, we can only try to attain his perfection.

"The only other girl at the *kuttab* was Aisha, the mayor's daughter, and she became my friend. It was at her home that I sang for the first time. I was six years old. She had told her parents I had a pretty voice, and her father wanted to hear me. My father came along, there was nothing he could do. I stood up on a sofa and chose a verse from the Koran. The mayor had invited the village notables; he was pleased, and he sent out for a *mehallabiah* with sugared syrup. That was my first pay.

"Bit by bit, my father agreed to take me along when he'd go to the village or nearby. We went with Khaled, and sometimes a cousin would join us, depending on how big the party was. People began to ask for me. It was a lot of traveling, and Khaled often had to carry me on his shoulders. He'd look at me in a funny way. Everything was going great for me, we were being invited further and further away. With the money, my father was finally able to buy a donkey. He'd go on ahead, and my brother and my cousin would run behind. And I'd sit there on the donkey, looking down at them.

"All through the delta, my fee was going up. My brother, my cousin, and my father hardly ever sang any more, it was enough for them to sing the chorus, echoing my voice. We took the train. I was so ignorant that for a long time I believed the carriages were sitting still and that it was the landscape that moved. Sometimes we'd travel all day, change trains, and spend hours waiting for a carriage that was supposed to take us to some wedding that had been cancelled in the meantime. When the train was delayed, my father would ask if we could rest in the lounge reserved for important people. I'd sing for the stationmaster—my voice opened all the doors.

"When I was ten, my father decided I should no longer appear in colorful clothes. He demanded that I wear the same gray galabias that my mother wore, and I had to cover myself with a cape. Khaled was even more finicky. Even the most enveloping outfit wasn't good enough, in his eyes. It was his idea to disguise me as a little Bedouin boy. He made my appearance his personal business. Every time we'd arrive at a wedding, a baptism, or a circumcision, he'd inspect me carefully and would hide even the tiniest lock of hair that was showing.

"By the time we got to Cairo, Khaled had become unbearable. He'd get annoyed for no good reason, he'd accuse me, criticize the way I spoke to people or even just looked at them. I didn't know what to do about him anymore. Saadiya says you have to understand him, he's my brother, I stole his seniority from him, and not just that, I even stole his privilege of being the boy from him.

"He can't even protest, because it's the heavens' doing, not mine. God sent me a gift, but what can be more unfair than a gift? I try to respect Khaled, to understand him—what else can I do? I'll never forget that he's my brother . . ."

There was only one thing I wanted, the same thing she wanted, and that was to start up again with our silent affair.

"Promise me . . ."

I promised. No sooner had I said the words than a shadow passed over her face. A bad intuition. She'd been afraid of losing me, she'd told me her story, there was nothing between us, the lie had become the truth. I was no longer a danger, she no longer needed to seduce me. I slipped my hand into my pocket and took out the latest poem, *You Share Your Charms with Others and You Smile.* And just then, in the middle of my own gesture, my heart broke in two. Maybe all that was needed was to reach out my hand. Her eyes were still filled with disappointment. In a flash, I knew change had been within reach and I had missed my chance, and I was terribly certain that such a chance would not come my way again any time soon.

7

SHE PERSUADED QSABJI TO COMPOSE FOR HER. This was a major accomplishment, because she refused the lute or any other instrument, all she wanted was the music. But for Qsabji the lute was everything. He was five years old when he received his first lute, his arms were too short to reach around it. He had been playing for so long now that his body had married the instrument; he'd become hunchbacked. But the moment he would sit and hold his lute, he lost his hunch, and his body found its place.

"*You share your charms with others . . .*" she sang, a capella. When she had finished, he plucked the strings and began a series of variations on the same melody, it seemed so easy. His instinct for music was so sure that he could pass from one mode to another, seamlessly. Child's play, or rather, he himself was like a child, immersed in his game, serious and light-hearted at the same time, concentrated and absent, having a good time, smiling, suddenly no longer aware that others were listening.

He stopped, beaming. "The lute is the echo of your voice," he said, "you sing to it and it replies. I've got nothing against your family ensemble, may God protect them, but you need a musical ensemble. Get rid of your family—listen, you don't need them anymore."

She shook her head. She couldn't do that, she would feel like she was betraying them, her father believed that the human voice was the only instrument created by God.

"Peasant girl, dog's daughter . . ."

From him she could take it. He made her laugh, he couldn't say no to her, he liked her, it was perfectly plain. And it was impossible for me to feel jealous, not of him. He brought people together, he'd granted me his friendship and the illusion that there were three of us involved; and to be three of us meant I could preserve my relation with her. But the moment he left the room, I was completely at a loss. I no longer knew whether she wanted me or not. I hated myself. Too slow, too fast, I fell out of step, I could no longer keep up with her. She recited the poems, gasping for breath like a drowning woman, quivering with the imaginary country I no longer inhabited. It did not matter how much, how deeply I listened to her voice, I remained outside. I observed her hands, the way she held her body—whether she was turning toward me or not—everything was like a sign. She would finish, drunk on her own sensual delight, and then her gaze would alight on me and flicker out. All I had left was the memory of her rapture, her untouchable nearness.

So it was with a sort of rage that I tore off what I knew and tossed it her way: I would have liked everything at once. I'm sure she could see how violent I was, but she didn't react, asked for nothing. My burning passion became the very stuff of my poetry. *Your Heart Has Betrayed Me, I Was Silent and My Tears Spoke for Me, The Separation Was Lasting, I Took Your Voice into My Soul:* never had I written so much. She accepted my verses without comment, willfully blind. She needed poems and more poems, that was all that mattered. She gave a concert the first Thursday of every month.

My stubborn hope was wearing thin, yet I could not give up. At the library, at home, I spent my time going back over every single moment. That was all I could think about. I bore the sorrow of a love affair which had never bloomed. And yet it was so strong.

I opened my eyes; my thoughts were strangely clear. It was

just beginning to get light. I'd found a solution, or rather the solution had come all on its own. I would write her a poem, the definitive poem, explaining everything, openly: a love letter. She would understand. Or not. But she would have to react, and I would know. I sat down at my desk, and the poem came to me effortlessly.

Three hours later I was at her house. She welcomed me as she did each time. I hadn't said a word but she could sense my impatience. She sat down. I read her the poem in one breath.

> *If I forgive*
> *And ignore your coldness*
> *How can I be free*
> *Of the memory of you*
> *Your gaze is dear*
> *The heart has no price*
> *Tell me to forget*
> *Have pity on me*
> *Or tell me to come*
> *Come drink this glass with me.*

I raised my eyes. She was staring at me, *the way she used to*. Her gaze recognized the desert of pain that had been her hand-iwork, she no longer denied it, there was contact between us. It lasted only a second, but I had caught her out; already she was closing up again.

Those are the very verses that Qsabji set to music, and no others, unlike anything he had ever composed before. It was a real turning point. She sang *If I Forgive* with such fervor that there was a riot. Never had I heard such wild acclaim. Her voice had reached the point which set pain free. It was terrible because that pain was mine, and she had understood it in a flash, had taken that pain of mine and proclaimed it on the town square, and had elicited an incredible response. Every man in that room became me, every man had drunk from that source and was aching with a love impossible to abandon. It was too much. The audience's reaction was out of all proportion, something else must be causing it. It went beyond the circle of love . . . or else everything was the circle of love—our situation, the era, the entire country. We wanted to be part of our time—independent, modern; we were in full pursuit of progress, then rejected it, then sighed after it. Perhaps *If I Forgive* expressed, unintentionally, our general state of mind; perhaps my peasant girl was the unconscious priestess of that feeling. There was something frightening about such a notion.

All the press were talking about the concert, an obvious triumph. Mansour Awad, the head of Gramophone, suggested recording *If I Forgive* without delay. He offered royalties of five piastres per record, or a lump sum of eighty guineas. Sheik Ibrahim, without hesitating, opted for the second solution, as to him it seemed a considerable amount of money. He could not imagine that this 78-r.p.m. record would be his daughter's first great success. *If I Forgive* would sell more than a quarter of a million copies, and she concluded all her concerts with that song: the audience simply refused to leave the theater until they had heard it.

The answer I was waiting for did not come right away, and when it did, I wondered if it was truly hers. Success had brought an incredible exaltation. For the first time, her feelings encountered an equally intense resonance. She was not surprised; this was merely the fulfillment of the prophecy. But I was the one who had written the poem. It was the fruit of neither cleverness nor of inspiration: I had written it with my blood. She had brought it on, she was singing it, and it was my very real suffering which was the cause of everything. She was closer to me, as if it were willed by fate. We were joined. The fire returned to her eyes, as did gratitude. She accepted me once again, and she was taking me with her, it could all start over again, perhaps.

8

AND SUDDENLY SHE WAS THRUST to the very first place. A French magazine, *L'Illustration*, presented her as the greatest Arab singer of the century, so great that compared to her all the other Egyptian artists were no more than "cabaret singers." She'd mastered the art of mixing classical singing with astonishingly modern melodies. That is what Sheik Abu al-Ela had seen in her, that fusion of tradition and renewal. Someone had understood.

I was in the tram on my way to Muhammad's, we had an appointment, like every Tuesday. The controller was looking at my magazine, and he recognized her photo. Is that her? That's her. He ran his finger over the incomprehensible French text, and he was astounded to see her there, surrounded by all that foreign language.

I found Muhammad impatient and distracted; I pulled out the poems I had written for him. He had become as successful as she had, perhaps even more so. He asked for more verses than I could write. He also turned to other poets, wrote his own music, accompanied himself on the lute. Work with him was different. He would take his instrument onto his lap, read the poem line by line and come up with snatches of melody, more mindful of the flow of the verses than of their meaning. That day, his fingers moved quickly, stringing together improvisations; his voice strayed from the text, came back, stopped abruptly then started again a tone higher. I was euphoric. But he never paused, went on as if in a rage to the next series of variations, and started the poem again from the beginning, singing all of it without a break. He finished, breathless, sweat on his brow.

"Does that suit you? Not too cabaret-singer?"

I said nothing.

"Who is that journalist? One of your friends?"

Again I said nothing.

"I think you're blind. You can see no one but her."

"And you, what do you see?"

"People, girls, the way the world really is. Have you met any other girls since you came back from Paris?"

I didn't answer.

"Well?!"

"But that has nothing to do with it."

"You shaped her, she no longer needs you. You can come out with me again, go to cafés, meet women . . ."

"I'm not like that anymore, I don't feel like it."

He got up and went into the bathroom. I could hear him running water and washing his face.

"Did you read the press this morning?"

"I don't have time."

"It's there, on the table in front of you."

In *Al-Masrah* there was a cartoon of her sitting on a donkey, pursued by the two sheiks of the family brandishing the Koran in one hand and banknotes in the other. The title of the article was "The true story of the diva from Tammay al-Zahayrah."

I was not aware that the young woman praised to the skies by *L'Illustration* could scarcely tell a C from an E. What is this renewal she is supposed to have brought to us? How dare anyone suggest that the poets are fighting over her, that the other theaters stand empty whenever she is performing? The secret of her success is not to be found in the beauty of her voice but in the intrigues of her numerous lovers. She is trying to supplant the Sultana, Mounira al-Mahdia, who was the first Egyptian

woman to grace a stage at a time when our only actresses were
Syrian or Lebanese; she was the first woman to reject the exces-
sive modesty of another era. This newcomer may claim to be
pure, but she did not leave her village for any reason other than
to escape her shame. Just before she left, she went to the local
police station in order to register a complaint for rape.

The newspaper promised to provide more details about this
scabrous affair in its next issue.

Muhammad had come back into the room. I looked up at
him.

"Her father mustn't read this."

"How boring you've become. Who gives a damn about her
father. What did you think? That her rivals would concede the
throne without any reaction?"

"But like this, it's disgusting . . ."

"Poor little girl. Don't worry about her, she'll bloom in this
atmosphere, you'll see, she's tough."

"I don't understand you, I get the impression I don't know
you anymore."

He didn't answer.

"Come on, let's go to her place."

"I'm going to work with Mounira-al-Mahdia. She wants me
to finish the music to *Cleopatra*. She's just bought a theater, the
Printania. I'll be Marc Antony, she'll be Cleopatra. It's better if
you go console your diva on your own."

I had never come without being invited. The door was half-
open, I pushed it further. The apartment was deserted, and
tidy. I called out: no answer. I walked across the living room.
On the balcony there was nothing, just the indifference of
things, heat, the neighborhood. I could hear someone crying
their lungs out, in one of the rooms.

The tulle curtains hindered me, but I was inside. In the semi-
darkness I could make out several forms. Someone in a night-

shirt, their back uncovered, lying on the bed. I recognized her from her voice, it was her. She wasn't crying, but laughing. Sitting on her thighs, Saadiya was massaging her shoulders. On either side, barefoot, their hair unbound, were two of the Abdel-Razzak sisters. And seated at the foot of the bed was Aziza, her friend from Alexandria. She was holding my peasant girl's calf in her delicate fingers; she wore a fine bracelet on her wrist. It shone out against the damp quilt, a sudden flash in the shadowy game, skin against skin, abandon, a woven landscape of legs, of hips. There was something there—organic, feminine, unveiled, all too human. Their breathing overlapped, the dampness in the air was laden with henna and sweat and it made me dizzy. Not one of the women reached for her veil, they didn't have the reflex, the fascination was stronger. I had broken all the rules, I was in their midst. Five women, astonished. It should have been shameful, but it wasn't. I could see myself in their eyes, incapable of looking aside.

Their lips were parted, they burst out laughing. On the carpet nearby, playing cards were scattered, reflecting the movement which had thrown them there. I could imagine the gesture, it was late afternoon, the sheiks were absent, it was too hot, they tossed down the cards, they didn't switch on the light, they lay down on the bed. More than their supine bodies, those abandoned cards, face up, were the image of their intimacy.

Their laughter was contagious. Their skin touching, breathless. In their eyes as they stared at me I could read desire. Not in hers; or rather, there was desire, but it came from her pleasure in their desire. The women's emotion had overcome her, I could tell, she could not pull away, she was caught in the moment. I could see how she hovered on the brink. She wanted to regain control, but her laughter was overwhelming. From her tears, the dimples in her cheeks, the sound of her laughter, I could tell she was someone else. The young woman I'd seen for nearly three years was only one of her possible selves. She had spent her time clenching her teeth to stay in control, using up an enormous amount of energy. The façade was crumbling now and behind it I was discovering something unrestrained and naughty and even a bit vulgar, to be honest: something alluring, like a sin.

I should have done something, after all. At that very moment. I should have broken the spell, stopped it from spreading. Or accepted it and entered it. There had to be something I could have done. I remained a prisoner of their bodies, in the tangle of sheets.

An hour later the apartment was full of people. Saadiya had brought out thick, bitter coffee. The little one was shut away in her room with her father, Safia Zaghlul, Sheik Abu al-Ela, and above all Abdel-Razzak bey, the man who had vouched for them. Her father was shouting. The word dishonor, Tammay al-Zahayrah, the word shame. Other voices were deeper, graver, resisting. Her father wouldn't listen to reason. To kill the journalist and go back to his village, that was all he wanted.

I had seen. And the force of what I had felt had paralyzed me, as always. If dogs were unleashed upon me, they would find no flesh to bite into, only words. Nothing to chew on but air. And disgust. Certain senses are too raw; with me it is my entire being. Everything assails me, everything is *too much*.

I heard her voice, drowned out by her father's: "Be quiet, God is punishing me for my weakness, I heard what you said and I have strayed from the path! If we stay here, next thing you'll want musical instruments to accompany you, you'll want to sing with your body, to show your arms and your hair—you who are a descendant of the imam Hassan, brought up on religion!"

Abdel-Razzak bey raised his voice, loud and stern, for the first time.

"Listen to me for once and leave God out of this. If you take your daughter back to the village, people will think that what the paper said is true. If you do that, shame will pursue you for the rest of your days. Is that what you want?"

Her father remained silent.

"You know me. You'll be compensated."

Still Sheik Ibrahim said nothing. But his anger had not been quelled, and it spilled forth once again. Tammay, shame, dishonor. I thought about those words—shame, dishonor—and I was somewhere beyond them. There was no end to the shouting. The same scene played out, over and over, for several hours.

Shortly before midnight she came into the living room. All alone, very pale, her eyes quite dry. You saw me as I am. Her gaze scarcely brushed over me, then looked away.

"I wanted to thank you," she said, "it was a difficult moment but it's all over. It's late, excuse us. You will always be welcome, all of you. I know you are with me. I wanted to tell you . . . I've decided to stay in Cairo, come what may."

9

S HE STAYED AND IT WAS WAR, and that war effaced everything else. When I saw the incredible brutality she was forced to face, everything else seemed meaningless, even the interest I took in my own suffering. *Al-Masrah* published new articles about her, insane rubbish, insisting on the story of the rape while overlooking the fact that they had promised to provide details and proof, speaking of the event as if it were a known fact; they did not hesitate to strike where it hurt most. The following week they attacked again, it was a campaign, their goal was simply to drive her from Cairo. Mounira al-Mahdia must be behind it, no one else had the necessary spite or influence: only she, the Sultana. She had begun by singing between tables, lingering too long for each caress, and now she wanted to be the singer of modern times and to block the route to the little peasant girl who hid her wickedness beneath her Bedouin cape.

Abdel-Razzak bey kept his promise. He ordered his lawyer to file a lawsuit and made his personal position known in an article entitled, "True Modernity and False." The fact that this man renowned for his secular opinions had lent such support was a formidable endorsement for my Bedouin girl. The article transformed the conflict into an object lesson around one basic question: what is modern, and what isn't? *Rose el-Youssef* took up the challenge. Mounira al-Mahdia had, commendably, introduced a lighter touch into a country which had become mired in its past—too serious, too contemplative, with too much discrimination against women. The newspaper opened its columns to another notable Cairo family, another pillar of independence, who responded to Abdel-Razzak bey on the major points of the issue. The entire press got involved, and it became an affair where everyone could follow the latest developments in their favorite daily paper. It was the topic of discussion in all the artists' and intellectuals' cafés; musicians and composers took the opportunity to air their own particular grievances. There were many skirmishes within the war. Politics were involved. Soon after independence, King Fu'ad had called Sa'd Zaghlul, obliged and forced by popular pressure. He'd gotten rid of him at the first opportunity and had appointed Rushdi in his place. Sa'd Zaghlul's partisans were now on our side, and those of the new president of the council, who was Mounira's protector, were in the opposite camp. The country was asked to choose between the Sultana and the Peasant Girl, as if between two possible reflections of itself. The general public got involved, of course, and the concerts at the beginning of the month (Monday for one, Thursday for the other) began to resemble support rallies.

How could I think of leaving her side when the game was so unfairly matched? Mounira had dominated the scene for twenty years, and her patrons had been Turkish, English, and Egyptian—and sometimes all three at once, depending on the era. She was too well-connected, had compromised too many people, and the power was on her side. My peasant girl had chosen silence, and made no further attempts to refute the slander: her singing would speak for her. She believed that by shutting herself away she would find peace. But for her family the philosophical debate about modernity was met with indifference. Her honor had been soiled, that was all they could say, because of her, and nothing could remove the stain. The entire city was talking about Mounira, but here it was forbidden to say her name. Still, even the words never pronounced lingered in the air, took on a certain density, the weight of a dead body. I watched as she weathered the blows, clenching her teeth, while her father looked on.

Fortunately, there was Saadiya, the mistress of curses, who swore and brought laughter in spite of everything. Her nanny's body seemed to swell up in the face of adversity, accepting and absorbing all the troubles. There were also the Abdel-Razzak and Aziza sisters. The evening in the bedroom had created a strange intimacy among us. When they saw me, they lowered their eyes and brushed up against me.

I had also suffered from the battle. I had lost my best friend, Muhammad. Since the day he had refused to accompany me, there had been no sign of him, and I had not sought to contact him either. He was rehearsing *Cleopatra* with Mounira, that was enough. His musical reputation would protect her, defusing from the start any artistic criticism and rendering her untouchable. *Cleopatra* was not just any opera. Sayyed Darwish had left it unfinished when an overdose of cocaine killed him. Mounira bought the rights, with an aim to revive the mythical work. The event would bury her past, crown her career and ensure her recognition as an artist. The audience was promised the vision of the bare-armed Sultana singing with Muhammad Abd al-Wahab amidst an amazing décor of the Egypt of the pharaohs.

Compared with such a dream world, the girl in black, singing unaccompanied on a bare stage, did not carry much weight.

Qsabji rehearsed her, leaving to his lute the job of telling her what to do. She was singing, but something was missing from her voice, and her eyes were focused elsewhere. Criticism had settled inside her and was corroding her from within. Wasn't she too much of a peasant, too much governed by her family, too much a prisoner of tradition? I could tell those were the questions which informed her stubborn silence, her boundless pride. She would say nothing.

She motioned to me to follow her out onto the balcony, made me swear to secrecy: she wanted to add a lighthearted song to her repertory. For a change.

"Lighthearted how?"

"Lighthearted! Lighthearted! The way it's pronounced!"

"A superficial song, easy to remember, or one with sort of risqué lyrics?"

"Exactly. I've had enough of lamenting and bitter regret. You've turned me into a professional weeper. Now I want something joyful, something lively, that's what I want. Give me a song that's lighthearted and even . . ." She blushed. "Yes, a bit . . . spicy. Is that clear?"

"I don't want to write that sort of song for you."

"You're an ungrateful wretch, you're completely out of touch with the times, and with me, it's no surprise either, the one time I ask you to do something, when I'm the victim of a plot . . ."

I spent the night writing the poem, eking it out verse by verse. The scene of the massage played again before my eyes, the women among themselves, the card game. *She was like that, too.* I accepted the feeling of defilement, forced my hand, succumbed to it. By morning, I had a poem: "*Simpering and swaying / That's my trade / Oh people, I love the way it feels.*" She didn't dare ask Qsabji to set it to music, she brought Sabri back to life and had him come from Tanta.

There we were the three of us again, but our shared secret did not bring us any closer. We weren't proud. She wanted to try it, in order to be sure. She decided, one evening when her father and brother were absent, to sing the song at the end of the program, just to see what would happen. Sabri and I were in the first row, and she hadn't warned us.

She began to sing, and a disapproving silence spread through the hall right away. Yet the audience was made up of faithful followers, a private event. My poem got the reception it deserved. Simpering and swaying. What was she thinking. She carried on, courageously, couplet after couplet, right to the last verse: *"The lover is back / And my heart rejoices, oh people / Through the Prophet."* There was a second's hesitation, a dizzying moment, a few isolated bursts of applause which fell silent, ill at ease. The audience seemed less scandalized than sorry for her. How could I have written such words? But she stood up to them. Showing no emotion, she launched straight into the next song, and finished her recital with *If I Forgive*, which was immediately greeted with an fervent ovation.

Backstage, she attacked Sabri and me. It was our fault, we'd pushed her into it: unbelievable bad faith. I didn't have the heart to reply, I felt too guilty. She never sang the song again; once was enough. The very next day *Rose el-Youssef* made fun of her grotesque attempt to be Mounira's equal on her own terrain. *Al-Masrah* wrote that she was a laughingstock.

Sabri chose that moment to make the biggest mistake in his life: he asked for her hand in marriage. She had just turned twenty-six, and there was gossip about her celibacy. He thought he was doing the right thing—otherwise he would never have dared. He got on the train and went back to his practice in Tanta. We didn't see him after that. I felt like his double: he had shown me what I must not do.

The smear campaign ended. The game was over, they'd won, we'd lost. The critics fell silent "out of humanity," the young diva was on her knees. That angered her more than anything. She believed that my lighthearted poem had dishonored her for good. It wasn't true. Virtually no one had heard the song, it had become an almost mythical rarity, and who still knew it had ever existed? She had acquired that little touch of spice she'd wanted, a blurry halo—and she hadn't even realized. The hostile city had defeated her, or at least shaken her. She was more alone than ever. Even her friends she no longer recognized.

The world went on turning without her. All anyone cared about was *Cleopatra*: the decors, the costumes, the dream . . . The president of the council had let it be known that he would attend the premiere. But she no longer existed.

As soon as I arrived I knew that it was a bad time. She introduced us. Ali Baroudi was in charge of the Misr company for the theater, and his mission was to support artists. He shook my hand, warmly, spoke to me about my poetry, and his tone conveyed the same elegance as his person, a somewhat aristocratic nonchalance. You could tell he was an important man because he didn't need to show it: his self-confidence and humility were self-evident. He pulled up a chair and invited me out onto the balcony as if he were the master of the house.

"We were discussing a concert in Baghdad, at the palace of Emir Abdallah . . ."

He looked at her.

"If you don't feel up to it, then forget it, go back to the village. Or go on singing disguised as a Bedouin, with your daddy, you might get two or three years more out of it."

She gave me a sidelong glance, her fingers playing with the collar of her blouse, or the top button. She didn't know what to say. I felt my presence was bothering her. But I couldn't leave now, that would have been worse. In any case I didn't want to.

"You don't know my father," she said with effort.

"You're of age."

"You don't know where I come from . . ."

"We all come from there."

She turned first one way then the other, helpless; I could see her fingers trembling. Ali Baroudi wasn't speaking as an envoy from power, but as power itself, the fraction of power which was not satisfied with the outcome of the battle with Mounira, and which had decided to get her back in the saddle. She

regained her composure. I could see in the depths of her eyes
that she was coldly evaluating her chances.

"I would like to thank you for your concern . . ."

"I'm not in the least bit concerned about you. You're making fun of me. You can send your father to kingdom come,
along with half of the human race."

"May God forgive you for what you have just said."

He gave a short burst of laughter, then took her by the
shoulders.

"Mounira is nothing. Forget her. You don't need to sway
your hips. What you have doesn't belong to you. It is in you,
but it doesn't belong to you. And you must give it . . . to the
country."

His face was close to hers. I could sense her weakness, her
powerlessness in his presence. He turned away, picked up his
hat and cane.

"The marriage of Emir Abdallah is in two months. Think
about it. But I won't take you to sing before the court in
Baghdad dressed as a little boy. You're not a little boy anymore."

10

HER DILEMMA WAS STARING HER IN THE FACE, and she dared not move. There was nothing I could do, except perhaps speak to her in this separate language, out on the balcony. Her gaze wandered; she was biting her lip. When she regained her senses and our eyes met, she knew that I knew. These silences created a new form of intimacy between us. When she suffered, I suffered.

My verses took on a meaning I had not intended. "*He had a tenderness for my heart / I plucked the rose from his cheeks / And drank the sweetness from his lips.*" Enraptured, she sang that poem to me as if she were addressing each verse to someone in particular. You had only to listen and she became radiant, with a surging joyfulness even she could not explain. She had been like that, almost the same, on the very first day. And even now she understood that she could play with me, but it was a new game. Through a disturbing transference, my inspiration no longer relayed my sentiments but her own, those she could not yet admit to. The attraction had been too powerful, I had invaded her and let myself be invaded by her. Already her eyes were measuring the opening. I felt a twinge in my heart: it had chosen for me. I would not love her in this world, but in another, where the relation is all the stronger because the body does not exist. I understood this shift from the way she smiled. I was taken. I could no longer withdraw what my voice had whispered to her. She was going to leave with Ali Baroudi.

My poem was entitled *The Beloved Has Come.* She did not sing it, but kept it as a memory for a future time. She asked for others from the same source of inspiration. She seemed confident I could write them. She wanted a miracle. For her next concert.

I began to write, every evening. With a feverishness that did not come from inside me. I would shut myself away in my room, forbid myself from thinking, and suppress my feelings, for they came like a milk spilling over; then I'd let go, surrender to the mystery as she did to her song. *Doubt Intensifies Love; Our Separation Has Gone On.* She read the poems and laughed. She was no fool. She'd slipped into the new game with suppleness and jubilation. But it wasn't exactly a game for me. Nor for her, all things considered.

The evening of the concert was upon us. At the Bosphorus. I had never seen her so nervous behind a closed curtain. She was delighted with the poems, but now there was the cape, and her headdress. They'd brought them to the stage, and she had to decide what to do. In the end she put them on, at the last minute and with a heavy heart. Her brother came to tighten the cloth beneath her chin and he pulled roughly, abruptly, as if he knew what was happening. All you could see was the oval of her face.

"*I plucked the rose from her cheeks / And drank the sweetness from her lips. / My beloved has come.*" A tumultuous response from the audience, immediately, from the very first verse, like arms opening to enfold her and welcome her. She absorbed the shock, surprised, full of wonder, as if it were the first time. The ovation rolled over her like a relentless storm. She caught my eye where I was sitting in the first row, took me for a witness, pleaded for help. I saw her moist eyes shining in the light. She stood up straight. "*I plucked the rose from her cheeks*": she took up the first couplet again and tossed it to their outstretched hands. The audience had understood. Something had happened, their diva was no longer the same. They recognized her laughing mood, it was their own, and they accepted it. She caught her breath in the midst of their acclaim, bowing with humility, withholding her pride. I watched as with an impulsive gesture she placed her fingers beneath the knot in her scarf to loosen it. There was a moment of suspense in the theater, then the applause grew even louder. She raised her head. Beneath the folds of her scarf on either side of her face you could see her thick hair. She began singing again. Word for word, she sang the poem which an obscure force had dictated to me, now set free on a new rush of inspiration. On her face I could see the same spell which had bound me in my room every evening. The very same spell. And echoing our private feeling was the crowd's acclaim. That night, the Cairo audience finished the song, took her in its embrace, gave her to the world. It was a fusion for her listeners too, or rather for her, for in her voice she had a new song, more than a song. Me-her-audience, trilogy of a strange alchemy. I had simply made a conduit of my body: the poem was born, and now it was circling around us, through the darkness of the theater. I immersed myself in the general inebriation. She was laughing silently beneath the applause.

My Beloved Has Come was greeted as her true response, as were the two other poems. They enabled her to return to the arena. Despite all the commotion surrounding the preparations for *Cleopatra*—or even because of it—there was a renewed tenderness for simple singing, for her voice. The simmering enthusiasm which had taken hold was so full of promise: people allowed a rush of hope to seize them, with the light-heartedness of beginnings, a willingness to believe that seasons change, that love can still come.

But even with her scarf untied, she had still been singing in a Bedouin's outfit. The audience pretended to think it was her charm, that it had become her charm. If she could have been satisfied with this version of events, she might have done so.

From the platform of the tram which took me to her house I watched the streets rush by, and the bright red, stroboscopic posters. I hadn't seen Muhammad again, and yet suddenly there he was, right in front of me, thousands of copies of him. Mounira knew exactly what she was doing. It was him, all right. Both of them. That was all you saw, anywhere. They colored the walls of the city, filled the atmosphere. A blue flyer had been pasted onto each poster: *Tonight—opening night.* The glue hadn't dried yet.

My diva had warned me she might be a bit nervous today. It was *Cleopatra*'s day, the day of that woman who had dragged her through the mud. But she seemed to be in a good mood, almost too cheerful. I brought out my poetry collections. I felt like reading Ma'ari to her.

Sounds rose from the street, shouts, people rushing, like a gusting wind. I raised my voice; the noise of the neighborhood grew louder. We heard cars starting up, shopfronts closing, running, sounds from farther away. We got up to see what was happening: a strange excitement seemed to have taken hold of passers-by. They would run up to each other, then rush off again. Saadiya burst out onto the balcony.

"God is great! Sa'd Zaghlul is dead."

The women clapped their hands to their faces. She wanted to go straightaway to her friend Safia, the wife of the deceased. In the street, people went up to each other, their arms dangling by their sides, in shock. That the Father of Independence had died, just like that, without warning—they had thought he was immortal. There had been no sign that he would disappear— no illness, nothing. She was wringing her hands as she moved forward, walking faster and faster. Yet just before she went out she turned to me and said, her voice low: "Like this, it's from God. Mounira will have to cancel her opening night."

And the opening night was cancelled, until after the funeral. Did anyone care? Another time had taken over, where history is made. It upset the normal order of things and of thoughts. We were burying the man who had set us free. In spite of everything. They tried to lend a certain class to the state funeral, but in vain. What took place was as simple as the emotions of ordinary people.

She was a friend of the widow's, and followed the coffin. Not a single artist or intellectual failed to show up. King Fu'ad led the mourners, accompanied by Crown Prince Farouk and every single person the Arab world considered a king, emir, or head of state. And by their side was the British High Commissioner, who (he too) had done everything he could to break Zaghlul. Then came the European diplomats who had strangled him economically; the landowners who had banded together when he had tried change the property laws; the captains of industry who had risen up against his timid social laws; the bankers, most of whom had preferred to side with the English, the king, and international finance. Fortunate in his death, Zaghlul no longer had any enemies.

Suddenly the people—Cairo, its distant suburbs—massed along the path of the funeral procession spilled over, a slow and peaceful high water, certain of the reason they were there. The ranks mingled. The workers forgot that despite his promises, Zaghlul had crushed their strikes and suspended the national federation of unions, the first one they had ever had. The peasants no longer thought of reproaching him for having done nothing to improve their lot. We were all overcome by the same feeling. Were it not for this man, we would not be independent. We would undoubtedly have become independent sooner or later, but history had decided that he would be the one, and we wanted to thank him for it.

11

A FORTY-DAY PERIOD OF NATIONAL MOURNING was declared. Flags flew at half mast, schools and administrative offices reduced their activity, cabarets and theaters closed their doors. The premiere of *Cleopatra* was in serious jeopardy.

I could see the certainty in her eyes. God was on her side, and he had always been; a higher force was intervening, relentlessly, in her favor—for she was the descendant of the imam Hassan, and bearer of a gift. That is what she had always believed. The battle was being fought not just on earth but also in heaven, and that is where she had a particular advantage. She was the *chosen* one. The world around her was magical, and she could move forward with her eyes closed.

She vanished. Safia Zaghlul had asked for her, and she packed her bags and went to live at her friend's house. We did not see each other during the entire period of mourning; we wouldn't meet again until it was over. The entire profession had been laid off. Actors, singers, and musicians wandered from one café to another. They would talk about politics, without much conviction; they would swap advice about odd jobs that could help them get by. The days seemed to drag on and on, and her absence exiled me from everything.

I used the time to correct the final galleys of Khayyam's *Rubaiyat.* Years of effort had finally yielded these two hundred printed pages, already part of the past. If she had agreed to sing them, she would have brought them into the present, she would have taken them into her breath. Right-thinking people had always viewed Khayyam as an infidel, even in his own time, but that was not the reason she had turned him down, I don't think so. We had begun work on the *Quatrains* in the same way as for the other poems, but once we were in them, I had exploded. Every level of the text, the absolute particularity of it, pleasure as a source of fascination, like a mystic had entered my exuberant body to find expression before her. She had come so close to the intoxication and the mystery that, too strong, they had frightened her. Or to be more exact, they had revealed something inside her which frightened her: a temptation that she had finally repelled. I handed the galleys in to the editor; the work was done.

The city seemed to be in the same state as I was, suspended. Qsabji dragged me along to the cafés and I followed. I couldn't take part in the discussions; everything slipped between my fingers. It was a sad sun which had risen over my life.

Toward the end of the forty days, there was a quiver of excitement. Advertisements announced the première of *Cleopatra* for the following Wednesday, the very evening the mourning period was to end. Mounira was wasting no time. She was giving the signal for life to resume. Poets were hired again, musicians took their lutes and citharas out of their cases. Deprived of music for over four weeks, Cairo changed overnight. Rehearsals started up again, wedding feasts were organized, melodies wafted onto the air from open windows, lines grew long outside theater box offices.

There was a knock at the door. I did not recognize the young woman who stood there, not right away. Her black dress was so elegant, it looked more like evening wear than a mourning outfit. She was wearing a large scarf which covered her shoulders and hid her mouth. I hadn't seen her in over five weeks.

She laughed at my surprise, immediately resumed her tone of mocking complicity, but she couldn't fool me. She was as moved as I was. She came in quietly, So this is where you live; she spoke in a low voice, her eyes were everywhere, on the photo of my father in its wooden frame, the wobbly coat rack, the darkened living room, the large table in the dining room where my brothers and sisters did their homework. We lingered in the shadow. She made an effort to rouse herself from a kind of strange indolence: "You see I've come, I need to talk to you." My mother came out of the kitchen, hurriedly untied her apron, shook her hand. You might have thought that my mother was the one with humble origins, and that my peasant girl was the princess.

I took her into my room, she left the door ajar. She saw the dust, the papers. I moved the piles of books, she touched my arm, sat on the narrow bed. I leaned against the wall.

"It's been a long time," she said.

"So it has."

"Have you written any poems about Sa'd Zaghlul?"

"Several."

"Thank God."

"Why?"

"Show them to me."

I shuffled through the papers on my desk. There was one, *If Sa'd Is No Longer in Egypt.* I read it to her.

"Have you got a copy? Can I take it?"

"Yes."

"Give one to Qsabji, he can set it to music, tell him it's for me. Come both of you to the house tomorrow at three."

"Can you explain?"

"No. Well, perhaps yes. But keep it a secret. Promise . . ."

I was silent.

"Safia Zaghlul will end her mourning on Wednesday, at her house. She's asked me to sing . . ."

The black crepe had been removed from the facade of the

Zaghlul residence, near the royal gardens. A silent crowd had gathered early in the morning outside the gates. To mark the end of the mourning period, to watch the celebrities go by. When I rang the bell, it had been dark for a while already. Valets in white jackets, exhausted, ushered me in. I got the impression I was arriving too late. Carpets muffled my steps. An old man guided me along the deserted hallways, until we reached a double door.

I went through the door. In the brightly-lit room I came upon rows of chairs, facing away from me. She stood in the middle of an improvised stage at the back of the living room, bare-headed, her hair tied in a chignon, dressed in a long green dress encrusted with golden sequins. She'd crossed the line. She was singing as a woman in public, for all to see, her head raised high. No matter how much I had expected this someday, I was still astonished. She'd pushed the provocation so far as to wear jewelry, a discreet necklace and earrings, set nevertheless with precious stones. Safia Zaghlul had lent them to her. Between her outstretched hands was a green silk scarf, held so tightly she seemed to want to tear it apart. But her voice did not falter. *"If Sa'd is no longer in Egypt / He has kept his home in memory / His glory in our songs . . ."*

Behind her, Qsabji was bent over his lute. Sami al-Shawa, the virtuoso from Aleppo, held the violin, and Muhammad al-Akkad the cithara. Qsabji, Shawa, and Akkad: no singer could dream of a more prestigious trio, the best musicians of the era. And yet they left her all the space, followed her line by line, offered a velvet setting to her sovereign voice, humbly harmonizing with each meander, as self-effacing as friends, as an echo. They pushed her into the front row, that little peasant girl who'd come up five years earlier from her obscure village of Tammay al-Zahayrah.

Above the spectators' heads, her eyes suddenly caught mine and did not let go. The room between us, full of people, had ceased to exist. As during our rehearsals, I began to articulate each verse of my poem, syllable by syllable, so that she could read my lips. Her clothes may have changed, and her brilliance, but not the way she sang. She was concentrating on each word and would not release it from her lips until she was sure she had given it the full meaning. In this case, she was singing about a man's death, and not just any man, and we were bidding him farewell. At one point, toward the end of the poem, her voice caught on the verse *"If Sa'd is no longer in Egypt,"* and she could not restrain a small sob. In the second which followed, the three musicians stepped into the breach, and together, with an amazing verve, they developed a series of variations on the melody. In the same instant she was blinded by a camera flash. It was like a signal. Saadiya began to cry, members of the audience followed suit. In the front row, Safia Zaghlul was sitting as rigid as an empress, all her emotion contained. She could not allow herself to let her guard down in the presence of her close enemies—the representatives of the palace on her right, of the government on her left. I looked for Sheik Ibrahim and Sheik Khaled, but could not find them.

On the front page of all the newspapers was the picture which showed her wavering in her black evening dress, surrounded by the three great musicians, her head flung back, the handkerchief outstretched like an offering. The headlines didn't mention her specifically, but announced in big letters the end of the period of national mourning. "Farewell, Sa'd!" read the headline of several of the papers, and it was what the photo, too, seemed to be saying. This woman; Egypt.

But I saw something else there: the image of a girl I knew and who that evening had thrown off her Bedouin disguise the way one throws off one's mourning clothes.

At the very moment when her photograph was on the front page of all the papers, very early in the morning, she was at the airport, ready to fly off to Baghdad with Ali Baroudi. I learned that he had taken her to a bank to open an account in her own name. She had received her first check book. Sheik Ibrahim had been stripped of all his powers. At the age of twenty-seven, the woman I loved had shaken off her paternal tutelage in order to pull herself up to first place.

I'd almost forgotten, but the première of *Cleopatra* had been held that same evening, at the same time, in the new Printania theater. Interested readers would have to look for the news inside the papers, in the Theater section.

PART TWO

1932-1938

1

SHE HAD ASKED ME TO GO WITH HER TO THE CEMETERY. I left her by the grave and walked away. Sheik Abu al-Ela had been dead for her for a long time already, no doubt. I saw her waver amidst the tombstones; her prayer was like a dance. Something was coming to completion. This strange trance was perhaps her way of paying homage to him, however late.

She had missed the funeral, all of us crowded together, astonished that we were so many. Sheik Abu al-Ela. We had all examined our individual lives, and measured the place he had occupied there; we were all there. He was our music master, a fragile soul, powerful in his fragility; a ferryman between two worlds. We walked with him step by step, with a tenderness that was much stronger than the tenderness that had surrounded him at the end of his life. He could sleep peacefully now. The legacy he had received had been passed on. But just behind his coffin was an empty space, where she should have been.

And now she was leaning on my arm, as if she were asleep, overcome by her thoughts. She let me lead her. We approached the cemetery gates, and she clung to me. She entrusted me with the weight of her body, without restraint. The poison spread through me. She was upsetting me; I rejected her. I could not believe in her grief; it was scarcely remorse, the emotion of an instant. She wanted to associate me with her pretense. I felt like pushing her away. But an impossible hope was rising like a desire to vomit, from the deepest, darkest place inside me, incredibly alive. Incredibly strong, nauseating. It was not even me: my body was beyond my control. She stopped and looked at me.

The colors of mourning emphasized her olive complexion and the blackness of her eyes. Her lace scarf gave her a murderous air. She was new under the sun, resplendent. Her rounded features were composed, her resolution sharp. She was an independent woman, and alone; she was thirty years old.

"Mounira al-Mahdia has invited me to her birthday party and I've decided to accept."

I stared blankly at her.

"What's the matter?"

"It's not . . . why . . ."

She stared at me uncomprehendingly. She was obsessed with Mounira, with the conflict which had lasted for over five years and which everyone else had tired of. Her art, nothing else. She had just returned from her first tour through Lebanon, Syria, and Palestine, the other cradle of Arabic music. Outside Beirut hundreds of boats had greeted her with Egyptian and Lebanese flags. In Haifa, she had offered the proceeds from one of her concerts to the fund against British occupation and Jewish immigration. Her welcome had been triumphal. She had even been given a new name: the Star of the Orient. There was nothing keeping her from a reconciliation with her rival. On the contrary, such a gesture would even propel her to the heights.

"What are you thinking about?" she asked me.

"Mounira."

"I'd like for you to go with me to her party tomorrow evening."

"I won't go."

"Why not?"

I didn't reply.

"The squabble was all about me, it's time to resolve it."

"I don't feel like it."

"You really hold a grudge."

And she was saying such a thing to me. When I had embraced her own spite to such a degree that I had broken off with my best friend!

There was a knock at the door. I was at home alone, I hadn't even switched on the lights. I went to open. Muhammad. In a tuxedo. With his cane in his hand. Smiling. As if it were only yesterday we'd parted. I was overcome by an insane shyness. He came in; how could we speak; he held me by both arms. We did not take our eyes from each other, embraced, burst out laughing, felt like crying.

"You're just a scoundrel."

And what could I have called him? I was so glad that he existed. I switched on all the lights. He didn't seem real, standing there in the middle of the living room. The promise that had always been apparent on his features had been fulfilled, and success was written there. Even the taste for pleasure visible in his eyes had matured. The years had been good to him: not a wrinkle. Muhammad.

"I've come to fetch you."

"You show up after all this time and–"

"I'm the one who vanished!"

I was silent. In our gaze, the five years that had passed hurtled by, then dissolved, without leaving a trace.

"Where do you intend to take me?"

"To Mounira's party."

"I can't."

"Because of her?"

"Would you like something to drink?"

"We'll have a drink when we get there."

He was waiting patiently. His body and mine: we were the

same age, just turned thirty-two, but his body was made for sensations. I would have liked to touch him, to push him, so he would stop looking at me like that. I didn't move. He gave a feeble smile.

"You've let her come between us . . . We are friends."

"I'm glad you came."

Suddenly I also wanted to go. Without thinking, I made my decision.

2

I FOUND MYSELF CAPABLE of a hitherto unsuspected nonchalance. The taxi dropped us off at Zamalek, in the posh neighborhood.

Nothing distinguished the silent house from its neighbors save the men gathered around the entrance. We went through a labyrinth of dark rooms. The garden was behind the house, set on a lower level, an enormous, unimaginable garden filled with laughter. I had heard about these parties, with their dimmed lights, Mounira's parties. From the top of the steps I could make out the basin and its fountain in the middle of the garden and the lanes which disappeared into small groves of trees; people milled about, shadows. A cool fragrance rose to one's nostrils, softened the heart.

Muhammad slid his arm under mine and we went in together, smoking cigars. The Sultana was stretched out amidst her cushions on a podium built in the middle of the stairway leading to the garden. My peasant girl stood on her right. She was wearing the diamond brooch which the king of Iraq had given her, and a low-cut black evening gown. She held the tips of her fingers out to greet Muhammad and scarcely looked at me. Mounira got up and embraced my friend. She ignored my outstretched hand and held me against her chest. She had missed me so much . . . I scarcely knew her.

I walked away. Mounira kept Muhammad at her side and motioned to the photographer. The aging Sultana, surrounded by two of the greatest stars of the moment: I imagined we were there for that purpose, for the photograph, so that she would be on the front page of the newspapers the next day. I had moved as far away as possible and was leaning against the wall at the foot of the steps. I wanted to be near the door, to be able to slip away.

Two floodlights were switched on, illuminating the space in front of the pond. The surrounding darkness grew deeper, and the guests lingering in the garden converged upon the scene. Muhammad came and joined me, holding his champagne glass. He leaned against the wall next to me. The musicians, carrying lute, violin, and cithara, moved into the light, surrounding a tiny young woman in a short-sleeved dress; she wore a red ribbon in her hair, she was almost a child. The violinist circled around her, lowering his instrument in a gesture of respect. She stood still. The audience sitting on either side of the pond encouraged her, but she didn't react, afraid of missing her cue. The music slowed, and she began to sing: there was an instantaneous sense of surprise, not only because of her voice but also because of the elegance of her pronunciation, the ease and fluency which reigned. The audience applauded, almost entirely won over. In the semi-obscurity I could make out the figure of my peasant girl standing stiffly next to Mounira. The little singer was not looking at them; her air of irrepressible freedom did not seem to be a local trait. My voice low, I asked Muhammad about her.

"Da'ud Husni discovered her. He's introducing her this evening, a lamb at the feet of the Sultana. She's not even fourteen years old, Asmahan, but that's not her real name. I've heard she belongs to an important Druze family, from the mountains in Lebanon."

She took a step toward the listeners on her right, sang to them, turned to the other side, came back to the center and raised her eyes to the middle of the podium. Her agility; her freshness and incredible slenderness. The fountain was at her back, nothing weighing on her shoulders, no pharaohs: she could release her song with utter freedom. She came from over there, from the other Arab world, the lighthearted Near East. Muhammad leaned over to me.

"Her parents probably think she's at school or in her dormitory . . . and she's here. Look at how her little body trembles to hold that note. Isn't she magnificent?"

She was, indeed. It was a form of escape. I was charmed. Muhammad went on enumerating her qualities in my ear: her silver bracelets ringing on her wrist, her smile which seemed to come from within as it broke onto her lips. I raised my head and felt my diva's eyes upon me: right on my face. She hadn't stopped staring at us for an instant.

Asmahan left the stage amidst the applause and went straight over to where her master, Da'ud Husni, was sitting. She pulled his sleeve; the old man stood up and nodded to everyone, visibly moved. He took the young singer by the hand and led her over to Mounira, who got up to kiss her. My peasant girl shook her hand.

The spotlights moved back to the stage. The music became more joyful, tambourines and flutes joining the orchestra. A dozen young women came on stage, scantily clothed, and were greeted with ululations. They were members of Mounira's troupe. Laughing, encouraging one another they began to dance. They went up the steps, approached the Sultana, and encircled her tenderly. Their dance was lascivious but also had something domestic about it, as if it were a present from young girls to their teacher, a birthday cake. They tried to draw her into the dance; she resisted. They invited my diva. She refused with an obvious, emotional shyness. One of the girls smiled to her, and her provocative gestures seemed to draw a sort of invisible thread; she took her hand, writhing her navel at the level of her gaze. My peasant girl retreated until she could find refuge in Mounira's arms; Mounira was laughing.

She was trying to defend herself as they gazed at her—the photographs were relentless, and the next day her audience would find her in the newspaper, among these half-naked women. Her father could no longer be indignant: he had died, two years earlier. Nor did she obey her brother any-more, and even Saadiya was absent. That evening she was her own chaperone.

The young women went back down the steps, leaned against the fountain and opened their arms. Their fingers touched. Water fell upon their naked shoulders, like a call. Men were on their feet, snapping their fingers and shouting words of love. The girls laughed like children. The thin veils which covered them clung to their skin.

My peasant girl had thrown her head back, and I had time to see the envy in her eyes—two perpetual sparks in the dark-ness. She was enthralled by the atmosphere of female sensual-ity and open, good-natured rawness. I could sense a long sus-tained sigh within her. If she let herself go, there would be no stopping. Her body, clinging to the cushions, expressed both fear and desire, one as strong as the other: the fear of desire.

"She loves women"—that's what everyone was saying. A gossiping buffoon's secret, well-kept. I couldn't stand hearing it. But there it was, hovering, around me and around her.

She loved women, that I knew, but not in the way they were insinuating. She had opened her eyes onto a world where men were like her father—tyrannical, stubborn, possessive. She sought peace among those of her own sex. I'm not getting mar-ried because I'm married to my art, I owe myself to my gift, to my jealous audience . . . what hadn't she said. She had broken the rules, she knew no others, and she was left without rules. What man could hope to dominate her when all the men were at her feet? And how could she possibly be attracted to a sub-missive man when, for her, virility was the ultimate quality? There was no way out. So she had preferred to give herself to the immaterial lover, the man in the shadows, the ovation which flowed over her every night. Day by day her celibacy ripened her virgin, violent sensuality, and she offered it forever to her audience alone. She did it all on her own, free of any male attachment. So quickly, so young. There was no one left to incarnate the models of her childhood, save herself—and she could not. If she had to be something, I would have said she was androgynous, man and woman at the same time, of neither sex because of both. And she was a mother on top of it, because her name was Om: the mother of all and a mother without children. And a saint because she was a descendant of the Prophet and bore the name of one of his daughters. But a woman all the same, to be sure, a woman belonging to no man, all vibrant yet untouchable flesh. I had bound my life to a living impossibility, a hermaphrodite divinity, a monster.

Muhammad tapped me on the shoulder. Three of the dancers were there, surrounding him. Their dresses were somewhat more decent; their wet hair was dripping. I could not remember any of their names; their faces, their damp curls all melted into a same youthfulness. He suggested they leave the party with us. They agreed to whatever he asked. The spotlights came back on, the girls leaned against the wall with us, between us.

The beam of light sought her out where she stood on the podium, the Sultana was urging her, the crowd were calling her name. She got up and went down to the stage. She would sing for Mounira. In a religious silence she spoke the words in her honor—respect, admiration, love—and each word made her greater. She began by showing how deep her voice was. *You Are Desire*, by Iman Shabrawi, her eyes never leaving Mounira's. Little Asmahan was sitting on the bottom step, her fists beneath her chin, fascinated. The audience seemed to be caught off-guard, moved. Without waiting for the acclaim to subside she immediately launched into *Like a Gazelle* by

Saffieddine Halabi, and rhythmic applause accompanied her from beginning to end. Now there were calls for some of her old hits, *If I Forgive, My Beloved Has Come.* But that night she would sing none of my poems, that I knew. Muhammad pushed us toward the door.

3

S HE WALKED TOWARD ME, her hand outstretched. I thought she would be distant and closed, but she was smiling with her head tossed back. On the balcony, as I was rummaging in my briefcase, she touched me.

"We have time to work."

I sensed some disquiet beyond her excitement. The world had opened and accepted her. She had gone onto a new battlefield, vaster, more complicated. Her problem was no longer that of reaching the top, but of staying there. She did not take her eyes from mine; she was there, really there, and she was trying to seduce me.

She asked me what I thought of Ahmad Shawqi, and I replied that the Emir of Poets did not wear his name in vain.

"When he was ten, Muhammad was singing in a seedy theater on the banks of the Nile, and that's where Ahmad Shawqi discovered him. Shawqi denounced him to the police, and they raided the place. Muhammad was furious, two policemen took him back to his parents. The next day Shawqi knocked at their door. He told them that Muhammad's voice was too beautiful to let it go astray; your son needs musical and poetic training, he said. Shawqi, the great Shawqi, wanted to take him to his home, give him a room, take charge of his training."

"I know all that."

"He denounced him, then he adopted him. Imagine the first time Muhammad came to Shawqi's place; imagine how powerful their relationship must have been. Muhammad became who he is on that basis, the basis of that deep relationship. Like you and me."

"So?"

"So—nothing, if you don't want to understand. A pair like that: they need to have blind trust, a bond . . . it might be something unclear, I don't know. But exclusive."

"You don't want me to write for Muhammad, is that it?"

"I'll abstain from singing poems by Ahmad Shawqi."

I said nothing.

"My voice will die with me, and all that will be left will be bad copies on 78-r.p.m. records. But what is this voice singing? One long poem. That's all that will remain."

"Are you offering me eternal life?"

"Be quiet."

"Listen, neither one of us is master of our relationship; it's the relationship itself which leads us, more than we lead it. We can't decide a single thing in that regard; the relationship will decide."

I would not split with Muhammad a second time, I did not want to, whatever the cost. She sensed this and was silent. I saw scorn in her eyes, but also something that looked like respect.

I said nothing to Muhammad but he realized that the reconciliation with Mounira hadn't helped a thing between him and my peasant girl. To put an end to this ridiculous quarrel he sent her a poem, *I Was at Peace*, and suggested he set it to music for her. She didn't reply. The poem was a gift, she could do what she liked with it. She gave it to Qsabji, who composed the melody. She recorded the song at Gramophone, the rival of Beidaphone, which was Muhammad's record company. "The Star of the Orient rejects the advances of Muhammad Abd al-Wahab," announced the newspapers.

Cairo very quickly grew accustomed to the violence of this

rivalry. Muhammad didn't want to talk about it, so others spoke about it for him. *Rose el-Youssef* supported him; *Akhbar el-Yom* took sides with my diva; the rest of the press followed suit. Once again two clans were formed, and the public was divided. In the end I was the only one who didn't belong to either camp, and I went on writing for both of them. This was something she accepted only with difficulty. My response was, *You Are Angry With Me*, which Qsabji set to music, and *My Paradise Is in Your Love*, to a melody composed by Da'ud Husni.

Muhammad had something else in mind: a major festival of Arabic music which King Fu'ad had decided to host in Cairo in order to reconcile the music of the East and of the West. The greatest musicians in the Arab world had been invited to share their art and embrace each other's traditions. For the ruling party, the event would serve to glorify Egypt: Pharaonic, Arabic, Islamic, modern, open to the West. Muhammad felt both strains of influence in his own blood, and this festival was the event of his life.

"The West has only two modes, major and minor, and look at the wonderful results they have achieved. And we possess an infinity of modal formulas. Just imagine if we could establish an oriental harmony! There would no longer be anything stopping Arab music from shedding its local character to become universal! All that's needed is to adopt a single musical scale. And in exchange we could begin to use the piano in our orchestras, and introduce wind instruments like the flute or the clarinet."

I couldn't follow, didn't really understand a great deal; she didn't seem to care. The issue filled page after page in the press. Musicians and composers were tearing each other apart by means of musical scales, and equal or tempered quarter tones. Like me, the general public couldn't follow. But there was a political angle to the affair. Traditionalists accused modernists of wanting to sell the Arab world to the West: "By inviting the Franco-English masters to come and teach a lesson to the little native pupils, the so-called partisans of progress are preparing a festival for colonized peoples." Muhammad had become the leader of the innovators. "Rather than being pushed into it by force and letting ourselves be invaded in an anarchical way by Western music," he wrote in *Rose el-Youssef*, "it would be preferable to find an intelligent way to negotiate the turn. Contrary to what the old turbans might think, the best way to preserve tradition is to give it new life and integrate it into a larger ensemble."

My peasant girl refused to get involved in the debate. Her stance enraged Muhammad. He no longer mentioned her name: she had ceased to exist for him.

But not for long. Her declared neutrality would serve her well. She received a letter asking her to do the closing act at the Opera Festival in Cairo, in the presence of King Fu'ad and all the foreign delegations. The invitation placed her above the fray, and she accepted humbly. She'd learned to play the new game.

She summoned all the poets and musicians she worked with. The festival was a world-class event, and she wanted everything, tradition and modernity, to be united in one person: herself. As I was used to writing in the utmost privacy, I stayed away.

During the weeks which followed, I could not compose a single thing. Time went by and nothing came to me. At night, shut in my room, I sweated over the page. I read ancient poetry, I tried to free my spirit. But in the middle of the night what I finally managed to compose were poems in a classical language, unsuited for songs. I kept them for my third collection, which was in a preparatory stage.

Rather than stimulating me, urgency paralyzed me completely. And yet I couldn't give up. The idea that my diva might not perform a single one of my poems at such an event was unthinkable. But how would I manage under such pressure?

Muhammad lost the round. The festival decided overwhelmingly to favor the traditional repertory, to the detriment of the debate on the future and the harmonization of musical modes. Worse than that, the most innovative musicians had been left out. Even Qsabji had not been invited! Disgusted, Muhammad left for Iraq. My peasant girl devoted her time to the closing ceremony. She was downright annoyed with me.

"If you can't write, look through your old poems. Maybe there'll be one from the time when I did inspire you."

I began leafing through the texts I'd offered at one time or another to the recording houses. I found one which seemed suitable. *I Loved You for Your Voice.* The poem was constructed in such a way that you would wonder right through to the end whether it was talking about the voice of the lover or of the country. I'd forgotten about it, and no one had ever sung it. I showed it to her. She accepted it enthusiastically and asked Qsabji to compose the music.

And then the magic was there again, right away, that capricious magic that bound the two of us. And Qsabji. Rehearsals were a moment of grace the like of which we hadn't known in a long time. She had only to listen to the melody taking shape to give herself. I loved you for your voice; indeed.

4

I RAISED MY EYES LIKE A DROWNING MAN. The huge opera theater was a sparkling globe, and we were inside it. Everything
seemed false to me. The gigantic chandelier hanging from
the ceiling shone a golden yellow light over the velvets and taffe-
tas, sliding over the worldly hubbub of voices, over princes,
emirs, dignitaries, leading experts of the music world. The king
and queen had just taken their seats in the first row. Like in a
puppet theater, the lights began to dim the moment they sat
down.

She appeared in the gap as the curtain opened, all at once,
an incandescent column, a white tower whose sequins caught
and radiated the light. Earrings, necklace, brooch—all dia-
monds. A bride.

Behind her, the musicians, instruments in hand. The opening curtain seemed to have surprised Qsabji just as he was moving. He didn't dare move any further, he was halfway between
standing and sitting, as if he were seized by an untimely lum-
bago. He alone seemed real, I wanted to wave to him in particular, but his eyes were blinded by so much darkness. The
applause subsided and he sat down, put his arms around his
lute, regained his composure. Among the other musicians,
Sami al-Shawa was on violin and Muhammad al-Akkad on
cithara. The trio who had accompanied her at Safia Zaghlul's
were together once again.

She did not raise her head until after the instrumental introduction, when the music receded briefly, waiting for the

moment when her voice would bring them back together all of a sudden, in the background. She began. *"If I could be his ransom / If I could / If he respects my love / He is . . ."* she held the last syllable, made it vibrate endlessly on her tongue, lost it as she exhaled. A murmur of approval came in response. She started again at the beginning, stopped at the same point, *"He is . . ."* began yet again, already entranced, and yet again, until at last the entire phrase was set free: *"He is . . . the king of my heart."* It was a poem by Al Masri that she had dug up; Sheik Abu al-Ela had set it to music, she remained faithful to the master in spite of everything. In Arabic, heart is *Fu'ad,* King Fu'ad, king of my heart, she had addressed her compliment to the prince with this play on words. She had won. I could see from the way she held herself, her smile full of pleasure. Her voice became more assured, more sensual. She finished her first song under a hail of cheers.

She held out her scarf to the audience. Other singers had tried to imitate her gesture, but it was only in her hands that the gesture became holy. A square of fine cloth, an object of sacrifice, knotting together all the waves: all through her concerts she would squeeze it, offer it to men with the tips of her fingers, tear at it with her nails. A trance came over her, so strong and radiant that she could move even this formal audience, little by little. She sang the four poems she had selected, managed to capture the inhabitants of the golden cave, to keep them tight in her fist, her silk scarf.

I Loved You for Your Voice she saved for the end. She squinted to see in the dark, saw me. She smiled at me, Qsabji's lute solo enveloped her. The dizziness reached equilibrium, her lips opened and her voice rang out like a liana being stretched— supple, long, solid. She was singing for the king, I was in the axis, all she had to do was raise her eyelashes slightly to move her gaze from him to me. I saw that long white flame on the stage, searching my eyes. When she finished singing, something inside me no longer responded. The audience were on their feet, but I was no longer there.

Muhammad still hadn't come back from his tour, but from Baghdad he had forwarded a scathing article to *Rose el-Youssef:* "Our worthy festival-goers went their separate ways without managing to come up with a single tonal scale. Yet that was the essential condition. The impact of the failure must not be ignored: Arab music has missed its appointment with history and is condemned to vegetate in an imitation of the past for the rest of its days."

The article was illustrated with a portrait of Muhammad, a grave expression on his face. On the same page was a large dazzling photo of my diva receiving the acclaim of the audience at the Opera. The contrast was striking. She opened the newspaper and closed it again. I could sense her secret jubilation. She probably had nothing against Muhammad personally. But she needed an adversary, the greatest possible, to live and carry on, incapable as she was of stopping.

"The poet who humiliated the Star of the Orient": the headline was spread across the front page of the *Rose el-Youssef.* Outside the newspaper stands, piles of newspapers spilled from their severed strings. I took one. I had a strange presentiment: the article mentioned me. "For the closing session of the festival, the Star of the Orient chose *I Loved You for Your Voice,* by her favorite poet, and the song received the welcome it deserves. What people don't know is that the poem was offered to Muhammad Abd al-Wahab several months ago, and that he declined it. His Majesty King Fu'ad, the foreign guests, and the Opera audience were treated to second-hand work." There was a caricature of me in a lopsided tarboosh, handing a rolled sheet of parchment to my diva. Muhammad in a bow tie calls out, "You're giving her my poem!"

Everything the paper said was true. The scene played again in my mind. We are in his house, both of us standing, he's going over the poem, then he puts it on the table, turns it down. It wasn't worth it anymore. The memory buried deep in a corner of my brain . . . that is where it had always been. Panic left me feeling curiously absent. I burst out laughing.

Muhammad was back from Iraq. He gave me a distracted look. I exploded.

"You're the one who told *Rose el-Youssef*, no one else could have!"

"You're losing your mind. Of course it was me."

"You're nothing but a bastard. As if you didn't know what they'd do with it, as if you didn't know them!"

"You're a bloody bore in the end. This woman is terrorizing you, making your life impossible. You're so spiteful that you knowingly gave her that poem. You were dying for a way to take your revenge, and you found one. And you won't even admit it to yourself!"

She was in the living room, the open newspaper in her clenched fists. She raised her eyes and shouted across the room: "Is this rubbish true?"

"I've come to give you an explanation."

"I don't want your explanation. I just want to know if it's true or not what this rag has written."

"A year ago, I showed Muhammad a text which was similar . . ."

"Similar?"

"No. This text, *I Loved You for Your Voice*. The same text. But I'd forgotten."

"Forgotten? This text . . . this same text—you did this to me?"

She'd dropped the newspaper and was wringing her hands.

She began to repeat the same phrase, hypnotically. I took a step in her direction, talking to her to try to break the cycle.

"Remember? You yourself asked me to go through my old papers."

She wasn't listening anymore. Her eyes gazing inward, she continued her soliloquy.

"That text, that very text. For my evening. You. A poem that Muhammad had spat upon. That same text."

She was frightening. Behind me, Saadiya was sobbing. My diva went on muttering the same phrase, her voice changing, becoming inhuman. I drew closer and grabbed her arms with my hands, to shake her, to break her delirium. She started as if I had burned her with a red-hot iron. What she shouted at that moment still rings in my ears today, still reverberates again and again inside my skull, never finding its way out:

"Don't touch me! Don't come near! Don't ever come near me again! I'm sorry I ever met you!"

5

T HE KING WAS IMPLICATED IN THE AFFAIR. She had to provide an explanation. "I didn't know this poem had been offered to someone else. I was deceived. I owe my excuses to His Majesty and his guests. I'm very sorry. I should have been more vigilant. There was no way I could have been aware of this betrayal."

"Let's start from the beginning again. The poet—"

"—I'd rather not hear his name. I met him eight years ago, and I trusted him blindly."

The sweat soaking my shirt smelled bad. I forced myself to reread what was written: *deceived, betrayal, not hear his name.* And she went on:

"The harm has been done. I can't repair it now."

"How do you explain—"

"I'm not explaining anything, I don't understand myself how this happened. He wanted to destroy me. I don't know why. Betrayal is second nature to him."

"You mean you won't work with him anymore?"

"I mean I do not know him."

A boundless rage was hardening inside me, rising in my throat, suffocating. "*Betrayal is second nature to him.*" She was saying this about me! I had hidden her in my eyes, I had made her with my hands! Here in this newspaper, in this interview, she was accusing me, for everyone to see! I sat down at my desk. I seized my pen, some paper. What I wrote was dictated by hatred.

Who are you?
To hurt my dignity
To humiliate my honor and my tears
Who are you
A woman who loves only herself . . .

I spelled it out to her, verse upon verse, the untouchable woman. To stay on my feet.

I signed the poem and slipped it into an envelope. The sun was beating down. At the corner newsstand I bought a stamp and posted the letter. I walked along the sidewalk, aimlessly. The dusty light filled my head. I went past a first intersection, then another, walking faster and faster. With each step I became lighter, as if I were about to take flight. A new feeling was progressively replacing the void that had been created. A dark liberation, exuberant and ferocious.

Muhammad opened the door. He had probably read the interview. He was searching for words, and I interrupted him.

"Don't worry about me. I don't care."

He went to fetch something to drink.

"I was keeping myself from living. That's all over with now."

He did not dare to reply.

"What are you doing today?"

"I have to leave for Alexandria in an hour. I'm giving a concert, this evening. Unfortunately."

"Why unfortunately?"

"I would have liked to have stayed with you."

"I'll come with you."

"Are you serious?"

"What is there to hold me back?"

We looked at each other. He caressed my shoulder, awkwardly. He was trying to understand what I was made of.

The evening was magnificent. His lute broke all the rules, the women besieged him. He invited two of them to stay behind. He took us to the casino, handed out chips, lost a great deal of money. At four in the morning it was too early to go to bed. He led us to a deserted beach, and what happened there seemed so simple.

Tuesday morning, on the way to the library, I stopped at the newsstand to buy *Rose el-Youssef*. On the front page I found the poem I had sent her, framed in black. *Who Are You?* with my name at the bottom.

6

I KNEW EVERY SINGLE DAMP SPOT along the beams supporting the ceiling: the deformed body, the dog's head, the pud-
dle of blood; they sprang to my eyes the moment I awoke,
and when I closed my eyes again it was too late. The instant
between dream and reality had crumbled. My nightmare lasted
longer than the night.

My suffering returned like the heat of an oven lit every
morning, something I had to live with. I was the June bug that
wiggles its feelers uselessly in the air, I would have liked to lose
the thread of memory leading to today. Or to skip the present
moment, so it would become the past, now and forever. But
that was impossible.

The words would begin to beat in my brain, swinging from
one side to the other: "*I'm sorry I ever met you.*" A sinister
nursery rhyme. I could hear it in her voice, and she would not
be quiet. I saw her—her black eyes, her scornful, angry lips. So
my rage would surface, as strong as my pain; stronger. It was
lashing my blood, giving me the strength to open my eyes. My
rage alone kept me alive.

When the light reached the edge of the bed, a faint scratch-
ing at the door told me it was time. For three weeks now, without asking a single question, my sister Salwa had been bringing
me my breakfast; I had stopped going down to the kitchen. My
mother was too old now, and Salwa had taken over the household. I waited for her steps to recede, then I opened the door
a crack, took the tray, and shut myself in again. Bitter and

sweet, the tea was welcome, the only thing I touched. I slipped into the bathroom, prepared myself hastily. Then I got dressed, pulled my beret on my head and went down to get the tram for the National Library.

As soon as I closed the door to my office I was isolated from the world. There were papers scattered before me; I sat and watched the endless flow of the Nile. My colleagues did their utmost not to disturb me, and when they had to, they always avoided my gaze. They all acted as if they knew nothing, but they all knew.

Then they left the office, and my bad dream returned. My eyes no longer saw the river; compulsively, my hands seized the smooth stone paperweight. I hadn't really grasped what was happening, and still couldn't. I'd come back from Alexandria—free, at last I was free. I'd read my poem, the newspaper had soiled my hands, I'd collapsed. Who are you. Her adversaries thought they had recruited me; how innocent. For me, the war was over. I had burned all my boats. I wanted nothing. Only my room, and to be forgotten.

I saw history unfolding before me again, a labyrinth, a forced march, I hoped I could find a breach, a detour, the possibility of another version: I always wound up facing the same wall. There was nothing for it but to start over.

The library clock chimed six o'clock and brought me back to earth: another motionless day had passed. Exhausted, the shadow that I had become headed for the family home, hugging the walls.

A dog's head, a deformed body . . . the spots on the ceiling began to move, changing shape and color. How many months had gone by, two? I hadn't written a thing. To translate my suffering into poetry had been an error. I should have realized long ago: the infernal machine had no other fuel. Pain, raw feeling. I would have done better to swallow my pain, turn my back, and leave. I should have. But every time I wanted to take some distance, she would run after me and take my hands. She'd tilt her head back and murmur imaginary words of love—my own verses. I could hear my own distress in her voice, and I was losing my mind. And every evening that distress, that sorrow passing from me to her: her entire body embraced it and tossed it out in broad daylight for all to see. Those who crowded together in the theaters and concert halls, who applauded her unendingly, took their sustenance from my substance. I was a happy idiot who felt like a lover. How many times did I go back to her for that instant of reassurance?

I learned to be silent, to disappear. Not a single verse, not a word. I would rather my pain were twisted into a pure loss, even if it ended up suffocating me.

And she was suffocating me. The blades of the fan rotated slowly above my open eyes. They did nothing to relieve the heat or my distress. Just once, three weeks after the scandal, Saadiya came. "Don't speak a word to anyone, as God is my witness, I came here in secret to get news of you, and set my mind at ease." Salwa had sent her away again, rather coldly, and later repeated her words to me. Perhaps it was true that Saadiya's love for me was sincere.

Since then, not a sign, nothing. Perhaps she too had understood. So much the better. She must have headed off again into her whirlwind, my hole had closed over again, she was surely busy devouring new faces. As for me, time had to go by. I had to keep telling myself that with each passing day I would be farther from the site of the shipwreck.

Someone knocking gently on my door: it wasn't time yet. Night had filled the room. Another gentle knock, and Salwa's voice:

"It's Qsabji. Do you want to see him?"

Him again. A long silence. Then the murmur again:

"You can't go on like this. It's been three months. God heals all wounds. It's the fifth time that Qsabji—"

A deep sigh from the other side of the door. Her steps grew fainter, vanished, then came back. Salwa again:

"He's left. He said he'll try again next week. And every week."

Another sigh.

"Do you need anything?"

"No."

I could hear my youngest nieces and nephews galloping along the hall, the children of my other sister: they thought my door was open. Salwa hushed them. The silence returned. I was bathed in my own sweat.

I did like Qsabji but I just couldn't bring myself to see him. He would have talked to me about her. One evening we were on our way out of the Bosphorus where she had been singing, and I walked along with my eyes to the sky and Qsabji, weighed down by his lute, looked down at the ground. After a long silence, he spoke as if to himself alone:

"You see, all that acclaim rising up to her from a dark hole, like a roar, there's something really violent about it . . ."

I walked along without speaking.

"Her body takes it in, registers it, night after night. But she's going to have to find a way to unload that violence somewhere else, to get rid of it . . ."

I'll always remember the way he looked at me, sad and bright, from beneath his hunched shoulders.

" . . . even to people who haven't done a thing to her."

Another evening he put his lute away during the curtain calls, very quickly, as if he were headed on to another appointment. A bit later I came on him sitting behind the wheel of his car, headlights off, outside the theater. He was embarrassed and put an abrupt end to our conversation. I stopped a few meters further along. I saw her come out of the theater and get

into a waiting taxi. Qsabji started his motor and, without turning on his headlights, followed the taxi. He was following her
to find out where she was going! He was attached to her, he
was jealous!

At that time the press was beginning to take an interest in
her most insignificant deeds and gestures. The papers had
announced secret marriages with Ali Baroudi, who'd taken her
to Baghdad, or with a certain Nabil Ibrahim, a landowner, or
with Abd al-Rahim Badani, an impresario, or with the sculptor
Mahmoud Moukhtar; or with me. All these supposed unions
were subsequently denied, but that did not prevent new
rumors from arising, week after week. It might have been
enough for me to trail her as well. I would have known.
Perhaps only a step away there was an entire parallel world.
Perhaps there was a man she was seeing, or even a woman?
Perhaps she turned into someone else? How many lives were
there within her life? Suddenly, I was frightened. I decided to
pursue the matter no further. I looked at Qsabji with rage and
envy, and jealousy too. For nothing on earth would I question
him. Perhaps he knew. This notion distanced him from me; yet
he had always shown me a constant friendship.

I had fallen asleep. The neighborhood was totally dark and
silent. There was nothing that could have woken me in this
way, with a start, in the middle of the night. Unless it was her;
her hand, still secretly searching within my heart. All this time
gone by, and nothing getting better. When would it come to an
end, when? I wiped the sweat from my brow, lit a match,
checked the movement of the hour hand on the face of my
watch. Darkness returned. Sitting in bed I contemplated the
ghost of my chair, of my deserted desk. I got up, went to the
kitchen, poured a glass of water. I stood by the window. The
city was deathly quiet. I went back to bed. It was too late: the
endless spiral had started again.

My hands sought the metal frame of my bed to cling to, to fight the dizziness. Enough. I had to be done with this, I had to breathe deeply, banish all the images, all the thoughts. I was slowly killing myself. The only solution was to squeeze my eyelids tight shut, clench my teeth, become abstract, sink slowly into the bed, forget myself one cell at a time, and try stubbornly to dissolve into the darkness of sleep.

Seated in my chair was a motionless form, facing me: a man. I closed my eyes and opened them again. He was still there, silent, a cigarette between his fingers. Despite the semi-obscurity, he might have noticed. He leaned toward me.

It was Muhammad. Leaving me no time, he pulled back the curtains and pushed open the shutters. A violent light entered the room, made of painfully pure air.

"What are you doing here?"

"And what are you doing?"

His voice echoed in my skull. Nothing on earth would get me out of bed. Salwa came in, humbly, carrying a heavy tray. Her fingers tidied up here and there as she passed. She went out without closing the door, creating a draft. I could hear her at the end of the hall telling my little nephew and niece to leave.

"In Paris, you slept on the mattress on the floor and I slept on the box spring with my lute. We spent the night like that. I was dozing and you were trying to write a poem. You read it to me and I improvised the music as we went along. You wrote, *"It's true that you are beautiful / It's true that I love you / But I must tell you / Above all / I love only myself."*

He began singing quietly, his voice so pure.

"I recorded that song as soon as I got back to Cairo. I'd bought it from you for fifty piastres."

He was looking at me. He lit another cigarette.

"Do you intend to live or not? It's been seven months."

I wanted to reply but my eyes filled with tears. He turned away.

"You got a beating and you fought back. Then you locked yourself up in your room. I don't understand."

He stubbed out his cigarette.

"I came to see you, and you didn't want to see anyone. I came back every day. You needed time, I gave you time. Nothing doing. The world doesn't exist for you anymore. You've been depressed, that's what. Come on, get dressed."

I didn't move. His lips were trembling.

"I'm going to die of boredom. Don't you want to get up?"

He stopped trying to make me talk, and paused.

"Qsabji told me she's leaving for Morocco tomorrow. The whole gang is going with her to the airport. I think if you went along, just like that, without thinking, she'd be overjoyed. And everything would work out."

He saw how I went pale.

"I'm not insisting. It's your business."

He held out his hand. I wanted so much to tell him. But he was leaning toward me, ready to leave. Except for a sprinkling of white hair on his temples, he hadn't changed. Sheik Abu al-Ela's prediction had come true for him too. He had become Egypt's foremost composer. His ambition to raise Eastern music to a universal level had come to a sudden end, but it had made him known throughout the Arab world. His voice knew no borders, he could do anything. He composed relentlessly, sought to incorporate foreign instruments, failed, started over. The Singer of Princes and Kings: that was his new title. Life remained a festive occasion for him. When he turned his back and walked away, I realized how much I had missed his vitality, his detachment, his craziness.

My door was closed again. Shutters and curtains shut tight, merciful darkness. For a brief moment I had thought that

Muhammad's visit had done me some good, but in fact it had only re-opened the wound. A past that went back beyond our break had burst into my room—those happy days, she's holding my hands before she goes out on stage, her eyes imploring me, she's holding my hands again afterward, full of wonder, I catch a whiff of her sweat from the concert, she's deeply grateful, as if she's about to throw herself onto my breast. I can see her in her home, offering Qsabji a tie spotted with oil, tying it around his neck, gravely explaining to him that it's the latest fashion in Paris, bursting out laughing at how intimidated he looks, even though all the while he's insulting her and trying to get rid of the tie. She is laughing. This woman was all my days, all my nights, nine years of my life. My body was racked with a painful nostalgia. Her absence had become intolerable. I was separated from her by an incomprehensible barrier, words that could never be unspoken. Once again the episodes of the crisis unfolded in my mind, a path I was forced to take, with no way out, a perpetual death sentence, for eight months now. Blind forces had ordered everything. Muhammad was my friend, as always. He had shown me that he was faithful; but I couldn't do it.

As for her . . . no. My anger returned, suffocating, a pain in my stomach, a sharp stake. The events leading to the abyss had followed one upon the other with such perfect precision. As if it were fate.

7

I OPENED THE DOOR AGAIN and headed quietly for my room. I'd tried to go out, but hadn't managed. I heard Salwa calling me. I turned around just in time to catch her in my arms, in the middle of the hallway. Her eyes were full of tears.

"Bad news?"

"No, good," she said, smiling. "You've got a letter from Paris."

She handed me a typewritten sheet, slid her arm beneath mine and led me into the drawing room; I hadn't been there for months. The Arab authors and composers of France were awarding me a stipend of forty guineas a month. I shrugged my shoulders.

She looked at me. A tiny, bitter laugh and she moved away, sank into the sofa with her back turned. I sat next to her. She was crying.

"Salwa, why didn't you tell me?"

It was absurd. Nobody had been able to speak to me for ages.

"How much is left of the inheritance?"

"The last guineas were spent two months ago, for Mother's funeral."

Her intonation was strange, flat, as if she could not swallow. I was floored. If I included my two nephews, there were six mouths to feed. Inflation had eaten away at my salary, and I hadn't sold a single poem. Salwa was in charge of the finances. She made regular withdrawals from the little sum our father had bequeathed to us. We had always lived very modestly; while I was gone, we had become poor.

"I'm sorry."

She turned around abruptly.

"What do you mean, sorry? What the hell are you talking about? Look at my hands!"

Her hands. Her nails broken, her fingers wrinkled, from squeezing the mop.

"You don't notice a thing! She's made a fortune thanks to you, millions, and yet you—she was only paying you two or three guineas per poem, if that!"

"Shut up!"

"You closed your eyes on her sordid miserliness, nothing was beautiful enough for her!"

Collapsed in a little heap on the sofa, shaking and jerking, grown prematurely old, Salwa held back her words with rage.

"Calm down. I'll find a way. I'll solve our problems . . ."

She pushed me away violently. Her eyes were dry.

"It's not up to you to deal with that. You've never known how. I'm going to tell you what I think. I think you married that woman in secret, like the papers said. I think you got married and then she jilted you!"

She couldn't stop talking.

"You're too soft. You don't even dare ask her for the money she owes you, and she rejected you the way a concubine is rejected and all you can do is stand there sniveling."

I still had my jacket on, and my beret on my head. I went like a sleepwalker to the door. She ran after me, calling my name. I'd already slammed the door.

The white and yellow lights on the opposite riverbank scattered their reflection across the entire river until they reached me. Sparkling, bouquets of palm trees, shadows of feluccas: the exoticism of the ordinary offered itself to me, gently, patiently. I was truly there, on the edge of the Nile, caressed by the warm air, stunned as if someone had punched me. The voice of the wounded man inside me was distant, strangely distracted. I no longer had the strength to suffer. I had been immersed in this love for too long; even my suffering had drained away.

I walked along the quay. This was the way to the tram stop, I came here every day without noticing it. People walking, passing by: I hear their laughter, the rustling of their clothes. White galabias, colored robes, promises. I headed suddenly to the right, into the deep narrow warrens of apartment buildings. The streets were emptier, the dust of the desert lingered in the halo of the street lamps, I was back in the material reality of the city, the humble, mineral reality which outlived everything. Salwa was like that, something so dogged about her that she could not be swayed, a blind and stubborn persistence. I couldn't hold it against her. She had been hiding the situation from me for months, and it hadn't been difficult to do. I had closed my eyes and ears, thinking only of myself. I had hardly realized that my mother was dying. Even at her funeral I behaved like a zombie.

Heat rose to my face, tears to my eyes: I started walking forward again, my life adrift. I had to go home, put an end to this. But the feeling of absence didn't leave me; a febrile energy continued to push me forward, like a desire to fall.

I raised my eyes. A horrid slum, dark streets, the rotting smell of gutters: my steps had led me into the outskirts of the working-class neighborhood of Imbaba. I'd wandered there by chance, no matter where I looked I saw nothing familiar. Only the darkness, hiding me. I walked slowly back the way I had come; the small streets gave me indifferent choices. I stopped again, hesitated, dead tired. I chose a path, began to move forward, a shadow among shadows, but the street seemed to stretch out indefinitely. The pavement full of potholes had given way to a dirt road winding its way among hastily con- structed cob-walled houses. Perhaps my distraught soul, to find its way, needed to be here, in the midst of these rubbish carts drawn by donkeys and which seemed to emerge as if out of nowhere; and these eyes shining as I passed, and all this pover- ty. There was no light, except for the flickering of gas lamps inside the houses. I paid no attention to curious gazes, to inter- rupted conversations, to the shuffling of children in the dark. This time I was truly lost. I went to the children to ask them the way. They ran away, then stopped, came back, began to observe me all over again. I turned first this way, then that. The dark blue sky was completely cloudless, curiously clean above so much filth. A fine crescent moon had appeared. She used to say, I love the moon when it is waxing, I love that which has a future. I noticed a glow on the horizon, the lights of Cairo, to which I had turned my back. I stayed a moment longer, bidding farewell. I set off again in the right direction—but was it the right direction? One small street after another, darker and darker. The labyrinth was running wild, I could no longer tell my right from my left. The men I met along the way seemed so ghostly that I did not dare go up to them. What would I say to them? Please, can you tell me how to get out of here? That was a question they were probably asking themselves.

I was astonished how big the slum was, like a fungus prolif- erating along the side of a neighborhood that was already poor—a disgrace that was not on any map. I hadn't even known it existed, nor when it must have sprung up. I had read, like everyone, that the population of Cairo had doubled in just a few years, that the rural exodus had grown rapidly since the crisis, but I had never imagined *this*. Such a concentration of misery without hope, these people crowded together, floun- dering, left to their own resources in the darkness.

The evening call to prayer rang out. It was neither melodious nor restful. A hoarse voice, full of violence. Not singing the sacred text, but shouting it, like a threat. As I drew nearer, the faithful came out of the anthill and walked along in the same direction I was headed, in an ever-increasing flow.

We emerged onto a vacant lot where a crowd had already gathered. In the darkness, the collective prayer recited its infinite murmuring. I stopped. A two-story house on the edge of the lot, lit by brandished torches, served as a mosque. From the balcony the imam had just begun his sermon:

"And the rest of us," he shouted, "carried off by the wind, we have nothing but the blood in our veins, boiling with strength, nothing but our souls shining with faith and dignity, nothing but our lives and this handful of piastres stolen from our children's food! We don't know how to act, nor whom we can turn to!"

The crowd responded with a relentless, chanted shout, which drowned the words of the preacher. "God is great."

"Here, in this country, Arabs and Muslims have neither a place, nor dignity. What have they done to put an end to their condition of salaried workers at the mercy of the English and other foreigners!"

New shouts interrupted him. The torches cast a shadow over the watching faces.

"With surprise and violence inside we observe the idle class lounging, sprawled in sidewalk cafés and spending their time in theaters and music halls. Who are these people? Egyptians like us, Arabs, Muslims! Some of them are cultured and would be better suited to take on our cause. But they don't, because they're fascinated by the West, they want to copy the way they live, the way they dress. They have only one occupation left in life: killing time!"

People began to give me strange looks. My tie, my suit, my beret. Their smudged galabias were a fair indication of their origins, peasants thrown into this incomprehensible melée, this land belonging to no man. Imperceptibly they drew away from me, and I found myself alone in the middle of an empty circle, in the middle of the crowd. I could feel their mute aggressiveness twisting my stomach. Without thinking, I turned on my heels to leave. The mass of people before me suddenly parted to let me through, as if to show me clearly the way out. I did not belong there. I moved forward through a thicket of hostile faces. I heard a few discourteous remarks and tried not to hurry. This dense body of people was driving me out, ignominiously. I felt that it would not take much—a misplaced gesture—for them to change their mind and close around me again.

I left the square at last and began walking quickly, almost running, bumping into people who turned around to glare at me. I was trembling all over. The city must be that way, a sure instinct was guiding me, my own body. At last I reached the first neighborhood with street lighting. In front of one house, the last one, twenty or so men were sitting on the ground, you could scarcely see them but for the whites of their eyes. I slowed my pace, involuntarily. The same faces I had seen outside the mosque, the same peasants. They were listening to music coming from the open windows, a scratchy phonograph. The voice bringing them together was that of my peasant girl. It was one of my poems. *My Paradise Is in Your Love.*

I put the key in the lock. Salwa opened at the same time: "Muhammad and Qsabji are here."

Holding my beret in my hand, I followed her into the drawing room. My two friends acted as if my pallor and my clothing were normal. They embraced me. Salwa left the room. The three of us sat in a circle. Muhammad made up his mind.

"We came because I have something to suggest to you."

Salwa came back with some tea and put down the tray.

"For three months," he continued, "I've been making a film,

The White Rose. A musical. We need short songs that will be an integral part of the action, performed in the film. Like the American musical comedies, but in Arabic. You'll be very well paid."

I shot a lightning glance at Salwa; she lowered her eyes.

"Where were you?" she asked in the midst of the silence.

"In the slum, Imbaba."

"The stronghold of the Muslim Brotherhood," said Qsabji.

I looked at him, not understanding.

"So what do you say about the film?" asked Muhammad.

"I don't know," I replied after a pause. "We'll see."

I didn't know what to add. I got up, they followed suit. They stood there, embarrassed.

"There's one other thing," murmured Qsabji in a scarcely audible voice.

"What?"

"Your diva—she wants to see you."

"Is that what she told you?"

"It's a different matter, today."

"Why?"

"Because she's in the hospital. She has to have an operation. Tomorrow morning."

"So?"

"Under general anesthetic."

Without a moment's hesitation, I put my beret back on my head.

8

QSABJI STOPPED THE NURSE. The door closed behind me. I walked across the bare floor. Between the four walls there was nothing but a hospital bed, and an out-stretched form, white on white. She opened her eyes to look at me. She was crying wordlessly, all at once, and I cried with her. For several minutes, both of us, unable to speak a word. From her iron bed, she asked me to forgive her, and she forgave me. I placed my hand on her lips.

"What happened is over with. It's all forgotten."

"Do you think the operation is that dangerous?"

"In five days you'll be up and about."

She took my hand and squeezed it nervously:

"Do you really think so? Are you sure? And you're not angry with me any more?"

"I am sure. And I'm not angry. Everything will be fine from now on."

The words burned my throat, but they were said. She dried her eyes and blew her nose. She believed me. She was laughing but could not stop crying.

"I want you to understand. You above all. We are creatures of God, and He is the one we return to. I'm not afraid. God gave me this voice, that's all He gave me. Even just for a second. Like absolute love. I am carrying your poem in my blood, I've become one with it. Do you understand?"

"Yes."

"My life began with the Koran, that's why. Whoever recites

the word of God puts himself in the same position as the prophet Mohammed, may God's salvation be upon him. He is standing and his lips pronounce the words which a greater force dictated. I have recited, and reciting has taught me an obsessive exactness. It's tyrannical, and it can hurt. At least accept this feeble excuse: I'm not acting out of selfishness, I don't take pleasure in offending others."

I accepted, I consoled her, I said that I believed her, whatever she wanted. I was myself again. But something hard persisted, something inconsolable, in my still-closed heart.

She could sense it, could not stop sensing it, even after the operation when she left the hospital. The way I had rejected her was as dense as a lead pellet, inside me, incorruptible.

The director of the radio station lowered the microphone to my diva's lips, masterfully, with an aristocratic air, but his fingers trembled with emotion. She gave me a long look. I could see how frightened she was.

"I'll give you the cue," he said.

He went out. Across from her there was no one but me. She had asked me to come for that reason, to be there, sitting a few feet away, her only audience. Qsabji, Shawa, and Akkad were sitting behind her. Her evening gown was for me alone, her deep eyes, her green silk figure, lengthened by the base of the microphone. Behind the glass the director had taken a seat amidst the technicians. He raised his finger, counted the seconds. A red light came on.

She threw her voice into the balance. The *Fatiha*, the first verse of the Koran, her country of origin, whence she had come, long breaths, no other God than God, her eyelids lowered. She did not raise them until the last word, questioning me with her eyes, an infinite panic. I nodded my head, a sign of deep consent. We were speaking the same language. I could see her face regain its composure, the shadow of a smile.

Qsabji played the first notes of the national anthem, *Biladi*, on his lute. Qsabji on his own, dazzling, even for such a martial tune. The violin, cithara, and tambourine joined in, my peasant girl in their wake. "*My country, my country, my country / You are my happiness and my life.*" She ended with a radiant smile. Everything had gone well. She had just inaugurated *The Voice of Cairo*, the only radio station that could be heard as far as the borders of Sudan and the Middle East, throughout all of Egypt, for the first time, through her voice.

The musicians took up their instruments again for *You Have Been So Hard with Me.* I had written it a long time ago, the music was by Sheik Abu al-Ela. She was staring at me, You see, I haven't forgotten a thing, I'm starting all over, from the beginning. "*You're so hard with me / Have you found in the depths of my heart / A remedy against the pain of you . . .*" She could see how I was resisting. Her voice began to implore, her eyes sparkled, there was something to be conquered. But I couldn't. I was protecting myself.

She sang, "*On that happy day / My beloved looked at me / After he'd been so cruel / His heart grew softer.*" It was my evening. I had also written that song, and Da'ud Husni had set it to music. Her rendition had an almost frightening intensity to it, and in her voice was an undertone of mute laughter.

"*You are near to me / My paradise is in your love*": every word in her mouth seemed chosen as if to speak to me. She was heading once again down the original path, the succession of feelings. It wasn't just about the past. At this very moment, she was extracting those verses from my body, projecting them onto the airwaves while her eyes spoke to me. In return, I was experiencing the vertigo of the abyss, the invisible multitude of all those who were listening, their dizzying echo. I was resisting my diva, she had taken up the challenge and was including me in the intoxication which possessed her, her dance steps with an entire nation, a love story being created across the country through my words and her voice.

She had kept the most astonishing surprise for the end. She motioned to Qsabji. He stared at me, a happy gaze, I could see the pleasure he took in surprising me. *I Loved You for Your Voice,* the poem which was the source of our quarrel. She was singing it there, for me, for the inauguration of *The Voice of Cairo,* and for all the world to hear.

It was on that evening that her voice first reached millions of people. Many were hearing her for the first time. *The Voice of Cairo* would change profoundly the way we lived. Until then we had only had local radio stations, and now all one needed was to turn the knob at any time of day or night to find music and news. Not everyone had a wireless, far from it, but there was always the corner café. For the price of a glass of tea, you could hear the 78-r.p.m.s. of Muhammad, Asmahan or Sheik Abu al-Ela broadcast by a radio station which reigned over us all and almost never shut down. There was even a program called, "By Request Only."

Every first Thursday of the month, the new station would broadcast my diva's concert live. On that evening the cafés were swamped, the backgammon was put away, the tables were pulled against the wall. The smoky rooms turned into so many little concert halls. In a stifling atmosphere, amidst the narghiles, her voice wafted over all those men in far-flung towns, across the delta, the entire length of the Nile valley.

That's what I was told. When it was time for the concert, I was invariably to be found in the front row, beneath her gaze. She was radiant on stage, no longer in anyone's shadow. She had a solid enough position now to control the flow, to play the part. She held out her scarf and whispered the secret into the ear of every Egyptian, the endless chant singing the pain of love. Her song was heard in homes and along streets, and in the surrounding air. The little peasant girl had the power to make an entire country live in the climate of her voice.

I stayed in the shadows, my head cool. Competition with the radio was having some dramatic effects: orchestras were laying musicians off, theaters were going bankrupt, doors were closing in the face of newcomers or unknowns. Fortunately, I had the National Library.

The price of my poems had still not changed. Despite what Salwa had said to me, I did not want to ask for anything. For the time being, I was making do thanks to *The White Rose,* Muhammad's film. I spent half my time trying to make ends meet from one month to the next, and the rest of the time following her. I would count my money anxiously, while my photo appeared regularly in the press. My peasant girl had been right about one thing. My poetry was finding its way into the narrowest streets, the tiniest villages. I was penniless, but almost famous.

I would never be able to leave this woman again, and I knew it. But henceforth I would no longer allow myself even the tiniest hope. I had suffered too much. Her success had carried her to the summit, I was there writing for her, and that was enough. She sang before me, offering herself; I could tell that my resistance excited her. In her eyes I read that she would never give up trying to make me yield, ever. A young reporter from the radio asked her one day what I meant to her. She replied: "He is my poet. His fire lights my way."

9

I HAD LEARNED TO ANTICIPATE THE TRAPS AND NOT FALL IN. You promised, you forgot me, you're neglecting me. I would wait until she'd done. My passivity was my rampart, I became smooth. She knew I was lying to her, and there was nowhere she could grab onto me. Every wound in her eyes was my victory. I only feel good with you, with you, with you. She did not want me, she desired nothing from me, she was just waiting for me to bend. I rebuffed all her advances, my back to the wall, a matter of life or death. She'd try again, looking for the breaking point, and this escalation led her much farther than she wanted to go, and me with her. I might have been lying, but I was not playing. I could not yield. My resistance fed upon my true, unshakeable love, as strong as that resistance.

She began asking my advice for everything. The organization of a concert, the launch of a new record, the dress she should wear to go out.

"What do you think? Should I accept a part in a film?"

This was the most dangerous topic of all. Muhammad had become the king of the cinema. *The White Rose* had been a triumphant success; I'd written all the songs. The film had sold from Morocco to Iraq, by way of Lebanon, and had exported the Egyptian accent to all four corners of the Arab world.

"You've got no opinion?"

"No."

I defused all the arguments she seemed to have prepared.

The last time I'd heard her talk about the cinema she'd sworn she'd never take part in a film. But I had sensed her desire, like every time. Forbidden fruit.

"They're offering me a role . . ."

I looked at her as neutrally as possible.

"What's the role?"

That's all she was waiting for. She ran into her room and came back with a blue folder. It was the synopsis: a decent story, something good; she was justifying herself in advance, as if it were me. She was virtually asking me for permission. The action was set in the time of the Mamluks; Widad was the young slave girl of a lord. He is desperately in love with her, and she loves him. Her heart is pure, she sings for him. And he is madly in love with her voice, and sacrifices his fortune to her. When he's lost his last penny he refuses to sell her, yet she is the one who insists. At the slave market the old man who buys her does not succumb to her body, but to her singing. He senses her sadness and returns her to her lover.

"If I've understood correctly, she destroys her men in complete innocence."

"Yes."

"And her voice replaces sex."

"You could see it like that."

"Well, it's right up your alley."

"Would you agree to write the screenplay and the dialogue?"

"That would be no trouble at all."

I set to work and was completely absorbed by the project. On the surface, I kept very close to the synopsis. Widad, a chaste, loving young girl, gave herself with her eyes closed. And with her eyes closed, she caused shipwrecks. She was the slave, and I wrote about her will for power, her perversity, her tyranny. I was telling the story, at last, in my way.

The producers around the table went over the text page by page. There was one thing that concerned them: there were no kisses, and they needed one.

"My partner takes me in his arms and holds me against his chest," she said. "That's the limit."

"A film without a kiss is not a film."

"In the scene around the fountain, I sing, he comes and sits down behind me, and I relax against him. There will be no kisses."

"No kiss, no film."

"Here's what I suggest. He could bring his lips close to mine, and then cut before they touch. That's all I can do."

The producers accepted and moved on to the belly dancers. They found a compromise. The dancers would have their bellies covered whenever my diva was on screen, and uncovered when she was absent. The negotiations continued in this fashion, every inch of the way, for four hours. In the end, she demanded that each point that had been discussed be listed in detail in an appendix to the contract, "Respect for Eastern Traditions." The other clauses guaranteed her forty per cent of the film's profits, an advance of five thousand guineas and the right to veto her male partner, the main actors, and the music and lyrics of the songs.

Widad was presented at the festival in Venice, and earned her a great deal of money. It was the first time she was really earning something.

She took me down to the banks of the Nile, saying nothing, to the island of Zamalek, Mounira's neighborhood. She stopped in front of a large plot of land on Abu al-Fida Street.

"Look, this is my land. I just bought it."

She'd invested everything she had in this place at the center of Cairo: a land of arrival, the dazzling symbol of success. She took off her shoes and began walking across the plot. I watched her, her bare feet reverting to a forgotten way of walking, a wild joy. She was no longer in exile; she had come home.

She changed. Every morning she was on the construction site, in theory to keep an eye on the work. She would touch the earth with her hands, breathe it in from her open palms; she wandered among the builders, giving her opinion on every detail. She had lived for more than ten years on the fourth floor of an apartment block: now she was back in touch with the only thing that has any value in the eyes of a peasant, and she was putting down her roots once again.

I had almost forgotten about Sheik Khaled. There he was, with the blueprints in his hand. He'd left off his turban and jubbah and was wearing a suit and tie. Officially he was in charge of finances but not a cent was spent without his sister's approval. Saadiya was far and away the most excited of anyone. She followed her mistress down the alleyways, repeating her orders, snubbing the masons; she stood in awe, recited formulas from the Koran to ward off the evil eye. Qsabji made fun of her. He told her that the land could only belong to God and that she must watch out for the imps hidden in the foundations. And she believed him.

The construction site on Abu al-Fida Street became a fashionable place. My peasant girl had set up a mat on the edge of the plot, and we would sit there every evening. Qsabji, Sheik Zakariya, and other musicians would bring their instruments. There was also a new composer, Sunbati. He had written the music for one of the songs in *Widad*, a song that had been a surprise hit entitled *Take Me to the Country of My Beloved*. He was a rather reserved man, clean-shaven, impeccable. He had begun his career by composing music for pilgrims on their way to Mecca. And now he was invited to the mat, one of us.

We would stay on long after the workers had gone home, to listen to the musicians. Sometimes she would sing to us beneath the dark sky. I closed my eyes; her voice filled the night. She was building her house. At last. She was thirty-four years old.

One day the villa was finished, "erased" as the masons say. Beige and blue, two living rooms on the ground floor, eight rooms on the second, a veranda looking out over the Nile, a large garden protected by a surrounding wall. We visited it together, she and I, all the empty rooms with their smell of paint and glue. She walked ahead of me, trying to convince herself that this was really her home. Frightened, breaking the taboo by crossing her fingers. It was exhausting for both of us. Just before leaving the villa she touched me on the shoulder.

"On the night of the housewarming, I'd like for you to be here at the entrance with Khaled and me, to welcome the guests."

She had asked me quickly, without blushing. My house is built, I want you to be here next to me, that's all. The knot in my throat melted all at once, releasing a sort of bitter liquid, a languor. She placed her fingers on my lips.

The villa. All lit up, welcoming. I was shaking hands. Writers, musicians, filmmakers, politicians, poets. Their eyes hid their surprise at seeing me there. Mounira al-Mahdia, who had just finished making her first film, *Al Ghandoura*; the aging composer Da'ud Husni accompanied by his protégée Asmahan; Qsabji, Sheik Zakariya, even Muhammad.

Saadiya reigned in the kitchen. Waiters in white jackets served fruit juice. We mingled with the guests. Obeying an invisible signal, they surrounded me. Heads of record companies, program directors, reporters. For months the press had refrained from writing anything discourteous about me. The Star of the Orient had spread her blanket above my head and I had become untouchable. People who had hardly said a word to me a few days earlier were now placing their hand against

my back. I put up with their undignified behavior, smiling with
perfect modesty. But mentally I spat on them, those people
who for so long had mocked my love for her.

I could sense what they sensed. In this game of bluff I was
playing with her, she had just shown her hand. She wasn't
cheating any more. On that evening she had introduced me as
master of the house.

10

THE RADIO HAD BEEN BROADCASTING military music all morning. At noon they announced the news: King Fu'ad had died, during the night.

There were not many people who genuinely liked the monarch, but his death could not have come at a more inopportune moment. One week earlier, demonstrators in rags had invaded Cairo to protest their hunger; there were millions of uprooted people. General elections had been set for the following Sunday, five days from now. Both the secular and Islamic opposition were launching a bitter attack against the British, who occupied the barracks in the cities and in the Suez Canal zone, and who imposed their will upon the country. The sudden death of King Fu'ad could bring about an explosion. The crown prince, Farouk, was only sixteen years old.

In the middle of the afternoon she called me at the National Library.

"Two envoys from the Palace are at the villa. I'm calling from the next room. They've decided to organize the enthronement, as quickly as possible. They want me to sing at the ceremony. What should I do?"

"They're going to lose the elections . . . if they are held."

"I know, but what should I say?"

"Say you need a day to think about it."

"They'll take it as an insult."

She hung up. And didn't call back. At six in the evening, before I left work, I called her. She was out.

The following day I called her again, and she wasn't there. Not a sign from her all day. An evening paper published a photo which showed her climbing out of an official vehicle at the gate of the palace.

The risk of things getting out of hand worried the leaders of the opposition and they launched an appeal for calm. The country held its breath, and nothing happened. Wednesday Fu'ad was buried in great pomp. The dozen or so kings and heads of state present at the funeral stayed on until the next day to attend the investiture of his successor.

I was reduced to following the ceremony on the radio at home together with Salwa. The ceremonial procedure was modelled on that of the British court. In the throne room, the prince raised his right hand and took the oath. His adolescent voice, somewhat tremulous at first, gradually became more self-confident. God, nation, motherland, and it was over. Twenty-one cannon shots were fired, then there were other explosions, a gigantic fireworks display.

Against this background was the voice of my peasant girl. *The Reign is in your hands . . .* I recognized the verses of Ahmad Shawqi. She was singing the Emir of the poets, Muhammad's great protector, for the first time. *Your Reign, young king, restores Egypt to herself.* I could hear that she was smiling. The music was by Sunbati, no doubt. It was neither Qsabji nor Sheik Zakariya, they would have told me. Shawqi the poet, Sunbati the composer, I was out of it altogether.

I rang at the gate. Two eyes observed me through the peephole, but I didn't recognize the face. I said my name. The gate slid open noiselessly. I was led into the first living room. There was no one there, and with all this European furniture, you would have said an exhibition hall. A waiter in a uniform brought me some tea. I asked if Saadiya were there, and his face lit up. I was a close acquaintance. He left off his mask and told me he was a distant cousin from Tammay al-Zahayrah, she had brought him here along with fifteen or so members of his family, and he was discovering Cairo. She had a visitor, I'd have to wait. He went to fetch Saadiya.

She came, stiff in her new dress. Everyone was dressed for the villa, and did not seem at home. She leaned against the armrest opposite me; she did not dare to sit down. She was pleased with the new house, very pleased even, and she seemed completely disoriented. She told me three times that her little girl had built a mosque in Tammay al-Zahayrah, and it had been inaugurated at the same time as the villa; no one could say that she was miserly or thought only about herself.

"Saadiya, what's wrong?"

She sighed again.

"Do you think it was a good idea for her to go and sing for the new king the other day?"

"I haven't a clue."

"The day before yesterday, the opposition won the elections. They say the Wafd will have the majority just on their own."

"People are unhappy."

"That, I understand. But don't you think it will be bad for my little girl?"

"It won't change a thing for her."

"That's what she said. But I can see she's worried. What a pity. Just when she had made an entrance at the palace."

My peasant girl came down the stairs with a European man. She accompanied him to the door then came back over to me.

"Hello!" she said gaily, "I knew you were waiting. I couldn't get rid of that visitor."

"Who was it?"

"An Italian. I'll tell you about it."

I followed her up the stairs. Sheik Khaled had moved his offices to the second floor. Several employees bustled around—it had become a regular little business. She led me out onto the veranda. There were garden chairs and a porch swing facing the Nile. I emptied out my briefcase and laid some papers on the table; we were there to work. I also pulled out the morning papers announcing the Wafd's victory.

"What do you think?" I asked her.

"About what?"

"This."

"I think the people have imposed a historic defeat upon the king and the pro-English parties."

"I think you're right."

A long silence followed.

"I am devoted exclusively to my art, I'm above politics."

"If you're sure of that . . ."

"What are you insinuating?"

She was suddenly white with rage.

"You think I can be bought by anyone? How can you think that? Listen to me. Governments come and go, along with elections, parties, even kings! And I'll still be here, to sing."

She picked up the papers, her anger had not abated.

"One last thing. You know who that visitor was that you saw? The cultural attaché from the Italian embassy, representing a new radio station in Cairo, Radio Bari. They'll begin broadcasting next month in Addis Ababa. He came to ask me to do the inauguration. The kind of radio station you like. Very militant, nationalistic, and anti-British."

"I hope you didn't accept!"

"Why shouldn't I?"

"Because Mussolini just annexed Ethiopia and Radio Bari is his mouthpiece! He's attacking the British because he'd like to take over from them. His radio transmitters are powerful enough to reach all over Egypt. I hope you're not going to put yourself at the service of the rivalry between the great powers? How would that make you look?"

"Like a singer."

"So you said yes."

"Not yet, but they're offering me a fortune."

She gathered up the papers, songs I'd written for her new film, *The Hymn to Hope*. I couldn't care less about all that now. She wanted to pass them on to Sunbati. She claimed in all seriousness that his music was perfectly suited to my poetry.

Radio Bari was finally inaugurated without her participation. The pro-royalist papers congratulated her on having refused to associate herself with an anti-Egyptian campaign; the opposition welcomed her anti-Fascist stance. Everyone seemed pleased. Except me. Just as I was nearing the goal, I'd slipped backwards, and I could understand neither why nor how. To reward her patriotism the palace had opened its gates: she was at all the official ceremonies, banquets, receptions for foreign guests. Sunbati was churning music out for her with a vengeance. Saadiya could not even remember ever having been worried: she was overjoyed. Her mistress was moving among princes and pashas. If she went on like that, she would soon be the Voice of the Monarchy.

11

Y ET SHE DID NOT BECOME THE VOICE of the Monarchy.
Far from rejecting her, the opposition went on to court
her all the more. The Palace had seen what was to be
gained from the elections, and appointed the leader of the Wafd
to be President of the Council. Representatives of the opposition and dignitaries from the court were jostling for power, and
they would spend the evening at her place, glass in hand. The
villa on Zamalek was an image of national unity, a battleground
of a particular kind. To enter the arena, to conquer and be conquered, or even become, herself, the object of this war of influence: that was all she could think of. Without me.

Receptions, society, jewelry all fascinated her, but above all
the royal family: those who secreted power merely by virtue of
their birth. She felt she had an equivalent power within her;
she too owed nothing to anyone, except God.

On Radio Bari, anti-British propaganda was scoring points
with each passing day. It was easy, the British were manipulat-
ing the King, driving the country to ruin; they were blamed for
everything. They were also condemned for their policies in
Palestine. Every night Egyptian Muslim Brothers crossed the
border to help out with the Palestinian uprising.

Eventually, the British made some concessions. They signed
a treaty with the government, limiting the presence of their
troops to ten thousand men at the Suez Canal. The news was
greeted with an extraordinary explosion of joy. No one paid
much attention to the military clauses of the agreement. All

eyes were focused on the spectacle of soldiers evacuating their barracks to the sound of the bagpipes. So, they're leaving? Thanks to my discreet pressure, said the palace, thanks to our unyielding opposition, said the president of the council, thanks to the fighters of Islam, said the Muslim Brotherhood, thanks to Fascist Italy, said Radio Bari. And for all of them my diva sang *Gather together, Oh Egypt,* a poem I had given to her.

Suddenly the press began writing about me again. My peasant girl left for a few days in Ras-el-Bar; one newspaper insinuated that it was to get away from my lamentations, it put it just like that, between two commas, in the middle of an article on life at court. She was the heroine of a melodrama. The clandestine love affairs she was reputed to have, her supposedly Platonic relationship with the king's uncle, her dubious attraction to the man who really held the reins of power, Hassanein pasha, known for his countless mistresses. Every day, every week there was new gossip. I began to suffer again. And I remained like a shadow across the door, feeling down, incapable of going either in or out.

My life became very strange. One evening I came home from work and Salwa told me that I had a visitor. A young woman I did not know; she was from Paris, she was waiting in the parlor. A friend had entrusted her with a letter for me. I ripped open the envelope and all it contained was a blank sheet of paper. I showed it to the young woman and she seemed as astonished as I was, embarrassed, as if it were somehow her fault. She gave me news. She had met my friend at the university, she was taking classes in Arabic literature while she prepared her thesis on Diderot. On Diderot? Her eyes grew bright. Diderot had understood it all before anyone else, in his days the Catholic religion wanted to control the lives of the people just the way our doctors of Islam do, he's talking about us, everything should be translated, the *Pensées philosophiques* to begin with, *La Religieuse, Lettre sur les aveugles à l'usage de ceux qui y voient,* and above all *Jacques le fataliste,* that luminous fable about human freedom. She told me all this, laughing, inexhaustible. She told me about the situation in Europe, she'd been living there for eight years now, now she'd come home and wanted to settle back in, re-conquer the city, maybe translate Diderot. She told me about the films playing in Paris, the plays; she talked about me. She had read my three poetry collections and was eager to see the next one, it was long-awaited. She did not say a word about my diva, and did not associate me with her in any way. I was a classical poet, the translator of Omar Khayyam, a lover of the Arabic language, the friend of her friend.

Her visit brought me no peace, no consolation, but only accentuated my feeling of exile. Another place, another body.

My peasant girl had gone out, I went to fetch Saadiya. I was told she was downstairs.

I had never gone downstairs. The basement was the realm of the personnel, that was all I knew. Light came from the cellar window and bare bulbs, the smell from the pantry rose to my nostrils, something damp and familiar. The space was very large, the same size as the house; to the left were the men's quarters, the women's to the right. Supplies of food were just behind, at the back, an incredible quantity of burlap bags, fava beans, lentils, sugar, flour, giant jars in a row sealed with waxed squares of cloth. It all came from the village, an integral assemblage of people, aromas, tastes.

White jackets and embroidered aprons hung at the entrance; everyone had to put their disguise on before going upstairs. As long as we stayed in the underground world, it was peaceful. I moved forward. There were water pipes lined up against the wall, decks of cards, boxes of dominoes, music. The wireless had the place of honor, right in the middle, on a tall piece of furniture at the end of the wide corridor separating the men and women. On the men's side a sort of small clearing had been arranged. I could see figures sitting in a circle on their heels, chatting, exhaling smoke from their nostrils. They got up when they saw me. I knew most of them—the waiter who had served me the first time, one of the porters, the gardener. I was in their place, at Tammay al-Zahayrah; they went off to fetch the only chair. Saadiya appeared.

She was queen of the basement, the mistress of the hold; she took me off on the landowner's rounds. She strode forward pushing doors open. I suddenly came upon girls having their siesta in each other's arms, or men shaving. Straw mattresses lined the large common rooms, with rows of mats on the floor. Sometimes there was a table, something to heat the tea, a platform of reeds acting as a sofa, an entire house.

"The people from Tammay who come to Cairo all come here—cousins, nephews, grandmothers, it's endless."

A family pension, and she was the landlady. If there was one place in the heart of the capital where things happened the way they were meant to, it was her place.

She even opened the locked door at the very end of the corridor for me. It was my diva's room, her downstairs room. It was furnished like all the others, two straw mattress on the floor, a wobbly table, a reed platform. A mirror hung from a nail at eye level—that was the only detail. And there was a French fashion magazine, with photos.

"She comes here when she's tired of upstairs," said Saadiya simply.

I was stupefied. A secret floor, in here, down below. Saadiya showed me the room as if she wanted to explain something . . . but she herself did not know what.

"Sometimes she plays cards with the girls and me, in the afternoon. Her mother, when she comes to Cairo, can't sleep anywhere else. My little girl has moved her home village here, and no one knows about it. We sleep very well. All we need is a rooster to wake us up in the morning. The palace . . . what can she be thinking . . . it's not the palace that will find her a husband. They'll always look at her as a peasant, and that's what she is . . . and a singer, even worse."

"What are you trying to tell me?"

She didn't reply. She was muttering, shaking her head.

"She's got some strange ideas in her head. I shouldn't tell you . . . She thinks someone from the palace will marry her."

"Who?"

"I don't know! You think she tells me these things?"

"Of course she does! Who is it?"

Saadiya did not reply.

"That Hassanein pasha?"

"Him or another, what's the difference? She's crazy. We're peasants, and that's the truth. No member of the royal family would ever . . . what's wrong?"

I'd turned on my heels. I'd seen more than I wanted to see, heard more than I cared to hear. Everything had fallen back into its dreary place. I just didn't cut it. She was no better. She too was exiled from a bygone past, from an impossible desire. Like me. Without me. Our exhausted love. I'd resisted her advances for months, or at least I thought I had. But in fact I'd yielded. At the door of her villa I'd yielded. Only now did I realize. Because the game was over, and all bets had been placed.

12

"A CERTAIN ABD AL-SATTAR HILALI, farmer in Qena, alarmed by information which has reached him on several occasions announcing the engagement of the Star of Arabic Song, makes it solemnly known that the latter is not in a position to marry for the simple reason that she has been his wife for fifteen years or more. In support of his claim . . ."

My diva tore the newspaper from Qsabji's hands, began to read it herself, her breast heaving.

"In support of his claim, Mr. Hilali has filed a complaint with the Cairo tribunal, demanding that his spouse return to the conjugal home and begin to live with him as in the past. To his deposition he joined a detailed description of the house he owns in Qena (two parlors, two bathrooms, six rooms with running water and electricity) to prove that he has the means to provide decent accommodation for his spouse."

There was a photo showing a peasant of fifty or more, posing in his galabia in front of his house. She had never seen him. Qsabji joked, "It's your fate, your past is catching up with you." She wasn't in a joking mood.

This time the press thought they were on to something tangible. Serious newspapers sent investigators to Qena. Hilali declared he was ready to swear on the generous Koran that this woman was his wife, as God was his witness.

"I never married this fellow, I don't even know his name, it's an attempt to cheat me, he's trying to slander my name, he wants money so he'll shut up and that's all." She repeated the same thing ten times a day as if even we needed convincing. The public only half believed her. Abd al-Sattar Hilali was demonstrating such aplomb that even the most faithful were perplexed. The more categorical my diva's denials, oddly, the more suspicious she seemed.

"Do you know this woman?"

In the dock, the peasant turned his head briefly in her direction, where she was sitting in the first row. Dark glasses, black dress, a scarf around her chignon, withdrawn.

"Naturally. She's my wife."

"Me, Mr. Hilali? I am your wife?"

"Just because you've been successful is no excuse for turning your back on your home. God won't accept it. Were you unhappy with me?"

"But this man is lying! He's making up stories that don't exist!"

"Mr. Hilali," said the judge, "Have you any material proof of this marriage?"

"Of course, everyone knows about it. Neighbors, the family, the neighborhood where I live. Everyone can testify."

"An official document, a marriage certificate, some paper signed by a sheik?"

"I must have that too. I'll have to look."

"The investigation we conducted in Qena did not enable us to find the slightest material element. Until proof to the contrary, the Tribunal will hold your claims to be groundless."

"You're making fun of me. I know perfectly well that I am married to this woman. And she knows it too, obviously. You ought to be ashamed. The oath you took was before God. And you, Your Honor, with all due respect, you're taking that hard tone with me because my wife has become famous and she enjoys the protection of the high up."

"Mind what you are saying!"

"It doesn't change a thing as far as the truth is concerned, Almighty God will vouch for me."

A broad forehead revealed by a turban worn on the back of his head, a wild moustache, his galabia open onto a white cotton singlet: Mr. Hilali would not back down. The tribunal dismissed his case, he counterattacked in the Court of Appeal. It was too much. Incapable of furnishing any proof, he was sentenced to six months in prison and a fine of one symbolic piastre for slander and infringement of privacy.

For the first time in weeks, my peasant girl regained her smile. The transfer of a coin from one hand to the other seemed to her an adequate symbol. And the six months of prison. But she was still shaken. Hilali had put his finger on her origins, mingled her image with his own. He'd soiled her, and she wasn't quite sure how. Now when she walked into drawing rooms, her step would not be quite so self-assured.

From his very first day behind bars, Hilali asked his lawyer to file an appeal with the Court of Cassation. His tenacity astonished me. I realized that this man was *truly persuaded* that my peasant girl was his wife. His fantasy had turned out to be more powerful than his memory. An unmarried peasant woman who belonged to no one: why shouldn't she belong to him, then? Now people were convinced that he was lying and were offended, as if the virginity of their own sister was in doubt. But behind the indignation I could feel that they were curiously understanding, almost complicit. Deep within, a silent voice gave passive support to Hilali, and longed for him to be the winner. This peasant's madness was something they knew only too well; but they had never dared.

The Court of Cassation handed down its verdict quite quickly, barring any new appeal on the part of the plaintiff. As if to put a final stop to the whole business, *Rose el-Youssef* commented ironically: "The Diva will take up with her world again and the peasant Hilali will stay in prison. He'll have time to meditate. He would have done better to seek advice from a certain poet, a specialist in the matter."

She found this very funny; I was at her house with Qsabji and the lawyer Abaza, who'd taken her defense. She looked at me, tried to control herself, she was so happy! This sorry story was over and done with, she was taking the plane in an hour to start on a new tour of the Middle East, just as the newspaper had predicted.

A bit later Sunbati arrived to wish her a good trip. She could not resist the pleasure of reading him the paragraph about "a certain poet . . . specialist in the matter." And she laughed again, with him.

I looked at them and felt all my strength drain from me. I saw things the way they were, and that they would never change. The Hilali affair was also about me, I'd had that intuition from the beginning and now it was clear. The feeling Hilali had inside was the same as mine. The same characteristics, the same family. We had lost, together.

I could let nothing show, I had to bury my hurt the way one buries the truth. I rose to my feet and said goodbye. I saw the surprise in her eyes, she didn't move, gave me a slight wave.

I went out into the street. To lean back against everyday life; to drown myself in it. Hilali at least had been consumed once and for all, had lost for good. Even when he was on the ground he hadn't given up. Now he was quits, for all time.

Salwa asked me what was wrong, took my sleeve, and led me into the kitchen where she had something on the stove.

She added a second place setting on the oilcloth, pushed me down into a chair, and served me. I didn't protest. I watched her eating, she was ravenous. Then she said, "You know Pygmalion?"

I looked at her blankly.

"He was the king of Cyprus, and he sculpted a statue of a woman that was so beautiful he fell in love with it."

"So?"

"So nothing."

I rose slowly to my feet. She stopped eating.

"What did you think of her?"

"Of who?"

"That young woman who brought you the letter from Paris."

"Why do you ask?"

"She just left. I've seen her a few times. We've become friends. What do you think of her?"

"Nice . . . a young little woman."

"She's got a degree in comparative literature from the Sorbonne. And she's unmarried."

"Salwa, there you go."

"What's the matter with her?"

"Nothing. I don't know her."

"Are you still hoping for something else from someone? Aren't you eager for some peace and quiet, for a woman who'd love you no matter what . . . for children?"

"Leave me alone. Anyway, I have no money."

"You've got enough to buy an engagement ring and two wedding rings."

"Are you implying . . . that that's enough?"

"Let me take care of it."

"No. I'll take care of it."

I went to find her. I told her my story, hiding nothing. She listened right to the end then raised her hand and tossed it all behind her shoulder. I began to see her every day. She was lively and fresh, and I felt a tremendous peace in her presence, as if nothing would ever again be serious. I trusted the feeling, light and unreal. My peasant girl was absent, and it was a rest for my soul. Even when the sheik came to the house, it did not seem real. The ceremony was very discreet, but it didn't prevent the newspapers from using it for their headlines. My diva came back from her tour three weeks later, and I was engaged.

She came down the steps from the plane, in her dark glasses, one foot after the other, careful not to let her heel catch. It seemed to take forever.

On the runway, she greeted the representative from the palace, from the government, exchanged a few words, and finally turned to us. She shook hands all round, as was her custom. Then it was my turn.

"So, is it true, what I hear?"

I wanted to reply; at that very moment an airplane started up one of its propellers and the noise drowned out my words. She held her skirt down with her hands to stop it flying up and motioned to the entire group. We headed for the V.I.P. lounge.

Refreshments were laid out for us. She was back in the whirlwind. I stood slightly to one side, glass in hand.

"What is going on?" she shouted suddenly to me. "By the look of you, you really have gotten engaged!"

"It's the truth. I am engaged."

She knew it, but to hear it from my lips . . . She remained poised. She had the right words, the right tone. Toasts were raised to my health, my long life, my future children. All I could see was that her eyes had clouded over. The noise of congratulations quieted down.

"I'd like to offer you a present. I'd like to sing at your wedding."

Her voice broke. No one said a thing; wax statues. She came closer.

"Let me kiss you, just this once."

She wanted to embrace me, I don't know what happened. Suddenly we found ourselves entwined, holding each other close, in tears, in the spotlight. It was the very first time. She pulled away, turned to one side.

"Don't worry, we'll go on working together. What there is between us is stronger than a marriage."

It was true, what she said. We were doomed.

PART THREE

1950-1956

WHEN I TURNED AROUND, there in the middle of the room was a little boy in pyjamas looking at me with a worried air. It took me a few moments to realize he was my little boy.

He said, I woke up and all the lights were on and I went in all the rooms and there was no one, I want my mommy, I looked everywhere and she was nowhere and in the end I saw you on the balcony and I thought you were a thief. I held his trembling little body close, kissed him awkwardly, repeated to him that mommy would be home the next day or the day after, mommy will come back and your brother and sister too, this is just a bad dream, and I felt like crying with him.

I put him back in his bed, he continued to cling to me. His eyes open in the half-dark, his closed fists tight against my shirt, he was afraid that if he slept he would let go. It didn't matter what I was saying, I just mustn't stop; I didn't know any stories for children, so I whispered poems to him, he couldn't understand but it was music, my constant voice against his warm cheek. After a short while his eyelids drooped and his legs began to twitch. I didn't move, my arm across his breast as he slept.

Hoda was a woman of few words. "One song too many," was all the note said that I had found on my return at midnight after the concert. It was on the little telephone table, not even signed. I had walked through the apartment, one room after the other, unbelieving, several times. She had really left, with the two little ones. I began turning this way and that, prisoner of a desert. I went onto the balcony and stared out at the sleeping city. She must have heard the concert on the radio, it was that song. Eleven years of untroubled marriage, dozens of songs, and this evening one song, one too many.

Samir opened his eyes then closed them again; his body perspired; I could touch it; curious stranger. That song—Hoda had believed it: what had she believed? Sitting at the foot of the bed I let the verses fall from my lips: "*Why did you revive my love / My heart had found peace / You lit the fire once again / That your own hands had once put out . . .*" I saw the words in a different light. "*Those happy days / We spent together / You have stayed inside me / With you I've spent my life . . .*" How long did it take her to decide, to write the note and vanish? Calm people are like that, they live for a long time and all of a sudden spill over. "*Why did you revive my love?*" and she had slammed the door. I could not yet fathom what had happened, an entire side of my life I'd never given any thought to was crumbling.

I tried to understand what had been going on in her mind, I forced myself. She must be at her mother's place now. It was three in the morning, I didn't care, I would have called at any time. But she was trying to tell me something by leaving, and I wanted to hear it first of all. I'd spent these years as if in a faint, with her on the one hand and my diva on the other, an unconscious, perfect balance. Eleven years. Outside, there had been war, a world war, the war in Palestine, and all that war had eaten away at our souls. The regime had evolved in the image of its king: obese and corrupt. My peasant girl stood behind the door waiting for it to open, and she sang. She had not abandoned her senseless dream: she wanted the palace to wed her. All that time, out of time, I was writing for her. Never at peace, either one of us. My poetry expressed longing and that longing, in her throat, became the country's. Her voice caressed rage and pain, nostalgia for a world still to come, and which failed to come. Both of us. We reached our hands out to infinity to close them around pure desire, an empty core. Perhaps art is nothing more than the trace left by this absurd endeavor, certain to fail. Khayyam had said as much, blind intoxication is the way.

And all this time, Hoda. Who carried on with life at ground level, busy, although I never saw her, good for running the household, raising the children, but as for true love . . . That verse, written for someone else, *"You have stayed inside me / With you I've spent my life—"*maybe it was that verse. It left no room for her. It took away what little remained of the paltry shared portion, my physical presence. With you . . . my life. That I had written it was not enough: she had sung it on the radio, to the entire country. Humiliation proclaimed, and not by just anybody. I had crossed a threshold. Hoda was gone. Her departure made her exist.

I gently pulled my arm away and stayed for a moment listening to my son's regular breathing. He was in a deep sleep. I took a pillow and lay down on the carpet next to the bed. His breathing calmed me. I'll call Hoda tomorrow, everything will be fine. I'll tell her I've understood.

She refused to take my phone calls; it was driving me mad. I drove Samir to school and went by her place—her parents' place, that is. Her mother received me in the entrance. She whispered that it wasn't a good time, Hoda had to calm down, that would be better, not for the time being, and she shoved me gently back out the door.

I shut myself in my office and spent the day writing her a letter; my wastebasket filled with crumpled drafts. At six, when I got back from the library, I could tell she had come by the house. She had taken all her belongings, and all the children's. Samir was there in his room, leaning over his homework. He answered my questions with monosyllables. His mother had picked him up after school, and told him that in a few days she would come to take him to live with her, she just needed time to get things ready.

I was careful not to react. I went into the living room, then the kitchen. All the household sounds had faded away. I asked Samir if he wanted something to eat, he answered no without raising his eyes, he was doing it on purpose. I opened the refrigerator door and closed it again. There was nothing I felt like eating. Back into the living room, a silence like mourning. I switched on the radio, a record by my diva was playing, "Ya Zalimini," *You Tyrannize Me*, one of my poems. I switched it off again.

Samir's grandmother came to fetch him, it seemed normal to me to let him go, how would I have managed with him? The cleaning woman also vanished, leaving her keys on the kitchen table. I needed no one. In less than a week, confusion had settled into my life. When Abaza the lawyer came to see me he found me in the middle of piles of dirty dishes. From his sorrowful expression I understood that Hoda would not budge. She had asked him to take care of our divorce.

She could leave, and take the children with her, do what she wanted, but divorce? No. I hated the very word. I left the lawyer standing there and turned on my heels. Without thinking, I did the only thing left to do. I forced my way into her parents' house to tell her that I loved no one but her. Her mother tried to come between us, I pushed her aside and went into Hoda's room. She sprang to her feet. This was the same Hoda, pale and cornered, I recognized her, her features had lost the very ability to smile. I leaned against the closed door, my anger drained away. I asked her forgiveness for all these years, you married a dreamer with his eyes glued to a star, I've hurt you, forgive me, there are the children, we are children, we can make a fresh start. I took a step toward her and she backed away. I've been unfair, I didn't realize, it won't happen again, believe me, I promise you. Her face was stormy, there was a suffering that would not let go, and yet she realized. What does sincere mean? I was speaking from deep in my heart, she could see that very well. But at the same time, from even deeper, I refused to admit that my vow would mean giving up my peasant girl. She mustn't ask that of me.

She did not ask. And she did not come back.

I began to guard the house, in the strict sense of the term. Every evening I'd come home to mount guard, to wait for who knows what. Once the door closed behind me I didn't open it again. People knocked, there were phone calls, all so much aggression, to my mind. I didn't respond, or only in the most evasive way; I made sure people wouldn't insist. I wasn't even depressed. I discovered the dark satisfaction of solitude, hours spent doing nothing, disappearing, lying on the sofa in the living room, no one watching me. It wasn't unpleasant. Or if it was, there were no witnesses.

Twice a week, Tuesdays and Fridays, Hoda's mother would drop the children off for the afternoon. I prepared a snack for them, I made an effort. They were there so that I could see them, I had to make every moment active and meaningful, and it was exhausting. Three hours later, when their grandmother came to pick them up again, I was almost relieved. I liked nothing but my walls. I had to make up for lost time. I'd never lived alone, or almost never, only in Paris, so long ago.

Abaza dealt with the paperwork, and I made things as difficult for him as possible. I dragged things out. I kept Hoda's departure a secret, nobody's business but my own. I saw Muhammad or Qsabji when I couldn't do otherwise, as if nothing had happened. It wasn't hard to pretend. With my diva, it was even easier. My universe was so well partitioned that I could be amputated of half of my life and no one was the wiser.

2

S HE WAS ROCKING BACK AND FORTH, distracted; she didn't want to work. Her body coming and going slowly, hesitating a bit more each time, losing its momentum, heavy and absent. It made me nervous. As long as we were dealing with poetry or concerts, nothing transpired, and I could prevent her coming closer. But if she set to dreaming, it was something I wasn't used to anymore, and I didn't want any more silences between us, especially now.

She raised her eyes and looked at me, with so much sadness. She'd found out about Hoda, perhaps Abaza had told her. I steeled myself, unwillingly; I could no longer avoid it.

"I wanted to tell you. I'm sick."

I breathed out. She was always sick. The slightest malaise and she would call Dr. Hifnawi. The doctor's presence had become as familiar as the very notion of a possible and in a way permanent illness. Her state of health was the topic of a regular column in the newspaper, on the same level as her rumored love affairs or secret marriages. When the alarm turned out to be false, no one dared to complain; on the contrary, she was congratulated, as if the fact of almost falling sick had spared her a worse fate.

"It doesn't bother you any more than that?"

"I'm sorry, I've been preoccupied."

"For a while now. I've noticed."

"What's wrong with you?"

"It's called an progressive goiter, a tumor in the neck. It may be cancerous."

She gave me a weak smile. I couldn't bring myself to believe her. Hifnawi had detected something strange in her throat, that was two weeks ago, he'd called a specialist, the palace had brought over two foreign professors and the king's personal physician. They had all made the same diagnosis. A possible cancer. I saw the effect this news might have; I didn't feel it. She spoke to me so quietly however. She had to choose between the Royal Hospital in London and the Bethesda Naval Hospital in Washington. Cancer, throat, vocal chords, risk of dying, of losing her voice. I said the words to myself over and over, trying to scare myself.

"You're not listening."

"It's not that . . . I can't."

She was silent. In her eyes as she looked away there was not even any surprise, only solitude, an unbearable solitude. Nothing, and no one, had come between her and whatever it was that would happen to her. She had said the words, and nothing had happened. To see her abandoned to this solitary confrontation roused me from my lethargy and I reached over to take her hands.

"Why didn't you tell me?'

"You always seemed to have your mind elsewhere."

It was not even a reproach. I remembered finding her brother Khaled seated next to her in the dark one evening, I hadn't paid any attention. Saadiya's red eyes, muffled footsteps, the silence in the house, a host of recent details now flooded back. But for all that I couldn't believe her, really believe her.

"What's to be done now?"

"I have to decide. They have to open up my throat and see, and maybe operate."

She was using concrete terms. To make them exist.

I closed the door behind me, leaned against it, breathless, my bones aching, I felt as if I'd been beaten. Hoda was gone, fortunately, and the children; there was no one for whom I was forced to pretend. I turned on the lights and slowly got undressed. I would find myself standing naked in front of the open refrigerator, by the door to the balcony, on the sofa, stock still in the hallway leading to my room. I don't remember getting into bed, I don't remember falling asleep.

I woke up completely calm. This body on the mattress, gone as far as it could; the space around, that was all that was left for me. Sunlight flooded through the window. I threw off the covers and lay there motionless.

She had always believed that a higher force was paving her way; now the stars had suddenly shifted. I was bound to her, that was no surprise, the same force had been leading me, the same force now let me down. I could not cry. I accepted the verdict in a strange way, did not exclude myself from it. Her vocal chords had vibrated to my own words, I was not innocent. I'd shown my loyalty to the point of renouncing wife and children, and had believed I could fly with one wing, yet believed nothing, merely faithful. Nothing could divide us, except death, or if she lost her voice. Well let her lose it then, let the curse be carried out. I could feel it beating, a sort of consenting fervor for misfortune, provided it was terrible. I'll write no more, I'll disappear, or else my verses will be nothing more than ink on paper. We've talked enough of love in dark halls, the world will vanish, things and people will become gray again, as will I, as will she, among them.

I went back to see her that very day. I took her in my arms and held her there without speaking. She understood that her news had penetrated into my body and that I had finally accepted it. All the awkwardness between us disappeared. The same calmness came over us, a dark and silent exultation. The illness put us back in touch with intense emotion, as during the strongest point in our relationship, or even stronger than then.

Before I went out I told her that Hoda and the children had left home; she didn't ask any questions.

The newspapers were given a medical press release, as the secret had become too heavy to bear. No one could reassure anyone, so the brunt of the anxiety was spread among all of us. If the diva was to have an operation, let all those who were in love with her find a way to bear the burden. Several hundred people gathered in front of the villa and the police had to put up barricades. Newspaper print runs climbed higher. The entire country felt threatened by solitude.

Hoda called me, told me she was with me but that she could not come back, particularly now. Her call touched me deeply. In a single blow I lost both the dream and the reality. I had never felt so free.

Every day the crowd grew larger. My peasant girl came out of her silence and gave an interview to the *Voice of Cairo*. She was not afraid, her fate was in God's hands, it is from Him that we have come and to Him shall we return, she was reassuring, laughing, and she asked that the siege of her house be lifted. People stopped crowding against the gate and went home. Prayers were said for her in mosques, in churches, in synagogues. The prayer was silent, the projectors were switched off, peace returned.

"It's not the operation which scares me, but the idea of leaving my sleeping body in the hands of surgeons who are strangers. I don't know them."

"Don't worry."

"What do you think of Dr. Hifnawi?"

"He's been coming to your concerts for years."

"He's Egyptian. I trust him."

"But he's a dermatologist."

"That doesn't matter. I want him to be there, to be responsible."

"He'll never agree to that."

"That's true. He said he'd have come with me if I were married because my husband would be legally responsible. So I'll get married. A white marriage. We'll break off after the operation."

"Who are you thinking of?"

"Mahmud Sharif."

One newspaper had claimed that marriage was the only recourse for her. They implied that there was an inadmissible relation between her illness and her long celibacy. The sickness hadn't lodged itself just anywhere, but in her throat, that very place where hope, passion, sensuality—everything she should have given to a man—were gathered. She had not married, and the signs had been reversed. Frustration, solitude and a poisonous chastity had hardened into a tumor. That was what was killing her. I could believe it. Or not. But it was true on a magical level. Her audience had always wanted to keep her for themselves, had forced her into a holy solitude. The only way they might accept the idea of her marriage would be if it were a medical act. And she went along with that. But Mahmud Sharif was an alcoholic, a second-rate violinist who was a member of her orchestra. He scarcely looked at her, with scornful irony. She let him get away with everything. He was a good-looking man, fairly coarse, and the dark shadows beneath his eyes betrayed an immoderate fondness for pleasure. He would arrive late for rehearsal, and when you went looking for him, you found him drinking with a friend, sitting on the curb of the sidewalk. He did not love her. And she seemed to be fascinated by his indifference.

"Are you against the idea?"

"It's none of my business."

"That means you're against it. Like everyone. But I too have a right."

3

ON THE RUNWAY A MAN CAME TOWARD ME with a nonchalant gait, carrying a little plaid cloth suitcase. It was Sharif. I'd had every reason to expect him but just to see him was upsetting. I didn't know whether he'd married her or not, she hadn't spoken of it. There he was, with his little suitcase. As long as it was with death that I was struggling for her, I could go along with it. But to struggle with him—no.

He didn't greet anyone; he was a lanky man, and not really awake. She came up to me, put her arm around my neck. Her body pulled away again, too quickly. She left us no time.

I'd taken a week off work from the Library. Wednesday, ten o'clock Washington time, five in the afternoon over here. Until then nothing could happen. I had to wait, four days, and I could not wait with the others. The country was going through the same emotions, a diluted form of my own. I stayed shut in at home, with the radio, with her. I never switched it off, day and night I was immersed in her voice.

In the middle of the night I awoke from a nightmare. I'd fallen asleep in Samir's room. I got up with a start. Mahmud Sharif was in my dream, that's all I remember, poisoning even my sorrow. If he had not been there, she would have remained whole for me, she would have brought me calm. I heard music from the living room, and went there.

Ana Bintizarak, "I waited for you": her voice was splendid, alive, it had ripened with time. "*You left your fire in my veins /*

I put my hand on my cheek / And I waited / Every second of your absence / I would have preferred not to love." That was what I was doing, waiting each second, that is what she had always done, I had gotten married, my fire in her veins, the poem was by Bayram but its verses spoke to me. I would have preferred, I really would have, not to have loved. All feelings were reversible.

Al Awwila Fil Gharam, "First in Love." Another song by Bayram. He'd been there constantly, for ten years, writing poems for her, almost taking my place. "*Passion's caught me in its net / Condemned me to submission / And to patience / But tell me, such patience / Where can I ever find it?*" Bayram had brought her the madness, the love which makes one lose one's mind. "*The nights have gotten longer / My mind has deserted me / And I'm asking tears to help.*" The music by Sheik Zakariya also played its role in the delirium. Bayram and Sheik Zakariya, the inseparable pair. They'd followed her throughout the exasperation of her feelings, better than I had. They were after her, all those men.

There was a knock at the door, I never answered anymore. But this time someone was using their fists. Qsabji was on the landing. Distraught, ashamed. I made him come in. He couldn't stand being outside anymore—his wife, the family, the waiting—it was Tuesday, the operation was set for the next day, he couldn't take it anymore. He was living in the same state of fear, his body here, his mind there.

I took him in. He was free to use any room he liked, to come and go, wander through her voice, which is what we both did, each on his own. Provided we did not spend time together. I didn't want to talk.

The Nights of the Moon Have Come, I'd written the words, and he'd written the music. Sitting cross-legged on the carpet, his elbows against his thighs, the ghost of his lute between his arms: he could see her with his eyes. She had invited us to

Tammay al-Zahayrah, she'd wanted to sing on the main square at nightfall. Her entire village was sitting close together, elbows touching elbows, and they'd surrounded us. *"The moon is on the edge of the Nile / Come and let's watch over the night / What we murmur between us grows ever lovelier / And caring for love / Makes the secret of life live longer."* The hour we had spent restored her original accent, her peasant's timbre. The previous night we had all met at the palace and she had received her decoration. Asmahan had just died in an automobile accident. It was wartime, there was talk of a settling of accounts between British and German services, and she was suspected of belonging to both. Another rumor maintained that my diva was the one who had sabotaged the vehicle in order to eliminate her rival . . .

I heard the door slam. Qsabji had gone out.

Wednesday five o'clock, it was time. The radio had invited a sheik to chant verses from the Koran. He asked each and every Egyptian to think about her . . . I wanted to break the radio. They shouldn't say anything! Such events required silence, they required secrecy. The special correspondent in Washington had a crackling, inaudible voice; the reception was very poor. I understood what mattered. The operation had just begun.

The radio gave news updates every hour, there was nothing to report, just that they were there. People too were there—in cafés, around their radio sets, around mosques. Night had fallen long before, no one moved, no one could bring themselves to leave, everyone was watching over their common soul. There was not enough space between the walls of my apartment; I would have liked to undress my very self. My mind was incapable of anything but a motionless, useless instant.

Midnight. The telephone ringing like a call for help. Qsabji. He was calling from the villa. Everything went fine, she's

regaining consciousness, the tumor was malignant, they operated, everything went fine. Now the news was on the airwaves,
a voice full of emotion, the Star of the Orient, God be praised,
to the tiniest village.

I went out onto the balcony, I'd run out of prayers. She will
sing. I'll write for her. The monstrous merry-go-round will
begin to turn again, feeding itself off suffering, crushing souls
on its way. The curse was too great for me, she would have had
to rise of her own accord like an invisible mountain. To whom
could I turn with my rage now? She was going to call me back
to her and I would hurry there, fascinated, rushing to my
destruction and rejoicing all the while, my body depleted. And
the nation would do a bit of pushing again, like the day before,
like always. All these men, this music that they received and
gave again, this sweat-drenched ecstasy. I must be consumed
again. It would have been better if she had died.

4

THE MEN GATHERED IN CROWDS along the road where she would pass, the women tossed rice as her open car drove by, a procession of vehicles accompanied her to her home, horns blaring. All people could think of was their joy. As if death had been defeated for good. As if everyone would live. At the gates of the villa the policemen seemed as excited as anyone, each of them taking part.

Hassanein pasha, the regime's strong man, her putative lover, was waiting on the steps to greet her. Everything unfolding as everyone had dreamt it should: her car buried in the mass of people, her white figure carried by devotion, her voice murmuring into the microphone of *The Voice of Cairo*, thanking, I would like to thank, what she was saying was of no importance, they recognized the voice, her voice, somewhat veiled perhaps, but it was her. They heard her and let out a cry, raised their arms in celebration; they would never be in pain again. As for me, I could no longer believe her inimitable movements, the way she would keep her chin against her chest, proud and submissive, motionless. She was there, with us, alive.

She kissed Saadiya, hid in the folds of her body, a homecoming. The living room had disappeared beneath baskets of flowers, bags of telegrams, jars of honey sealed by peasants' hands, and just as much again from the cellar to the attic. She wanted to sing right away. She had to try her new throat. She insisted on sitting in the middle of the mass of gifts. She sat down. Her voice, limpid, laden with an unfamiliar gravity, drowned the room. She sang for herself, seeking reassurance as she went along, striving ever farther, catching a note, alternating bass and treble, forcing the extremities. Such a voice.

Qsabji came to the rescue, rolling his body around his lute. She burst out laughing, then wept. *Ask the Glasses of Beauty If They Have Touched Her Lips:* Ahmad Shawqi's mystical poem, of course. Hassanein pasha was beaming. The palace had gotten her back, intact, she would be able to carry on. Mahmud Sharif was at the back of the room, staring at her with a distant, feverish air; I'd known him to be offhand in a different way. I observed him with a sense of dark joy, an evil pleasure, I didn't even try to stop myself. He seemed to have tasted of the bitter fruit, he was discovering the meaning of it; he was beginning.

At midnight, Hassanein pasha asked everyone to leave so that she could rest. But she was in high spirits, could not possibly go to sleep, tonight was her night. He gave in, irritated, and left with his followers. She had recovered her strength, her old smile, there was nothing to hold her back and we were among friends: she sang until dawn.

She called me the next day, at the library, at home. I didn't call her back. She called again, but I let it ring.

Hoda had invited me to have dinner at a restaurant in town and I couldn't refuse. I saw her arrive, in a lightweight dress, there was a spring in her step, she was thinner, perhaps more fragile. She spoke to me as if it were over between us, our story belonged to the past, we simply had to get along because of the children. She spoke with ease, almost cheerful. But I felt good.

When I came back to my street, I saw Muhammad leaving my building. I watched as he drew nearer, elegant and hurried as ever. At the last minute, without thinking, I flattened my back against a shop window and let him pass on by.

At ten in the evening I decided to go out for a walk. Saadiya was coming up the stairway, there was nothing I could do. I went back up with her.

"Why don't you come anymore? Why don't you telephone her, she's called you ten times, she needs you!"

"She doesn't need anyone."

"She's not well at all."

"What happened?"

"The day after her return, Hassanein pasha and the king's uncle came to the villa. Both of them."

"What did they want?"

"They said: you went and married that violinist without saying a thing to anyone, nobody knows what he went and told you, you were sick, it's understandable. But you're not just any woman, you're the voice of Egypt, you are Egypt. As far as we're concerned, your union has never existed. And if it does in fact exist, you have no choice but to repudiate that man as discreetly as possible."

I said nothing.

"They are powerful. They gave her ten days, no more, and if she persists, it's simple, she'll be banned from the radio, that's all it takes, she'll disappear just like that."

"What did she decide?"

"She wanted to talk to you. The ten days will be over tomorrow. They're supposed to come at noon. They told her they'd bring a sheik with them, for the divorce."

"But what have I got to do with it, what can I change?"

"You don't understand. You are the only one she's ever loved . . . I mean, in that way. But her lover could never be a man."

"So tell me, who then? Who could be her lover?"

I was shouting. She didn't answer. I could no longer keep calm. After a long silence came her humble voice.

"So shall I go?"

I was resisting with all my strength.

"Saadiya, I'll be of no use, it's all too painful for me. Tell her you didn't find me."

She came herself the next day at the end of the afternoon. She came after the battle, defeated. Her gray dress seemed to imprison her, she wore dark glasses, she wanted to disappear. I asked her to come in, she slammed the door behind her. She asked me to draw the curtains, it was too bright. I darkened the room, window after window. She was there. Sitting on the edge of the sofa. We had never been alone like this.

She raised her head, distracted. Nothing had happened, I wasn't supposed to know. We had to talk about her next concert, that's why she'd come, it was scheduled for fifteen days from then.

"I've written a poem, I'll show you."

"Never mind. I already know what to sing."

Her voice was so weary. There were moments of absence, she was making an enormous effort, holding onto the railings of her former self.

"I have to work, I need to work. That's the best thing we can do."

I didn't respond.

"I want to sing the *Rubaiyat* of Khayyam."

I was silent.

"I feel ready. Khayyam can fill my throat. The pointlessness of worldly prohibitions, the exaltation of a solitary path toward God: I don't see what else I can sing."

She'd taken off her glasses. She no longer lowered her eyes. I'd remained standing. Without thinking, I murmured, "'*The most worthy is for this heart to beat / And to burn in the furnace of love*' . . ."

"'*And there is no greater waste / Than a day spent without love or desire.*' You see, I already know the verses."

"You're not afraid?"

"What should I be afraid of?"

"Of the guardians of the faith, guardians of the law—they're always the same. Khayyam insulted them in every other quatrain. You'll be attacked the way he was. By the powerful, by doctors of religion, even some of the opposition. The Muslim Brotherhood will not accept it, for you to sing about drunkenness, they'll accuse you of weakening the feeling of submission, and Islam is submission."

"Submission to God alone, yes."

"'*Oh friend! Destroy the bases of the prayer and those of fasting / Drink wine, thieve if you will, but do good.*' You would sing that?"

"No."

"You see, nothing is finished."

"What are you looking for, what's left for me to do?"

"You sing the verses of Ahmad Shawqi, and people start to call you the Religious woman of Islam, people listening to you all night long: you console them in their bitter poverty. Above you there is nothing but the generous Koran."

"I want to sing the *Rubaiyat*."

She was at the end of her tether. Slowly, I sat down next to her.

"'*I've been cloaked in the mantle of life with no say in the matter / And it will be removed without my knowing / Either why I have come or where to find the way out.*'"

"Tell me some more."

"'*The heart is broken by the love of beauty / One's breast tight with what remains unsaid / My God, how can you allow such thirst / And water flowing sweetly at my feet.*'"

She repeated the words. My God, how can you allow. Only these verses allowed her to express what was bottled up inside. Her body grew calmer, folded over itself. I went on reciting.

"'*Rise and fill a cup of wine / Before destiny comes to fill that of our existence.*'"

"Perhaps I could say just cup, rather than cup of wine, do you think I can? The deeper meaning would be the same, I'll sing."

"*Snuff out the blaze in the heart with a glass of wine / For the days pass like clouds.*'"

"I'll say, '*Snuff out the blaze in the heart with . . . the honey of your lips / For the days pass like clouds.*'"

She questioned me, as frightened as a child. She inclined her head, waited, whispered between her lips: "Yes, they do pass like clouds. And I would like to fill my cup before fate comes to fill that of my existence."

I left her to silence. She was ready to succumb to this ironic melancholy dominated by an obsession with death and with the vanity of the world, ready to succumb to a terrible madness which was luring her like a betrothed, ready to lose herself provided it be heard in her voice.

She had said yes. After all these years. When all was lost. She was accepting Khayyam, in her soul. She was as abandoned by all, as abandoned as I was, so close. We had no one but each other in the world.

5

LIKE EVERY SUMMER, those who reign and govern had fled the furnace to settle in Alexandria, the second capital. They were followed by those who compose and write, those who own and direct, all the members of that small population which believes itself to be the world. For two months Cairo was abandoned to its inhabitants, the obscure, real millions. For a time the city would be theirs, as the heat created an illusion of vacation, even for them. And for me, for I refused to follow the seasonal migration. This vacant space suited me, as did summer, where nothing could happen.

She too went to Alexandria. She had sung the *Rubaiyat*. The changes she had made didn't alter the outcome: a tempest had been unleashed, against her in particular. She had not tried to make excuses. Omar Khayyam's verses belong to the history of mankind, but also to the present; the fever which animates them also animates us. Only those who understand nothing about love, only those who trample it underfoot might be offended. She had brought this on deliberately, with a malicious, suicidal joy. Let them knock her down, if they dared. Hassanein pasha had immediately cancelled the concert she was meant to give at the summer palace. Rather than give in, she made matters worse. She used that evening to sing the *Rubaiyat* in a working-class theater in Alexandria, a free recital. The palace did not attack her directly. They merely let it be understood that she would be forbidden from appearing on the radio as of the fall. The same weapon, once again; she'd yielded a first time, she'd sacrificed Sharif. No doubt she did not love him enough. But it had been such a bitter experience to capitulate to them: now she wanted to go to war. That was the best we could hope for. An apocalyptic ending for her and for me, with my translation of Omar Khayyam no less—our rebellion.

I was alone, the city was lonely. No one tried to pull me out of my almost voluptuous sadness. Hoda had left with the children, I didn't even know for where. The unchanging taste of tea at dawn, on the balcony, the air still laden with the relative cool of the night, the radio quietly playing in the background: I wanted nothing else.

The radio. There was military music on the radio. A first announcement: "During the night of July 23, 1952, the Free Officers have seized power with neither blood nor violence. The revolution has control of the palace, and of the headquarters of the radio, of government and of the armed forces. Oh children of our courageous nation . . ." A coup! The military had taken over the places emptied of power! Faraway sounds, children shouting, noises of water, silence: it was as if history were unfolding in another country. The sun above the horizon; an ordinary summer's day.

I grabbed the phone. The operator told me in a frenzied voice that he was alone, overwhelmed, surrounded by soldiers who didn't understand a thing, all his colleagues were down in the street, he wanted to go there too. I managed to get him to write down the number, Hotel Cecil, Alexandria, Room 36. An indefinite wait. I went out.

I found people down in the street, hardly awake. Who are these soldiers, what's going on? We went to find news, every man for himself. In the street the crowds were getting bigger, blocking the squares, spilling out onto the side streets, without any particular aim. Any change was welcome. An incredulous joy spread from one group or another, then was immediately silenced. We were walking. Tanks were positioned at strategic intersections, so it was true. People were reaching their hands out to the soldiers as they leaned out of their turrets—their sons, their brothers, as stunned as they were.

On the square opposite the Ministry of Defense, nothing but a strange silence rose from the crowd. Even the armored vehicles seemed to be adrift on this pregnant sea of people, unaware of what it was giving birth to. There were no slogans or banners. The apparent ease with which the coup had taken place had left people speechless.

An officer with a tannoy in his hand climbed onto one of the tanks mounting guard. "In the name of the Revolutionary Council . . ." He was drunk with several sleepless nights. Poverty, corruption, humiliation, the war in Palestine: his broken voice rang true. The crowd began to move, to be roused, like a swell forming. The officer was shouting. "A few months ago, in January, you invaded the streets of Cairo and set fires, two hundred and seventy-seven fires in a single day, and you stopped the firemen from intervening. We, the armed forces, your children, we understood your distress. What the people began on that day, we are finishing today. The foreign occupiers will no longer make the laws in Egypt, the peasant will no longer work for an absentee landlord, the courts will no longer side every time with the boss against the worker, and the country will at last be free to grow and open to the world . . ."

There was no turmoil. Only the tense faces of the workers, burning with a desire to understand and to believe. It all sounded too beautiful. They refused to release their joy, a joy they could never reclaim.

Hundreds of bearded men had gathered around the tank. As soon as the officer had finished, they all shouted *Allah akbar*, the ritual call, to the rhythm of their breathing, their fists raised toward the sky. The Muslim Brotherhood. The crowd responded, their cries spreading through the entire area until they came to me. Heads were raised, and hands. The rage which had been building, year after year; the frustration and all the darkness in people's souls, thousands of hearts were now coughing it out in unison. In one single cry. Allah, God, greater than joy or pain, life and death, greater than all that, always. That cry as familiar as the galabia on their backs, passed on from generation to generation, which one could never mispronounce—even that shout eventually got weaker and died, absorbed by the ocean of perplexity. There were no dominant watchwords, nothing to explain the extraordinary shift. The king had not been ousted, merely suspended; a delegation of the new rulers had left for Alexandria for discussions. That meant the game was not yet over.

Just as I was putting the key into the lock, the telephone rang, and I fumbled with the key.

"It's me," said the voice.

"So you know. What's it like where you are?"

"Terrible. Like a curfew. They're all locked up in their hotels and villas and their knees are shaking. Yesterday everything belonged to them, even my voice. (She laughed joyfully.) I'm caught in the rat fortress, I beg you, if you're still my friend, get me out of here!"

"But what's stopping you?"

"Seats on the plane! The airport has been besieged."

"But you . . ."

"They don't know who anyone is anymore, I tell you. It's marvelous!"

She laughed again, her joy unmitigated, like mine. And there was something else there, an accumulation of weariness and sorrows.

"Find a way but come back. It's all happening in Cairo."

"Tell me."

"Everyone is struck dumb, there's so much hope. I missed

independence day and now I feel it's being offered to me again. Thirty years later the wheel is miraculously back at zero, like a second chance."

She didn't answer. She didn't believe it. Or not for her, and not for me. I didn't know what else to say. My heart was beating fit to burst out of my chest. If they succeeded, the officers would be the first Egyptians to govern Egypt since the pharaohs.

This would not give her back her love, nor me my peace. Reality was still forbidden to us, and our dream was carried on others' shoulders. Our only revenge, our only joy—a miserable one at that—was to imagine the royal family, and the king's uncle, Hassanein pasha. It was their turn to swallow their arrogance.

"Come back. I'm on my own here."

"I'll try. Tomorrow at the latest."

She laughed again. All her youth in that laughter, all the sadness, all the history. She said she had to hang up. I held her back.

"One last thing—"

"What?"

"Nothing . . . I'm happy."

"Me too." A moment of silence, then, "Do you think it's true, I mean, I don't know . . ."

"*Inshallah.*"

6

S HE HAD COME BACK. She wasn't seeing many people. She
was vaguely preparing her next concert, assuming that
the new leaders would organize one when the situation
became a bit more stable.

She had no idea what was going on. For four days not a single one of her songs had been played on the radio. The idea
that she might be in disgrace had never even crossed her mind.

The king had abdicated. Not a single shot had been fired.
General Naguib spoke in the name of the victorious revolution. He was a prominent military man, a member of the bour-
geoisie, he had integrity, was respected by all. Behind him was
Colonel Nasser, the real artisan of the coup; I'd met him once.
He and a few other officers had been the only ones to perform
bravely during the war in Palestine, and my diva had invited
them to her place to thank them. And now they were punishing her.

The radio headquarters had been transformed into a verita-
ble bunker. Two tanks in front and in back, rolls of barbed
wire uncoiled on the pavement, soldiers on every floor. Cairo
was once again the capital, in the middle of summer. The
Revolutionary Council was working in the furnace, like everyone. That fact alone would have been enough to make them
popular.

Hoda called me, mad with worry. From a distance, things
always seem more impressive. She asked whether I wanted her
to come back, but I could guess what she really wanted. She

gave me her address, and she no longer knew how to hang up.
Nor did I.

I found the villa buried in a silence of mourning, the gates
wide open. White sheets had been tossed over the furniture.
She had learned. Saadiya was sitting alone in a corner of the
living room. She got up and came toward me as if she did not
know me.

"There's no one, they've all left."

"What are you talking about? Everyone left for where?"

"They went to Tammay al-Zahayrah, she's fired everyone,
she asked them to leave, she doesn't want to see them anymore,
they left right away."

"Where is she?"

"She's not here!"

I went toward the stairway leading to the basement, but she
got there before me. Her right hand clung to the banister, with
the other she leaned against the wall.

"Go away. Leave her alone."

I pushed her aside. She ran behind me.

"She won't see anyone, not even me!"

I kept going.

"And in any case, she's not alone!"

"Who is she with?"

"They've humiliated her and hurt her, and all she wanted
was to support the revolution with all her voice. Why don't
you just go?"

I went down the stairs. The village atmosphere rose to my
nostrils. I went to her room. I could hear whispering, the
sound of cloth rustling. I pushed open the door. They were in
bed. I recognized the young woman, the radio announcer
who'd interviewed her in Alexandria. The mattress on the
floor, everything stripped bare. In this place. This place where
nothing could hurt, the belly where she drew her ambiguous
strength. Two women stretched out beneath the rough blan-

ket, in an animal immobility. It did not bother me, but it was something else that I could not take. That this was her reaction, when faced with the test. To send everyone away, shut herself away downstairs, re-immerse herself in the climate of her origins with such despair, such delight. The dark room. To be beaten, to be banished into an inner exile, banished from everywhere. But not this dark abandon.

I didn't move. The announcer was looking at me, I could hardly see her face. and my peasant girl was hiding hers in the crook of her arm. So I began to speak quietly to her. I reminded her of everything she had sung over these last few years, and on whose side she belonged. I spoke to her of her voice, the soul of the people beating in time, she was above everything, the most beautiful voice in the world, and her name would continue to shine long after that of kings and colonels had fallen into oblivion. She said nothing but I could sense that she was listening, a vibration in the air; we were bound. I stayed like that for a long time, standing in the cave, murmuring. She turned back the blankets.

"Our history is part of the dying of hope, no one needs us. Go home."

Her body was dazzling, she no longer had the strength to restrain so much rage. Her voice broke.

"Do you think they can really prevent me from singing forever?"

I did not need to answer.

Saadiya came running in. The telephone; the private line. She got quickly to her feet. I followed her to the room upstairs. She held the receiver away from her ear so that I too could listen:

" . . . Lieutenant-Colonel Nasser," said a deep, friendly voice.

"You have raised our heads," she said, with incredible poise.

"Yours was never lowered, except before God."

A silence. He continued,

"That is my honest opinion, I've always thought as much. For more than a year the clandestine meetings of the Revolutionary Council have been held the first Thursday of every month. We were in peace time, everyone was busy listening to you. Across from me is the journalist Mustapha Amine, your friend. I was completely unaware of what has been happening, he's the one who notified me. I called the head of the radio. I told him that the Nile and the Pyramids also existed under the old regime, and there has never been any talk of outlawing them."

"You make me out to be much greater than I am."

"You will be even greater. You were the voice of Egypt, now the revolution will make you the voice of the Arabs. In the eyes of the entire world, you'll see."

7

T HE HOUSE WAS IN A STATE OF SIEGE—soldiers, plain-
clothes policemen, dark glasses everywhere, people you
couldn't recognize. The front rows were filled with uniforms, the Revolutionary Council were nearly all there. A row of
empty seats separated them from the crowds in the audience,
who were spilling from the balconies, bursting with joyful exuberance, waiting for the curtain to rise. The boxes and the
orchestra had been invaded by crowds from the working-class
neighborhoods and suburbs, who were feeling progressively
more at home. It was the siege of the Opera, or rather its resti-
tution to its rightful owners who had come to hear their poets
and musicians. Only two stars—but what stars. Muhammad
Abd al-Wahab for the opening act, the Star of the Orient to con-
clude. The new leaders had understood.

I made my way around the security services. Saadiya's wary
eye peered through the chink in the door. She made me wait
the time it took for her little girl to put on a coat: no one must
see her dress, it was a superstition. The diva appeared in the
middle of the dressing room, a tiara on her hair, an ivory tower,
an idol. Her gaze was worried.

"How do I look?"

Her eyes did not leave her reflection in the big mirror.

"You are magnificent."

She shrugged her shoulders. The little loudspeaker in the
dressing room announced five minutes to curtain. I kissed her
hands.

"How long do you think Muhammad is going to sing?"

"Calm down, you're not on until after the intermission. It will be fine."

She held onto my hands.

"Do you really think so?"

"Of course. Don't worry. I'll be in the orchestra. Let me go or I'll miss the beginning."

"Wait. Look at me one more time."

Her make-up was a little bit shiny.

"Don't change a thing."

"But maybe . . ."

"Nothing, I assure you. I have to go."

Backstage was an invasion of cables, producers, radio technicians. I was in their way, and they wouldn't let me past. I glimpsed Muhammad sitting in front of his musicians, facing the closed curtains. Without thinking, I went toward him. He waved to me. The stage director pushed me back into the folds of the curtain just as it was opening.

I could see the hall. Muhammad stepped forward in the darkness, his lute in his hand. He was the friend of my adolescent years. He was over fifty now, almost bald, still here. Year after year he had brought his music to the stage. He had composed his *Hymn to Freedom* right after the war in Palestine, and King Faruq had banned it. He was too disreputable, he had been the adored child of the palace, and had seen his image reversed at the last minute. And now, his *Hymn to Freedom* had become that of the revolution.

He was performing it on stage for the first time, and the crowd with him: a clamor, an ancestral expectation. The new departure, the real one, was this evening. Much more than a concert, the lights and ovations were celebrating the magnificent opening of an era which would reconcile us with ourselves. The revolution was only two months old, and had kept its promises. There was no need to spell out the project which limited farm holdings to 90 hectares: a massive expropriation from the major landowners, the land to the peasants. A plot of land in the valley or the delta meant emerging from the dawn of time.

Muhammad was singing about this freedom, and the audience was overjoyed. In the folds of the curtain, I would have given everything to take part in the promise, with all my being, but something was excluding me. The profusion of exuberance before my eyes brought home the emptiness of my life. A vital incentive was missing, I don't know what—Hoda, my wife. She had brought me the children to look after today; I'd spent the afternoon playing with them, a pretext to touch them, feel their growing bodies. She had come back to fetch them and they ran to her. Sometimes you get out of a story the way you get out of a train, and you suddenly discover that it keeps going without you, that it is already far away in the distance.

I felt someone pulling me by the sleeve. She could not bear to wait in her dressing room, and now the cheers and applause had acted as a magnet, she had come to join me. She was backstage from Muhammad!

"The poem I'm going to sing is your poem. You'll be with me."

I lowered my head. I could feel her body against my back, her tense breathing against the back of my neck. Muhammad yielded to the ovations, they didn't want to let him go, so he sang one last song, a short one. We listened to him in the shadows, motionless.

The musicians were putting away their instruments, she took my hand and led me behind the closed curtain. Gently, she opened a crack in the heavy red velvet.

"Quick, tell me who's who."

I pointed out General Naguib, in the middle, with the most medals, always indignant and virtuous. During the war in

Palestine, he was the one who sent the press the notes signed "the unknown soldier" to denounce the palace as bearing the greatest responsibility for the defeat. Everything had come together during that war, it was in Palestine that the officers had met and discovered their common ground. I pointed out Sadat, Nasser, and Amer. She stepped back. She was discovering her new playing field, her next partners. Just thinking of it her body became animated, quivering, leaning gently against me. She didn't realize. The revolution, the proximity of the leaders filled her with an animal, sensual excitement, and she was sharing it with me, quite unawares. She leaned more heavily against my chest, and I withdrew. I had never felt so alone. She gave a hushed laugh:

"Watch out, they're getting up."

She drew aside.

"I've got to run. They're coming backstage."

She stood motionless before her audience, her arms outspread, offered in silent jubilation. A low-cut green dress, the color of Islam, jewelry, tiara: nothing could be beautiful enough for this evening. Backstage, Nasser had taken her and Muhammad by the arm, he wanted to make them promise to work together. "You can unite the people. That is what they need most at present." Muhammad was enthusiastic; she had merely lowered her eyes. As always. She hadn't changed.

That was the one thing she liked. She waved to Qsabji, held out her scarf. But the audience, carried by her enthusiasm, could no longer restrain themselves: when one sector fell quiet, the other started up even louder. Her laughter was unrestrained, and the applause doubled in volume. She was woman, another name for Egypt. A strange play of mirrors between the audience and herself, we are Egypt, you are Egypt.

The orchestra began to play. "*Egypt in my mind and on my*

lips . . ." She had to pause when the audience, worked into a frenzy, released a torrent of shouts, "Long live Egypt!" From their lips came cries of "God is great!" wanting to sanctify her, the movement bringing the crowd ever closer. She greeted them again, the applause and shouting were reaching the intensity of a riot. She broke the circle: "*Egypt in my mind and on my lips . . .*" and the theater roared one last time; "*I love her with all my soul and my blood / If only all believers could cherish her / And love her with the love that is mine / Sons and defenders of the homeland / Who among you loves her as much as I do?*" The choir was meant to give the reply, Sunbati had carefully arranged the music, but the audience in their delirium changed the arrangement and, a second too late, reading her lips, they roared the words which I had written: "*We all love her as you do / As much as you, as much as you / With all our soul and our blood / We love her so much we'd sacrifice our children.*"

And me—for what had I sacrificed my children?

8

T HE VILLA WAS INVADED BY UNIFORMS, EVERY NIGHT. The rows of caps in the entrance—it looked like a general staff meeting. The revolution had set up cooperatives to distribute land to the peasants; a project of free, mandatory education had been embarked upon; and greater protection was granted to young girls by raising the legal age of marriage. Everything had been turned upside down, it was what we'd been waiting for since independence. But it wasn't a reason to live surrounded by soldiers.

The Arab world had watched as Faruq fell. The king of Iraq was trembling, as were the British, the French, and the king of Saudi Arabia too. Egypt was setting a bad example, and they attacked her relentlessly, calling her all sorts of names. Just to hear them made me part of the revolution. I was one of them. Ready to defend most of their major decisions, the agrarian reform, and all the rest. The military men had put the lever where they should. But I didn't feel at ease with them. Or with anyone else for that matter.

I had begun to hate my apartment. I spent the day at the library and in the evening I put off the moment of departure for as long as possible. Where could I go? Muhammad was in the midst of a new love affair, Qsabji was with his family, and in the cafés there were no familiar faces anymore. And even if there had been someone there, I preferred to be outdoors. I'd put my beret on my head and go for a walk all alone. I walked interminably along the quays, I sat on benches. Cairo was beginning to change: more populated, dirtier, more real. I stayed at the edge of the whirlwind, indifferent, as if I didn't exist, without curiosity. I would wait for the day Hoda came to leave the children for the afternoon, and I would prepare myself so they would not see what I had become.

Hoda, Hoda's body: I'd wake in the night with her absence in my arms. It was on my skin, I could touch it, a wrenching, ravishing tingling. With my head on the pillow I lay in the dark looking at long-ago events that I had experienced somewhat distractedly, and which only my senses had recorded. Hoda. She had given me to the tangible world, she had opened me to the flavor of life. I pictured her as she had been, and in the way I had never seen her. I had let her pass me by.

On the rare evenings when I went to the villa, my diva greeted me warmly, too warmly. As if she owed me something, as if she were the one who had dropped me. She gave herself away, her mind was elsewhere. And she went into that other place. I stayed behind in the shadows, where her suitors and those who were disgraced drifted. I was neither one nor the other, I was nothing. A mistake. She moved about in full sunlight, smiling, exuberant, the only spot of color in the middle of all that khaki. Sometimes I thought I saw the expression of a wounded animal in her eyes. She was already in the game, in its center. She had already been celebrated by the former regime, and she'd hosted social gatherings, but the leaders of the revolution were of peasant stock, from the same earth as she. The universe of her origins was now in power, at home with her, an exclusively male tribe for whom she was fiancée, wife, sole mother. No matter what I did, I could never belong there.

If anyone asked my opinion, I was actually rather in favor of General Naguib. He had promised to restore the political parties which had been dissolved right after the coup; he had promised to remove censorship and organize real elections. I'm a child of the city, perhaps that's why. But it was not

Naguib who had the wind in his sails, it was Nasser, and the officers who were close to her.

Telephone, in the middle of the night. Saadiya's voice. Through her sobs I managed to understand that Sheik Khaled had suddenly fallen to the ground and was not moving. She was alone, her little one had gone to America to receive an award. I got dressed. There was nothing left to do, he had died from a heart attack. I had never liked him. He'd spent his life taking advantage of my attachment to his sister. Even now, surrounded by doctors who'd been called too late, he did not seem any more likable. Saadiya clung to my arm. I looked at her. She was all wrinkled, drained of strength. I understood that she was not crying for sheik Khaled. I was crushed by the idea of the solitude to which my peasant girl was condemned.

Sheik Zakariya had broken off with her because he felt he was being too poorly paid; when he left he forbade her from using his music. Qsabji was no longer composing for her. He limited himself to accompanying her on the lute in the midst of orchestras which were getting bigger and bigger. She was preparing a film on the life of Rabi'a al-Adawiya, the great mystic of Islam. For the texts she'd chosen to work with another poet, Taher Abu Fasha. A new wave of lyricists and musicians surrounded her. From the older generation, only Sunbati remained. His music exalted patriotism, and he had become her official composer.

She began talking to me about it as we went up the stairs and out onto the veranda. The British were still occupying the Suez canal zone, and she needed a song demanding their departure, a hymn to the evacuation that everyone could pick up.

"Ever since I've known you you've been critical of the British. Why don't you write a poem . . ."

"Could you call such a thing a poem?"

"What's the matter with you?"

"I don't know. The revolution, that's all well and good. Maybe people need to be mobilized, but as for me..."

I rummaged in my briefcase and handed her my poem. She shook her head. I read it myself. She interrupted. On her face was a shocked anger.

"And how do you think I feel? You write, I sing your love songs, and . . ."

She got up abruptly and went to lean against the stone parapet. She stood staring at the Nile. On the verge of tears. I had thought that she felt fulfilled by all the honors and recitals; I hadn't understood a thing, hadn't felt a thing. The void. We hadn't even managed to be alone together. She came back over and sat down.

"Read some more."

I picked up a collection and opened it at random. Ma'ari. The poet who had died a thousand years ago still spoke mysteriously to her, and to me. "*I distract from hope a wayward heart / As if I did not know I was perishing.*" "*What we live is a dream / Dreamt by what has been destroyed.*"

She did not move. I let a few seconds go by. She was so still that I wondered if she hadn't fallen asleep. I started a new poem but after a few verses, I gradually lowered my voice. I fell silent. She opened her eyes.

"Why doesn't Hoda come back to live with you?"

I didn't answer.

"I'm going to get married."

"What?"

"I'm going to get married."

"With whom?"

"It hardly matters."

"What do you mean it hardly matters?"

She didn't reply.

"You're not going to get married for my sake!"

"I too come back to an empty house every night."

"Tell me who it is."

"You know how little respect I have for men. Without them the world would be a quieter place, more chaste and faithful."

"Stop going on like that."

The silence became prolonged. It was completely dark out now. She was murmuring.

"You and I—we can't leave each other, the past is holding us prisoner. We're unhappy. We have to put it behind us. So, there we are . . ."

She said nothing else. I wanted to help her.

"You've decided to get married."

These simple words spelled out the reality by its name, resonating like an acceptance. She was talking quickly.

"In America I stopped off in Washington to see the surgeons who had operated on me. I didn't tell anyone but I've been undergoing treatment for some time now."

Her voice was becoming rougher.

"It's nothing, I just have to keep an eye on it. A routine treatment. For the last six months Dr. Hifnawi has been coming very early in the morning to . . . give me the injections."

"And?"

"In the beginning, it was very difficult for me to undress before him. But bit by bit I got used to his presence. That's it. I've decided to marry him."

"Who? The doctor?"

"Yes, the doctor."

Her tone was so pitiful, I was ashamed of my reaction. She was getting married for my sake. For her and for me. She was trying to break the curse with her own hands, all on her own. The force which united us, inhuman. I threw myself at her feet, and she stopped me. She pulled me to her and took me in her arms.

9

THE OLD SHEIK WAS BLIND, and didn't know whose house he had been led to. A car had gone to fetch him at the time of the dawn prayer, at the last minute. In the living room of the villa, he had resumed his immemorial rocking, he was at home. Obedience and submission, the woman is the residence of man, and he is her residence, her *sakan*, united in this life as in their final hour. Words fell from his lips, his face as transparent as the wing of a firefly, a gentle smile.

We all arrived at the same time, to lend a hand to the clandestine event which was taking place. They sat next to each other in armchairs. She threw anxious glances in the direction of the open door. Her nervousness protected her from the ceremony. She had put on a white silk dress. To her left was an old uncle who would act as her guardian, and speak in her name; it was the law.

The sheik took Hifnawi's hand and placed it in the uncle's. He placed a handkerchief over the three joined hands of the men. He asked the guardian if he would take this man as his husband and the witness replied that he would. With this word, he gave her. The sheik then went on to say that the marriage would be contracted *with the power to the woman*, a rare clause which gave her the ability to divorce; she had insisted upon it.

All that remained was the *Fatiha*. Glory to God, Lord of the worlds, merciful and forgiving; the sheik had lost his voice. He was still smiling, his throat whistling when he took a breath, his thin body about to dissolve in the air. King of the day of prayer, You are the one we adore, You are the one who gives us succor; he was exhausted. Each of his words seemed to be supported by a cavernous echo. Show us the path of righteousness, the path of light, the sound was getting louder every second, giving the prayer a terrifying gravity. I looked behind me. Huge white shapes had invaded the living room, standing stock still around the chairs, their hands outspread before them. The household staff, Tammay al-Zahayrah, the inhabitants of the basement had come up to attend the secret marriage of their queen. Underneath the handkerchief I could picture a sort of puppet theater, generations of ancestors, souls committing souls in others' names. Lead us far from the path which gives rise to Your anger, the path of the wayward. Amen. Saadiya burst into tears, the small crowd gathered around the bride. She turned this way and that in the center, in the well of emotion.

The procession of cars headed for the central station, the streets were still deserted. We accompanied them onto the platform, to the train, the pair of them. Their trip would last a day and a night. In a sleeping car. A suite had been reserved in their name, Mr. and Mrs. Hifnawi, Hôtel de la Grande Cataracte, Aswan. She did not want to be in Cairo the day the news would be spread all over the papers.

As I left the station I watched the cars drive away without me. I began to walk. Along the Nile, through the gardens of Ezbekia, walking inside myself. Passersby bumped into me, hurried by, soldiers, students, workers, their steps leading them all somewhere. Cars, trams, the city at work. At the library, I could not even say why I needed to take time off.

The day went by without me. At dusk I went and knocked at Muhammad's. He knew nothing, so I let him in on the secret. This man who as a youth had sworn never to marry was already on his second divorce. And his most recent love affair had ended. That evening he was as single as I was. He took me out to the cafés. And when the cafés closed for the night, he took me into the bars. We weren't looking for company, we just wanted to drink, glass after glass, and celebrate. The Arab world has always considered real life to be without women. We were not like that, we belonged to a generation where the influence of the West had brought about a greater mingling of the sexes. But that night was different. Atavism had been revived, the ancient familiarity among men. Bar after bar, until dawn. I went home with an impression of having buried my bachelor's life.

I had trouble putting my key in the lock, the door opened. Hoda. The children. I thought they were not coming until late morning. Already there. Everything I had prepared in my mind became pointless, everything I'd promised myself to say to her. She saw me stumble and she laughed. That was the first thing she did. A happy, engaging laugh. I wanted to explain, she told me to be quiet. She helped me in, closed the door, sat me down on the living room sofa. The house was beyond recognition, yet nothing had changed; there was a sound in the air, sap rising. The children ran in and all three stopped short when they saw me, intimidated. Hoda came back from the kitchen, she had wanted them to see their rooms again before leaving for school, that was why. She was virtually offering her excuses. She asked them to go get ready. I thought she had gone for some strong coffee but she was holding a bottle of brandy. She sat down next to me, poured a tall glass for herself, drank it all, poured another. And there, with her lips moist and delight in her eyes, she announced her intention of catching up with me.

The news of her marriage was only revealed a week later, in a modest column. The headlines were devoted to Nasser's escape from an attempted assassination in Alexandria. A man had fired at him, a certain Mahmud Abd al-Latif, described as an elite marksman who belonged to the Muslim Brotherhood. Nevertheless he had missed his target; the security services had overwhelmed him and he had immediately confessed to his deed.

The assassination attempt aroused unprecedented emotion. Well-organized crowds stopped Nasser's train from Alexandria in every station. In Cairo, a human tide was waiting for him, banners unfurled. The cries of the crowd rose in volume; the radio broadcast was live. A podium had been set up inside the train station itself. The announcer described Nasser stepping up to the microphone and waiting for the clamor to abate. He had to start over several times before the crowd finally fell silent. In every town in the country work had come to a halt, cafés were full to bursting, people squeezing in, standing between the tables, clustered at the doors, to listen. "Oh children of our nation"—they recognized his voice—"this is your revolution, working for progress, for the future of the country, but there are among us people who seem to prefer the past. Obscurantists who veil themselves in the cloak of religion in order to kill, reactionaries paid by the Arab monarchies and by colonialism. In the beginning we tried to bring them in with us, we suggested they take part in the government, and they refused. The country went forward without them, and they no longer knew what to do, so they turned to crime. When dealing with such people, politicians who have only democracy on their lips are useless. Terrorists understand nothing but the iron fist beating down upon them. We will make sure they are no longer capable of doing harm, by whatever means it takes. The Arab people has the right to defend its revolution, to crush those who attack it, and those who corrupt it!"

At that very moment, while he was speaking, the headquarters of the Muslim Brotherhood was stormed by the demonstrators, and set alight beneath the indifferent eyes of the police. I was astonished. At the time of the coup, the Muslim Brotherhood had qualified it as a blessed putsch, and there had even been rumors that Nasser was one of their secret members. They had refused to participate in the government, that was true, but they had offered him the enormous social base which had been theirs since the war in Palestine. What was even more surprising was that they seemed to be totally caught off guard by the repression. Thousands of their members had been thrown in prisons where they found themselves alongside communist militants who'd been incarcerated before they were, and whom they detested. They cried foul, said it was a provocation, and accused the police of having organized a phony assassination attempt, but who was listening? Their newspapers were forbidden, their leaders had fled or were already in jail. Nasser was head of state, minister of the Interior, the regime's strong man; he controlled all the security services. The only title he did not hold was that of president, which still belonged to General Naguib. The clumsy sharpshooter had given him a decisive advantage. The people suddenly acclaimed him as the man of history who had defeated the monarchy and restored dignity to the nation.

She came back with the first train. The assassination attempt had left her beside herself. As if they had attacked a member of her own family, or herself, or everything the country had gained thanks to the revolution; the land above all. Her indignation was as violent as it was sincere.

She had expected the city to be in flames, a bloodbath, and she found perfect calm. On the airwaves of the Voice of Cairo, they were playing only Muhammad; in record time he had composed *You Who Are So Dear to Us* in honor of Nasser. The very evening of her arrival, after a few hours of rehearsal, she sang, live, *Gamal, Example of Patriotism.* "*You faced the fire with your faith / There is no greater courage than yours . . .*"

Sunbati had composed the music, she had turned to Bayram for the lyrics. The song addressed Nasser by his first name; I could never have written it. I was in another world altogether. With Hoda. We were concerned only with the present. To make her understand, I'd increased my invisible gestures. For her, for the children. As if nothing could ever separate us again.

Gamal, example of patriotism. Three weeks later, to virtually universal indifference, General Naguib was placed under house arrest.

10

W E WERE SITTING OUTSIDE, she and I, in big wicker armchairs. We'd deserted the veranda. The ritual of work sessions which had been ours for so long had been broken, and we'd come down into the garden. Perhaps another ritual was about to begin, we didn't know. We leaned far back into the chairs; it was a perfect time of day.

Boys and girls were lying in the grass, five or six of them, a few meters away, we could hear snatches of their conversation, their laughter. Friends of Mahmud, her favorite nephew; she'd given him Sheik Khaled's old room and treated him like a son. She was staring at his supple, almost skinny, body on the lawn, without seeing it, but she never took her eyes from him. He shared the name of that other Mahmud, Mahmud Sharif the violinist.

Blissfully, the political fever had abated. The magazines had suddenly remembered her marriage with Hifnawi. She'd opened her villa to them, introduced her spouse, and posed for their cameras; they'd come up with the predictable story ("Love at last!"), and she'd politely pushed them out and closed the gate. In the days which followed, women hurried to the doctor's office: his union with the diva had granted him almost magical powers. He worked ten hours a day, we never saw him. The villa in Zamalek was once again her territory. There had never been such peace.

The light had changed again, we were nearing the border. She laughed for no reason. Her silent reverie had led her to a euphoric conclusion. She laughed again and I laughed with her; our good spirits fed on themselves and on the freshness of the air. We had overcome all the obstacles, hedged, used a thousand detours; we were nearly there, in this garden. She was married, and so was I. The circle of appearances protected us. We were above board. There was nothing left to stop the all-consuming fire from rising again, our passion intact. The words had come back to me; I'd dared to write them, she was going to sing, once again, of the sublime wound. We didn't need to hide anymore.

The adolescents were watching us out of the corner of their eyes, watching her especially, their friend's aunt, an unbelievable oddity. Some of her glory had fallen onto my shoulders. I had resumed my place. With me I'd brought her first long-playing record, Khayyam's *Rubaiyat*, twenty minutes on each side, forty altogether; almost the entire concert. The tyranny of the seventy-eight rpm records was over.

The National Theater could hold three thousand people. There were ten times as many all around the building; with great difficulty police barricades managed to keep the passage open. On either side nothing but a sea of arms reaching toward the car doors with shouts of love, or simple shouts, a crush of people. She waved to them, smiling at all the furor.

The same gestures, all over again. King Fu'ad had once asked her to launch *The Voice of Cairo*; now Nasser was asking her to inaugurate *The Voice of the Arabs*. The new radio station was so powerful that it could be heard from Baghdad to Casablanca, from Damascus to Khartoum. The revolution would now speak to people wherever they were, from brother to brother, going over the head of regimes. We were no longer Egyptians, we were Arabs. The great speech that Nasser was about to make that very evening on the main square of Alexandria would be broadcast live, right after the concert.

The car stopped at the theater doors, the barricades gave way. In a split second the windows were covered with hands, noses, mouths, flattened bodies. Against the windshield a single body made of fragments of men shouted incomprehensible words of love. The atmosphere grew heavy, the car was rocking back and forth. Hifnawi removed his eyeglasses and put them in his pocket.

Truncheons went to work. The police squadrons were striking with a vengeance, people did not seem to feel a thing. They would fall and get back up, there were always some who came back, the same or others, a bottomless well of grasping, desperate hands. All the sap of a too-fertile Egypt, its demographic pressure. One young man of twenty, his head streaming with blood, allowed himself to be led away by the forces of order; he looked back, shouting to her, "You are my life!"

Still more policemen stood elbow to elbow in a line at the foot of the stage, their eyes worried. Their nervousness anticipated violence and encouraged it. People were shoving in the aisles, climbing the walls. So much youth, all this vigor which had come up from the nearby province, the poor outskirts, could not be contained in one single space; all this hot blood running wild. This was a far cry from artistic ecstasy with one's hand to one's ear.

She came on stage, facing the ovation, the frenzied enthusiasm. The policemen held onto their truncheons, pressed closer together. She did not see them. Above their heads she threw her body toward the audience, responding to their invisible embrace with her empty hands. Her voice alone could control the flow of the clamor and its echo. She started toward the microphone but this had the opposite effect: the cries of the crowd were ever wilder, the wave of heat exploded. She stood her ground, thrust her chin forward, her body, the fury of the theater was inebriating, she provoked it and gave herself to it with her eyes open. She put her lips to the microphone and began to sing. Her breath went through the wires, into the air, over half a continent. Aden and Tripoli, Damascus and Benghazi. "*The memories are in my dream / Like a diamond on the wings of the night / How could I forget them / How can I steady my heart / They are the story of my love.*" I had written this poem, *Zikrayat*, "Memories," the way one pays a debt long overdue, the way one proclaims one's passion without shame. I was right. It was not patriotic hymns that the famished crowd needed, it was love songs. The theater melted all at once. Tenderness, pain, words that make one cry. Silence had solidi-fied, she tossed out each verse and took it up again, kept one, sharpened her voice on it, introduced another, then a third, began to juggle with them. The words explored the scales of waiting, overlapping and whirling like dervishes. The intimi-dated young men listened religiously, they didn't dare say another thing. The voice held them under its charm, they were children, she played with them. On an impossible variation, the shouts of the connoisseurs echoed and provoked a near-riot, but this time my diva didn't let them get away with it. She went one step further and imposed silence by the authority of her singing alone. She held the multitude on a tight rein, she was the one who decided when to let go and when to tighten up. The Voice of the Arabs, her own voice. It was my very own love that she was telling to the world.

The concert was a relatively calm one. Afterwards we found her in her greenroom, drained, still trembling from the excite-ment. On the radio, there was a short spell of military music, then the very solemn voice of the announcer, "This is *The Voice of the Arabs* . . . broadcasting from Cairo," as if he were going to faint at the end of his announcement. All the loudspeakers in the the-ater were transmitting the program; the crowd outside the build-ing had not moved. Now, the clamor of Alexandria was unleashed upon her, the radio had picked up the relay. My peas-ant girl had gathered the Arab people, the *Rais* was getting ready to speak to her, live. The announcer informed us that the large podium had been set up at the foot of the statue of Sa'd Zaghlul, before the crowd, before the sea. The shouting, in unison, of thousands of voices was part of the message. Nasser came on stage, he was wearing civilian clothes, a dark tie and a gray suit, he was the head of state, the Egyptian voters had just elected him.

"Oh children of our great Arab nation . . ." His inimitable voice echoed from the walls. Very low, not in the least declamatory, warm, almost tender. You might have thought this was an ordinary man preparing to pour his heart out to you, to reveal his problems and ask each person to be a witness. "We are millions, and imperialism wants to strangle us; we are tens of millions, one single Arab nation, from the Gulf to the ocean, bearers of an eternal message. One language, one culture, one civilization, unlimited resources—but what do we lack to claim our freedom? I will tell you: all that is lacking is for us to unite, to believe in ourselves, to raise our heads. Raise your heads, Arab brothers!"

Shouts, more shouts, from Beirut to Algiers. Even I felt an inner shock, an imperceptible shift, as did everyone. Nasser let the furor die down then began again. It was a marathon he was running. He spoke for two whole hours—on the summit in Bandung, on the war of independence in Algeria, on the Third World, on the price of cotton. He explained everything, and the words made sense coming from his lips, but their music too, coming and going, the rope pulled tight, the rope left slack; a collective trance. Because we had turned to the East to ask for the weapons which the West had refused to give us, the forces of imperialism had cut off our credits. The project of the Aswan High Dam was threatened, and that was to be our masterpiece, we could not possibly give it up. They were trying to bring us to our knees and make us change our tune through monetary means. But we knew where to go for money. And at this time, facing the crowd, Nasser gave us the news, the incredible yet simple news. I guessed it just before he uttered the words which could henceforth never be revoked: the Suez canal had been nationalized.

11

I HAD ALWAYS SAID that it was only a little sea which separated us from Europe, that we were from the same mold and that eventually there would be a bridge between us. *Your friends*: there was always a touch of spite in her voice. I'd made them believe, Taha Hussein, Abdel-Razzak bey, an entire generation of intellectuals and artists had made us believe. The Mediterranean will be an inner sea; a same cloak will cover us. All signs were born, on one side as on the other. The English and French bombarded our airports, attacked Port Saïd, marched on Ismaïlia. To punish us. For wanting to control our own resources, for wanting to become a modern country, like them. They had responded with war. A real war. The dead and the injured numbered in the thousands. What was worse, Israel had gotten involved, Palestine was no longer enough for her, her soldiers had come as far as the canal we had just nationalized. We'd sunken ships, obstructed her, what else could we do. The feeling that was consuming me was consuming everyone. For the first time, I was disgusted by the West, masquerading as democratic but in reality colonialist and nothing more.

Your friends. What could I say to her? My son Samir, if he were two or three years older, would have been a soldier. Already, he'd made up his own mind, and he'd been to demonstrations. Egypt was in her rights, and all the damned of the earth were supporting her, India and China and Yugoslavia, all the Arab countries; all the illiterate. Civilized people were aggressors. She was right.

My friends. Moreover, they had mistaken the era. The Americans and the Soviets had taken them by the ear and obliged them to back off. The time for European colonialism was over. Nasser, the man they had wanted to kill, had become the hero of the Third World, the idol of the Arab world. I rejoiced with her. Gunboat politics had collapsed, and the unequal battle had, miraculously, turned in our favor. We had won.

How could I explain to her that we had also lost? She thought we'd been betrayed in our minds; the promise had weakened our souls and corrupted our minds. It had been too close a call; the English and the French had dominated the economy, and it was normal that the regime wanted to have better control over the country, normal that they nationalize the big foreign companies. But she didn't realize. The decision stripped Egypt of a good part of its substance. Not just money but men, too, and not only the propertied classes. Thousands of Greeks, Italians, French, Maltese and British; all the minorities. Nothing to do with politics. Garo, the Armenian tailor who made my shirts: his shop was in Champollion Street. Saltiel, who for thirty years had worked in the office next to mine at the library. Paolo the dentist, Madame Iroula the boss of the Greek restaurant on rue Kasr el-Nil street. They belonged to another era. They had no influence. By the time the first shot was fired, they had vanished.

Alexandria was packing its bags, entire neighborhoods. The silken thread which had woven layer upon layer of this town, of every color, a splendid, fragile cloth. A real place of flesh and stone, a melting pot where all our desire for openness and diversity, all our tolerance, had been laid. A mass of ordinary, frightened people, interrupting their lives to pack their bags.

There were many Jews among those who were expelled. They had been living in this land since the dawn of time, were as Egyptian as I was. The recording industry and the cinema would never have known such a blossoming were it not for them. The composer Da'ud Husni was Jewish: he had trained Asmahan, and my diva herself performed his songs. Zaki Mrad, his daughter Leila Mrad, and a host of other singers, composers, and musicians. An entire patrimony, a huge part of our culture had been torn away.

It broke my heart. And yet Nasser's speech had been secular. His references to Islam had been limited, fundamentalism had been banned. The designation Arab does not refer to a religion. But Israel had cast doubts upon the loyalty of the Jews of the East, and our State was not sure enough of itself to consider all citizens as equals. That was our defeat. Implicitly, we were accepting the logic of the community—the most to be feared, capable of destroying any sense of solidarity of opinion as easily as frozen water breaks a stone. Wrenching scenes were unfolding on the quays of Alexandria. In the working class neighborhoods, people were celebrating the departure of those who had exploited them.

The exodus left us quite alone. But where could one protest, to which newspaper, with whom? The masses occupied the streets, their vigorous, fertile bodies, soldiers, a multitude. Revolutionary fervor had reached such a pitch that any dissident opinion was tantamount to complicity with the aggressors, treason. Carried by her own momentum, Egypt had closed herself to Western ideas, art, culture, let alone politics. Politics—to live as human beings—that was for them, not for us.

The result of the adventure was a more independent country, but it was also harder, poorer, more hostile. We might be free, but we were on our own, and with one less helping hand. We had the canal, it was ours now, and ours alone. We had won, after all. The revenue from the canal would help us to build the Aswan High Dam, to work, to develop the country.

If there are those who want to leave, then let them do so; history crushes the innocent, that's nothing new, we have no choice, we have to look to the future, that's what she said. She was singing to celebrate the victory. *"By God, for so long now, my weapon / I have missed you in combat / Speak and say that you are ready / Oh war, by God, for so long now."* Everyone took up the refrain, in the Egyptian cotton fields, on the banks of the Oronte in Syria and of the Tigris and Euphrates in Iraq, and the Rif in Algeria, the Palestinian refugee camps. An empire where Nasser was the absolute father. And she was the figurehead.

And who was I in all this? I loved my country as much as she did, as much as they did, as much as the Arab world. But an ineluctable chain of events, possibly ineluctable, had induced us to crush our own selves. And that spoiled my joy.

PART FOUR

1965-1975

1

THE AIR IN THE ROOM was dense and soft, rich with the particular smell of newborn babies. The little creature lay motionless in the semi-obscurity, on his back, his eyes open upon sensations which have no name. I raised the mosquito net and leaned close. He stared at me. I've come to say goodbye, I'll come visit you tomorrow, I'm leaving you with your mother and father, I have to go now, she'll be singing later on, she will, in two hours, you see, I have to be with her. He opened his toothless mouth and drooled a droplet of saliva onto the pillow. My grandson, made outside of me, in a parallel world to my own. He had caught hold of my little finger, and would not let me leave.

I'll tell you later, for the time being she's waiting for me. As for you, I love you like an unhoped-for gift, you are my flesh . . . but my soul still belongs to her. I can't help it, you're not the son of that love.

He was holding on as best he could, he just wouldn't listen. I went on talking in a low voice, his eyes were listening to me. You see, I could have told you that it was my youth, a long time ago; I could have told you about a violent love grown calm, one of those loves on which, at last, one can rest a grand-father's gaze. But it still consumes me like on the very first day, just as if I were young, what can I do. Watching lovers frolic on the opposite bank of the river, that's not yet for me. I'm on that riverbank too. I suffer, and I hope, just as they do. My love has never had a body, perhaps that's why, that's why it can voyage through time. Nothing has changed or corrupted it, it has escaped. And when it calls me, you see, I have to run to greet it.

His right hand clung to my finger, and with the other he reached up and touched my nose, his tiny fingers closed round the hair of my mustache. I did not dare move or speak. Tears rose suddenly to my eyes. It wasn't a game anymore. I'd never spoken of my love like that, to anybody. He was gurgling now, and never took his eyes from me. I took his hand between my lips and nibbled it. He let out a little cry of surprise, arched his body, laughed, wiggled his feet in the air. I looked at him with a hopeless, longing gaze; he restored my gaze to me. When my son Samir came in the room, he found me like that. He lay his hand on my shoulder and reminded me of the time for the concert.

In the taxi my heart spilled over with love for the child. Tarek. I gave him his name for the first time, I acknowledged his autonomous existence, stronger than anything. As the car sped through the town, this emotion mingled with another, a rising stage fright, something which happened before each recital, but this time more than usual. I'd been attending her concerts for over forty years, and nothing had cured me. "*How can I be aware of what is before or behind me / When the light of my beloved is not before or behind me?*" These verses by the Persian mystic Rumi were a perfect description of my state of mind. All it took was for her to go away, and she went away often.

She sang in every region of Egypt and half the Arab world. *The New Dawn*, to celebrate the fusion of Egypt and Syria; *Baghdad, Citadel of the Lions*, when the Iraqi monarchy collapsed; all the love songs. She truly believed, she truly resonated, she incarnated the tremendous transformation. She sang in Hulwan, the city which overlaps into the desert. The smelting furnaces had been lit for her. She sang at Aswan, *It Was But a Dream*, on the dam's construction site, the site of the new pyramid. Thousands of half-naked bodies, a teeming mass of earth-colored galabias, as far as the eye could see. She sang for the man with his bronze body, the peasants who had become workers, builders, soldiers, lost men, torn from their land. They heard their own suffering in her voice, and she was a homeland for them. She stayed with them, reassured them, Don't be afraid, you are changing our future with your hands, I too was a peasant, look how far I've come, and what about you, here with me. "*My eyes have grown used to you, I've left you, My heart has grown confused*": she spoke to them of what was elemental, the pain of love, my own verses, gone far from me. The words of others too; one of her songs was entitled *How Handsome You Are*, quite simply. You are the new heroes, your bodies aroused from sleep to work the steel, to move through the air, to wear an iron mask before the spray of sparks . . . how handsome you are. These were her new lovers.

She came in again, her silvery figure moving through the uproar, and the applause flowed behind her like a long train. The crowd was shouting her name, and another, bursting their lungs: Muhammad's. My friend was seated three seats over from me, and he gave me a sidelong glance, very moved, his back bent under the torrent. People were chanting in unison, stubborn in their ovation. He stood up, nodded, pointed to my diva to divert the applause to her. The audience did not yield, nothing could stop them. Muhammad finally gave in and went on stage. The concert had not yet begun, and we were about to see something unimaginable, the two of them together hand in hand, their arms raised before the crowd.

She turned to Qsabji. The old lute player embraced his instrument, an almost anachronistic figure before the shining orchestra, the forest of violins, the rows of cellos, flutes, bass, tambourines, and above all that famous, and omnipresent, electric guitar. Qsabji was startled, as if he were a dreamer brought back to earth. We all knew he was recovering from an operation, and this was his first appearance. In the midst of an enormous swell of applause in his honor she grabbed his hand. Qsabji. From the front row I could see the spotlights shining in his eyes. Muhammad took his other hand. The three of them greeted the audience, over and over.

Working with Muhammad. She had finally decided to honor the promise she had made to Nasser; he had insisted. The news had spread quickly, everywhere; no one could believe it. Reporters gathered details as they lingered around rehearsals, spoke to musicians, snatched secrets. There was not much that they could find out, only that the song was entitled *Inta Omri*, "You Are My Life," by the poet Ahmed Shafiq Kamel . . . and that a dispute had broken out over the electric guitar. Muhammad insisted upon the guitar: he said that his audience was younger than my diva's, and he had to have modern instruments. She took it very badly. But he would not give in. She asked for my advice, I replied that music was not my department. She asked Qsabji, who also dodged the issue. My feeling was that if the musical renaissance ushered in by Hamuli at the end of the last century had served no other purpose than to import electric guitars, it meant that we'd lost for good. But I didn't say anything.

And now, here we were. Before us the Star of the Orient was getting ready to sing music by Muhammad Abd al-Wahab. The feeling which overcame me was close to panic. The two of them. And other lyrics, not mine. My two parallel worlds had joined, and I had been mysteriously excluded. The image of my grandson suddenly struck me, I don't know why. She was already gesturing to the musicians.

They began the long introduction. The two audiences were finally united. The same faces of dark leather, the same patience of mummies, the same eternal eyes, nothing differed. Yet they were two distinct groups, two sides who had been glaring at each other their entire life. Now they had been inextricably thrown together by the simple grace of the ticket machine, and all they could do was glance at each other and wonder. There was a wariness between them, and a shyness as well, the wariness and shyness of a historic reconciliation that no one had even expected anymore.

The instrumental introduction was drawing to a close, so she rose to her feet and went up to the microphone. The concert was being filmed for television, the cameras had to be placed more than fifty feet away, and she had refused to sing "with a finger to her temple." In any case, not many people had televisions. The radio remained the uncontested sovereign, it followed her wherever she went.

The applause died down, and the silence which followed was not a usual silence. Not the unanimous, homogeneous fervor, but a curious tension, an expectancy at the point of bursting.

Her lips parted at last. With her first breath, the tone was remarkably contained: "*Your eyes brought me back to days gone by / Taught me to regret the past and its pain.*" The orchestra kept very close to her voice, following all the curves, coming and going, playing close to the nerve. "*What I saw / Before my eyes saw you . . .*" and the music held even closer to the movement, crescendo, yet casual, like in a film when a too-quiet tune begins to hover. My diva stepped back, began from the beginning again, injected some calm, lingered on one meandering phrase which led to another one, stopped on the third verse which she broke up into fragments: "*What I saw . . . What I saw . . . before my eyes . . . Saw you . . . Was only a lost existence . . .*" The violins rose shrilly with each passage. When they reached the climax, "You are my life!" erupted like a flame, her voice held the last syllable and drew it out, dwelled on it and magnified it, causing it to stream over the audience's heads and their raised arms. Suddenly let loose, the audience overflowed with endless enthusiasm.

206 · SÉLIM NASSIB

I recognized Muhammad's remarkable brilliance. His music had knowingly led the audience from one level to the next until the final, inevitable ovation. She had molded herself to the exercise with obvious pleasure, her voice had crushed the structure in order to soar free of any obstacle, and the two idols had miraculously formed one single god. The people responded with their cries: you too, you too are my life . . . And now she was starting on the first three words of the following couplet: "*The beautiful nights . . .*" improvising as her inspiration saw fit, entering a dialogue with the docile orchestra, who again provided a loving reply. "*The beautiful nights, desire and love, for so long / My heart set them aside for you.*" The fervor rose to the boil, overflowed in wild applause. Solidly anchored in the middle of the stage, she received the tempestuous acclaim with open arms, and sent it back with equal force, repeating the two verses in their entirety, extending certain phrases at whim, playing on words, and smiling as she turned the knife in the wound.

She ignored the riot, looked only at me, drew closer. She made a sign to me with her chin, and her little laugh seemed to make fun of my pallor. When her lips approached the microphone she murmured, her voice hoarse, "Taste the love with me, taste it . . ." and the audience fell to pieces. She laughed again, pure provocation, took the verse again, taste with me, until there was nothing left but the one word, taste, which however she pronounced it sounded as suggestive as possible. She was over sixty years old, and now she dared, there was no more shame. At last. And I who was the other side of her mirror, her whole audience concentrated into one single person, I had not waited in vain. I was her life.

2

TAREK WAS TWO YEARS OLD. I'd gone on talking to him about her, relentlessly. I would pick him up at his parents' and take him along the banks of the Nile. While he played, I would tell him about her concerts; I could no longer tell them apart, they'd all merged into one interminable concert. I wanted to explain to him—I don't know what exactly—but it seemed essential. This thing that had happened between her and me, this secret: it should serve to light his future. I was in a hurry, I no longer had so much time, soon I would have to keep silent . . . because he would begin to understand.

Everyone said that Egypt was about to take off: the national revenue had doubled in ten years. You could not yet feel the effects in everyday life, perhaps it was even the opposite. The movement which had yanked the peasants out of their villages to thrust them into a better life had reached a sort of saturation point. People, suddenly, were exasperated by slogans, by speeches, by the omnipresent police force, by socialism, better tomorrows that never came. Workers' strikes were on the increase, brutally repressed, and there were student demonstrations, demanding the restoration of civil liberties. Egypt had never had so many students.

Her voice soothed all the anger, all the sorrow. She would come onto the stage in a white dress, a yellow dress, a green dress, and people would throw out their hearts to her, she'd take them into her warmth, breathlessly, for a long time. At midnight, when the scheduled program was reaching its end, she still wanted to sing, and she'd start *Ya Zalimni*, "You Tyrannize Me," a long poem I'd written for her fifteen years earlier; or *Amal Hayati*, "The Hope of My Life," Muhammad's second song. This part of the concert was for fun, improvisation was welcome. People in the audience removed their jackets, rolled up the sleeves of their galabias. Their idol would sweat out their distress, wallow in it, release it. She knew that the Arab people remained glued to their radio, that the streets were deserted, that the leaders avoided making the slightest declaration because on that night, their people only had ears for her. But after midnight, all the glory was no longer of any significance. The breath and smell of the men there before her was enough. Her fame had become somewhat abstract. Even the honors, even Nasser, even politics. I knew her. That the dream of Arab unity had fallen short after four years, that the fusion between Egypt and Syria had finished in a rancorous divorce: she could not really sense the reality of such events. All that mattered was the stage. She abandoned her body to a trance, as if that were the only way she could feel she existed. Through the trembling of her belly, the intoxication of her own voice, the shouts of love which covered her in return. Only the space crushed by light enabled her to put her awareness of things to sleep. And then, only then, with her eyes half-closed, would she release the brakes and let herself go until morning.

I told all this to Tarek. She speaks, and repeats, for each person as if he were alone with her: *Far, far, you and me, you and me, all alone . . .* You, the man seated in the darkness, who causes me to weep, causes so much pain, if I had known I would not have loved you, you who are my life, the hope of my life, that is what love is like, why can't I wake up from this dream where you are holding me. She says she has been waiting for him for nights on end, nights on end, and why doesn't he come, why, why . . . Her voice comes and goes, marries the melody which suddenly unravels in an apotheosis, and thousands of chests can breathe again, together.

The orchestra does not leave them the time to shout their fill, they go straight on to the next couplet, the point of departure for a new circular intoxication. But the words have lost their meaning. In the dizziness of the theater, she is now playing on one syllable, one fragment, modulating her voice on one letter. The poem is nothing more than a pretext for abstract variations on sounds shot with emotion. The man listening has lost any sense of where he is. From time to time he feels himself shouting with the others, as she passes through a deeper intonation; he hardly realizes. Very quickly he falls silent, and his silence is a word. Far, far, you and me. Whirling, ritual ceremony, he is caught in the spiral and can't break free. He has no more family, or mistress, or children, his brother hasn't been arrested, it's not so hard to make ends meet. Tonight he won't go home to sleep, he has time off. His body buoyant, he lets himself be carried off by the mystery, You and me. Far from the eyes of power, far from domestic troubles, in an intimate realm. At home there is a woman waiting for him, or no longer waiting for him, who may love him, he isn't thinking about her for a second. He is here, in the dark hole where only commerce with the goddess matters. To listen to this voice he would gladly stay the entire night, his entire life.

But he suddenly recognizes the theme of departure. Again she tells him she is waiting for him and why doesn't he come . . . That is when he knows the party is nearing the end, something he refuses with his entire body. Outside, dawn has not yet come, sing some more my divine woman, I kiss your feet. The orchestra plays faster, he is on his feet. The voice is not yet silent, here comes the explosion. He leaps up with the others, his arms closing round her from afar, closing over the void, just a few more minutes. He would have liked to shout to her that it isn't true, he isn't like that, not he, because he also loves and suffers and waits . . . and perhaps for a moment happiness is possible.

Tarek began to tap with his little rake against the parapet, shouting incomprehensible sounds, just to make noise so I'll be quiet, in the end. And yet I could see in his eyes that he understood.

I didn't remember her concerts. Except for one that I will never forget. She had sung *El Atlal,* "The Ruins," one of Nagui's most beautiful poems. But the words alone would not have been able to express so much sadness—sadness is not the word, the wrenching feeling that has no name, and which each person recognizes when he or she feels it. *"My heart, do not ask where desire is / It was a palace of dreams and it has crumbled / Give me a drink and drink with me on the ruins . . ."* We had believed; we are still at the gate of the world. We're not going to cry, but we'll drink, pour something, drink with me. We burned, after all, didn't we; we loved after all. Better than that: *"Has love ever seen any as drunk as we are / We went along the path beneath the moon / And our shadow walked ahead of us."* Hope was something good to experience. But when we woke up, all we found were ruins: *"The world as we know it / And lovers going each their own way."*

The world as we know it. With no lightness, no openings. Sad, military, closely watched. She shouted: *"Give me back my freedom, untie my hands / I gave everything, and kept nothing for myself,"* and an insane furor overwhelmed the theater, a deliverance from deep within. People were shouting and crying for something vital which had been lost; they would have liked to know what it was.

With the invention of the transistor, her voice was able to go everywhere. Give me back my freedom, untie my hands: those words were heard by Mustapha Amine in the prison where he was locked away, his ear glued to the radio. He thought they were meant for him. Despite her repeated appeals to Nasser, she had not been able to obtain the liberation of the journalist who had intervened in her favor immediately following the revolution. The sins of those who wield a pen would seem to be the most unforgivable.

Untie my hands. Everyone recognized on her lips the very weight on their own chest, their own disappointed hopes . . . or not even. What she was singing expressed the essence of the thing, the very state of mind, a profound nostalgia for no visible object.

The audience no longer tried either to applaud or to please her. She was outside herself. A feeling of mournfulness overwhelmed us. It was nothing to do with the poem, or the pain of love, or politics. Or perhaps it was all those things at once, grown terrible because of an absence which, from the very first instant, had kept us on the verge of tears. Behind my diva, Qsabji's chair was empty. And on the woven chair lay his lute, nothing else, placed delicately face down, its neck in the air.

3

I N THE DARKNESS a man had placed his hands against the metal grille of a closed shop. He was shouting God is great, God is great, banging his forehead against the metal curtain. That night, on his own, he represented the entire Arab world.

War. We thought we had won. We had lost so utterly that everything was lost. Everything we had been trying to do for twenty years, for forty years, our every endeavor had led to the most total failure, there was not even any point talking about it anymore.

He was banging his head so hard that he had begun to bleed. Nobody was paying any attention. The shouting crowd went by without even noticing him. They had other things to do. There were those who tore their hair, or screamed continuously, or twisted their mouths with fear. Where could they run? There was nowhere left to flee.

We had believed it was enough to get our independence, to distribute the land, nationalize the canal, industrialize the country, call for unity among Arabs, and take the lead of the Third World. We thought we had won. Or at least were in with a chance.

I went up to the man and tried to get him to stop what he was doing; he was much younger and stronger than me. He had his back turned, he wanted nothing more to do with mankind, all that mattered was this metal curtain, the space between his arms. He went on banging his head, totally unaware that I was pulling him by the arm. I caught a glimpse of his expression, so troubled that I was ashamed. Like when you push open a door and encounter a nakedness, a somewhat disgusting yet all too human intimacy. I stepped aside and excused myself. But he hadn't even realized, he'd lost all awareness of anything else. He wanted to bash himself into oblivion, but couldn't do it.

"Oh children of our nation, we have grown used to sitting together and speaking together in moments of joy as in moments of bitterness . . ." That broken voice, still ringing in my ears. He had been so proud, had defied imperialism, Israel, half the planet, had brought about the fall of the Iraqi monarchy, had sent his army to fight against the King of Yemen and the oil sheiks. Oh children of our nation. He wasn't speaking to anyone else, only to us, looking us straight in the eyes, sitting together, talking together. His face filled the entire television screen, black and white, or rather, gray, lines moving slowly over his face from top to bottom. Oh children. Then came the fateful words, words we all heard at the same time throughout the entire Arab world, words we would never have believed coming from anyone's lips but his. "We must recognize that it is a major, serious defeat . . ." For five days, on the radio, announcements of victory had followed other announcements of victory. Perhaps they had been exaggerated. But this! The leader himself announcing it. Major, serious defeat.

His lids drooped over his eyes, his fine mustache was trembling, we had to believe him, what else could we do? He gave the details, told us about the war we had lost. The entire Egyptian air force destroyed on the ground in less than six hours; Sinai, Gaza, and the West Bank occupied, the Golan Heights invaded, and the most terrible news of all: Jerusalem.

It was a disaster, thousands of dead and wounded. But it was when he said, "Let me return to the ranks of the people and carry on with my task like any ordinary citizen . . . Let me . . . like anyone among you," that we finally realized. This defeat was of the kind that leaves nothing behind. The father was throwing in the towel, hanging up his apron. Only that could make us realize the extent of the disaster. It was no longer just about a military defeat. It was much worse than that. On the radio, the Israelis had announced the organization of a major concert of classical music to celebrate their victory; they were already moving on. The world had started turning again, without us. We had fallen back into our past.

How long does the body need to say no? And no to what, anyway? Just plain no. Unaware of having taken any decision, I saw myself rushing down the stairs along with my son Samir; we hadn't even stopped to talk about it. All of Cairo was doing the same thing right now, and in Beirut, Damascus, Baghdad, Alexandria, Algiers . . . When we got out in the street, it was just after six in the evening, and the clear light was changing by degrees, as if there were an eclipse, so quickly that I had the impression that the light would fade completely. This darkening of the sky, just as the dazed inhabitants came out of their buildings, was like the end of the world. I was one of them, pushed to the right, then the left, carried along under the gigantic shadow, moving forward into chaos, deafened by a voice calling hoarsely in my ear, "Nasser! Nasser!" until I suddenly realized that the voice was my own.

I let myself be carried along to the left, then stopped and leaned against a wall to catch my breath. The flood of people went by, grazing me as they went. I heard the echoes of the crowd reverberating all around me. Countless spontaneous demonstrations crossed paths in the intersections and squares, on the bridges, and spilled into each other. Left to its own resources, the city was going round and round, getting larger by the minute. I had lost my son. I was alone now.

Perhaps the man banging his head was right. The best thing,

no doubt, would be to do likewise, or to sit on the curb and cry. For twenty years we really had been trying to stand tall: "Arab brother, raise your head." And there in the space of six hours, six days, we had slid all the way back down the slope. Our fall had been too quick, no one knew how to live with such a rout from within; how to live, defeated.

Blindly, the crowd gathered to converge on the presidential palace as they chanted the name *Raïs*. In other Arab capitals, crowds were heading to the Egyptian embassy, the seat of government, the house of the mufti. They were shouting, No! That was the answer to the question. Night had fallen, and the street lighting had not come on. In the darkness the human tide had invaded the center, all the centers at once, a merging mass of figures shaken and startled, the only light that of the fearful whites of their eyes. Asked to choose, the Arab people had, instinctively, paralyzed all their cities. An enormous, spontaneous strike. Their only strength was their size, the mass of bodies. We would not move until Nasser revoked his resignation.

I was trying desperately to go against the current. Streets were no longer streets, actual distances no longer made sense. The Nile corniche was blocked, so it was impossible for me to go down Ramses Avenue. I set off down the long, narrow Rue Champollion without recognizing it, passing various demonstrations which carried me along with them. Shadowy buildings, empty of people, lurked over us on either side. All the windows were painted dark blue, because of the war. The blind city, at the mercy of the uproar, had abandoned its houses in order to take to the street. At one point, exhausted, my knees trembling, I leaned against a parked car. Concentric shouts immediately assailed me. To be alone like that, in the middle of a gigantic nervous breakdown, was impossible. I began walking forward again, moving with the people and their pain, fighting alongside them, against them, taking the same overflowing emotions into my gut. It was too late to say I, me, I personally think that. We were we, there was nothing for it. Immersed once again in the shapeless miasma of our burning, self-suffocating origins.

I was no longer able to slow down or use my elbows to get out. The current was too strong. Or I was too old. For hours I walked unsteadily alongside the sons of Egypt and of the Arab world, bouncing from place to place, becoming, in spite of myself, a part of the same monstrous flesh. *Tawhid*, "to unify:" that had been Nasser's obsession, to unify the Arab world in the way God is one; my diva, with her voice, had known better than anyone how to do it. But it was only today that it was really happening. Tossed among the sea of shoulders, I moved to the same rhythm as the blind crowd. Nasser. Nasser. His name was the karma of this procession through the darkness, these nuptials exultant with misfortune.

And yet, there was another name which continued to guide my steps, another compass. There I was in front of the villa, and I have no idea how I managed to get there.

A human mass blocked the entrance. All facing the same direction, thousands of men waited below the illuminated windows. It would be an insurmountable task, beyond my strength, to make my through the crowd. I had walked half the night only to fail her in the last few meters. I had no stamina. Trapped in the last row, I could feel tears of helplessness welling in my eyes. Behind those walls, she was behind those walls, only thirty meters away. I wanted to take her hands and kiss them, to wash my face in her open palms. That was why I had come all the way across the city on foot.

I stayed there against the parapet, exile in my throat. My face was not familiar but my name was famous. For the first time in my life I decided to make use of it. I am who I am, her poet, and I dared to say it. Several braggarts immediately surrounded me. They shoved the passive crowd aside and cleared a passage for me. We made it to the gate. A line of soldiers, very young men, stood protecting the entry, and the untidy state of their uniforms was another sign of defeat.

All the lights were on and the living rooms were deserted. No one came to greet me. Upstairs I found nothing but a succession of empty rooms. The house seemed to have been abandoned in great haste. I went toward her apartments.

Mahmud opened, her nephew Mahmud. Without a word, we fell into each other's arms. In the little waiting room, by her closed door, were a dozen or so people: Sunbati, Bayram, Sheik Zakariya, a few other close friends. They were looking at me. I had lost my tarboosh, my hair was disheveled, my collar was on crooked, and my shirt was not tucked in on one side. I shook hands and sat down, there was an armchair free between Sunbati and the old Sheik Zakariya. I was glad that he was there, Sheik Zakariya, he had patched up his quarrel with her at the last minute, a quarrel which had lasted for over ten years. In one corner was a radio, the volume on low, nothing but catastrophic news. No one was listening. We already knew the most important thing. Unfortunately.

The bedroom door opened and Saadiya appeared, her face swollen, her hair so white that it looked blue. She was followed by Dr. Hifnawi, his stethoscope round his neck.

"She's all right," he said in a hushed voice. "I gave her a tranquilizer. But she can't see anyone."

He came to shake my hand then and, not knowing what to do, sat down with us in the circle. Bitter tea was served. In a low voice, I asked Sheik Zakariya what had happened.

"She suddenly didn't feel well. I had just arrived and she came up to me. An old woman, all of a sudden. As if her own body had suffered the defeat. She said, 'You see . . .' and then fell over. With Hifnawi and Saadiya we carried her into her room."

Sunbati leaned over to me.

"It's a plot, a plot that's bigger than we are."

He nodded his head several times, the way one does at funeral wakes.

"Our own allies, the Russians, have betrayed us. The weapons they sold us were inferior. Just tell me how we can be responsible."

I didn't feel like talking. What could I say, in any case?

"Why the Russians?" asked Sheik Zakariya, almost distractedly. "There was nothing in it for them."

"How the hell do we know. The Russians and Americans must have worked something out behind our backs. I'll give you this, you give me that . . . that sort of thing."

I stopped listening. The shouts from the street were still ringing in my ears. Better not to even think about it. Tarek was only three years old. He was going to grow up in the world of the defeat. Weariness brought on a sort of waking sleep in me. I slumped down into the armchair. The political discussion had begun in hushed tones, but now it was getting louder. Arguments overlapping, the Americans' fault, the Russians' fault, the entire world's fault, we had expected enemy planes from the west and they'd come from the east . . . must have been an aircraft carrier, American of course, top-secret, a plot I tell you, bigger than us.

"Those who don't know how to dance claim that the floor is uneven."

I opened my eyes. These last words had been Sheik Zakariya's. So much sadness. And anger, too, which I shared. To hear us, you'd think we were not to blame for anything. It was not their victory, it was not our defeat. We'd had nothing to do with it, we were not there, it was not us.

4

IN THE MIDDLE OF THE NIGHT NASSER went back on his decision to resign. From one end of the Arab world to the other, radios, televisions and loudspeakers relayed the news, but the cities remained blocked. No one wanted to believe his decision yet, it was too soon, first of all the tragedy of abandonment had to be played out to the end.

And it was. Not until the next day, in the early morning hours, were the people persuaded. It was like a happy, exhausted ending, after a long ordeal. The war was not over, the Israelis were pursuing their conquest of the Golan in Syria and at the same time, the Arab people were expressing . . . their joy. They had lost the match, but not their shepherd. They had rescued the most important thing: this man, our leader, the incarnation of our unity. If we were rushing headlong to the abyss, it might as well be with him, the failed father, but a father all the same. I too was relieved, I could not deny it. I was a part of this nation. This proof of loyalty at the most difficult moment was our only consolation.

That did not alter the fact that the shipwreck had occurred. After a day or two the enormity of the defeat resurfaced, we learned of disquieting details, crushing errors. We learned the truth despite the ever-watchful censorship, stronger than ever. The radio was relentless. The catastrophe required us to close ranks, that was exactly what the enemy expected, wrenching scenes on the public square. As a family we had to present a united front, we were vanquished but had not lost our dignity, we had lost a battle but not the war. However dark the gut feeling provoked by the night of the resignation, the return to propaganda was even more sickening.

Whose fault was it then? The question remained, like a tiny pebble in one's shoe. The conspiracy theory didn't quite hold water, so something else was found. "We spent our time singing 'Oh night!'" wrote one (left-wing) newspaper, "eating beans and laughing at the jokes we'd made up about our leaders, while at the same time, over there, behind the dunes, *they* were preparing for a real war. We would not have suffered such humiliation if we had learned to mobilize ourselves, to grow, to become modern, and serious."

That is how the allusions began, and the exaggerations grew over the days which followed. We were dreamers, our temperament had been our downfall, our taste for pleasure, our immoderate love of words. And who endorsed this atavistic behavior, this criminal nonchalance, who'd been encouraging it for decades? "We will not proclaim the innocence of art," replied one of the newspapers leading the hunt. "We must admit it: our Eastern art is one of the causes of the catastrophe. In other countries, art gives life to the soul and the mind, and galvanizes consciousness. But here, all things carefully considered, art has become a permanent incitement to indolence and contemplation. How can a nation prepare for war if it sits until four in the morning listening to a singer on the radio?"

She no longer left her room, no one had seen her. We did not know where to go, so we'd formed the habit of meeting every day in the little parlor in front of her door. Hifnawi was back in his office, the household employees had vanished, the only one left was old Saadiya, who received the guests. She played go-between, informing her mistress of our presence, bringing us her replies. Her little one thanked us for our visits, she knew we were close, it was not the attacks she'd been subject to which made her sad, but the defeat itself.

Some articles claimed openly that the war had been lost by an army of musicians and poets born of the previous generation and who, on the pretext of artistic ecstasy, had caused the Arab nation to stray from its higher duties. Although I rejected such accusations, they affected me deeply. The intoxicating laments for impossible love: that was me. My living passion was itself a palace of dreams, the contemplation of which had brought on the catastrophe. That was it. No matter how much I denied it, protested along with the others, it was my fault. The fault of the much regretted Qsabji too, and of Sheik Zakariya, Sunbati, Bayram, Muhammad Abd al-Wahab. We had wanted to revive an ancestral dream and pass it on, a dream which had been modernized, and we tried . . . It seems it would have been better to train soldiers, specialists, war technicians. The absurdity of the conclusion was perfectly obvious. What sort of people would we have been if we had turned our back on our culture? For me, the reason for the drama was exactly the opposite. We had not managed to go far enough, to revolutionize our heritage, to bring it to its ultimate conclusion. That was, precisely, where we had failed.

But how could we have done things otherwise? The war over Suez had been imposed upon us, had dealt a decisive blow to the cosmopolitanism which had been our wealth. The necessities of the battle became the decisive argument. We had interrupted studies on the time of the pharaohs, on language, on the Coptic contribution to our civilization. The fabric had worn thin, society had become more fragile. And then what? Perhaps there was no solution? Perhaps we were doomed from the start? I could not accept such an idea.

I took Tarek down to the Nile. To the same places I used to walk with her. The fact of having made all those secret confessions to this small boy during the first two years of his life had left me almost shy with him. Now he was three and a half, but that was not the only reason. I could no longer talk to him of my immense love, the love which had led to the defeat. It was enough just to listen to him talk, filling me with silent wonder, while my heart was heavy. He was beginning to have friends, he used all the words he knew, and then some; it was never-ending, so fresh.

One evening on the way home I bought a newspaper. On the front page there was an open forum, and a commentary signed by one of the leaders of the Egyptian left. The title spoke for itself: "I accuse the Star of the Orient of having been the opium of the people." Without taking the time to read it, I picked Tarek up and jumped in the first taxi.

She threw open the door to her room and faced the small group who filled her parlor. She was holding the newspaper.

"The time for lamentations is over, the mourning has gone on long enough. Now we have to start fighting again."

She spoke with such energy. Anger had restored the color to her face, her body had recovered its poise. Anger erased all her wrinkles, and would sweep everything in its wake. She turned to face me, and then melted. She drew near, slowly, asked me if she had got it right, was this really Tarek, and I nodded my head. She wanted to take him in her arms, but she had shout-ed so loudly only moments earlier that Tarek burst into tears and snuggled even deeper in my arms for refuge. She said, "You can cry, go on. I've sung enough for your grandfather. Now I'll sing for you."

She had decided to leave. The weapons may have been defeated, but people's souls were still proud. She would tour the country, one town after another, anywhere affected by the defeat. You say that voice puts the people to sleep: just wait, you'll see, that voice will wake them up.

I was due to begin my retirement three days later. I'd been entitled to it for over a year, but I'd been delaying it as the months went by. I'd spent over fifty-three years in this library, practically my entire active life. My colleagues had organized a farewell ceremony. The entire music world had been invited, along with writers and poets, Tawfiq al-Hakim, Naguib Mahfouz . . . I expected it to be a sad event, the beginning of the end. But when the time came, I was as cheerful as a young man. Right afterwards I had to rush off to the central station. I had no more work, I was free. She'd invited me to go along on her national tour. Almost a honeymoon.

"Stay, you are the dam which protects us / Stay, you are what remains of the people's hope / You are Nasser the victorious / You are beloved by the people." Those are the words the poet Saleh Jawdat had written during the night of the resignation, and now she was throwing them to the face of the world with her very first concert, in Damanhur. She sang them with such conviction that the audience was trembling. Nasser the victorious? Victorious over what? How could they say such a thing? It was our old sickness, coming back. Taking the word for the thing. In the train, I'd ventured an allusion to this notion. "What else do you suggest?" she'd replied. "A tour devoted to self-criticism and self-denigration? I will never be the voice of defeatism. The people are full of despair, don't know where to turn. First we have to unite them and give them confidence. That's the most urgent thing. Afterwards, we'll see."

Rebroadcast on all the radio stations, her recital was first and foremost a response to the defamatory criticism. I do not drug my people. On stage, there was no more sensual, lascivious modulation, no more circular breathing patterns relentlessly returning to the same musical phrase, no indulgence, no complicity. The audience greeted this deeply serious voice with an almost silent devotion. They too were trying to behave. It was no longer a question of slipping away into the night with one's hand on one's ear and one's head held back. In the end, I didn't care. She could do as she pleased. Speak her lyrics, hammer them, declaim them. For me, that wasn't the point. Slumped in my front-row seat, I was quite simply thrilled to see her there. A few meters away, still standing, still alive. And sensing at my back the rumbling of the audience as they responded, their cry of pain.

Just as she was attacking the second couplet, she had a moment of weakness. She broke off, leaned against the chair and motioned to the orchestra. The instruments fell silent. You couldn't hear a single sound. And there, in that silence, she took up the microphone : "As God is my witness, like each one of you I believed that our house was destroyed and that misfortune would forever be our lot. I shut myself up at home and did not want to see a soul." She had never done such a thing, speak to her audience, still less speak about her personal life. "But one can't stay forever in the darkness. One day I wondered if my voice, this gift from God, was not meant to serve anymore. If there was nothing more I could bring to my wounded homeland, to the mother of the soldier who died in combat, to her child orphaned by the war. The answer is this evening, my presence here before you. I have decided to sing everywhere, to mobilize your hearts and your faith, to say, wherever I go, that we have lost only the first battle, and to win the next one, we must unite and we must change. With the help of God. I ask all the women of this country to imitate my example and donate their jewels to the war effort. All the money raised by these concerts on my tour, the total box office earnings, I will give for the defense of the country."

A few awkward bursts of applause followed. When silence fell again, she slowly removed the earrings which the emir of Kuwait had offered her a few years earlier, along with her necklaces and bracelets. Her gestures were those of a woman humbly undressing in public. Two men came onto the stage carrying a flag by each corner, and she dropped her gift into the folds of the flag. There were not many women in the audience, filling only a small, separate, square on the left-hand side. The flag made its rounds, and nearly all the women removed their jewelry to toss it in like a ritual offering. As for the men in the audience, who were suddenly on their feet, she began to sing the national anthem, *Biladi* (my country), her voice full of tears. Since the defeat in June, this was the first time that Egyptians had dared, be it with rage or timidity, to raise their heads again.

The Damanhur recital brought in 283,000 guineas; the one in Mansurah, 120,000, and in Alexandria, another 100,000, not including the women's jewelry. She sang *Stand Up With Faith* and *Hope Has Become Action, and The Dream Is Fighting,* but above all the famous couplet from *Al Atlal,* "*Give me back my freedom, untie my hands,*" which each time elicited the same scene of riotous adoration. She went to the destroyed city of Port Saïd, to Ismaïlia, which had been affected by the war of attrition, and in Mansurah she offered ten thousand guineas for the reconstruction of the city. She set up a National Union of Egyptian Women in order to help wounded soldiers and their families, and organized a drive for sewing machines which she distributed to the canal-zone population, who had lost everything. She went everywhere, but nowhere could she find rest. As if the name she'd been given, the Opium of the People, could not be erased no matter how she tried.

If anyone was pleased, it was those in power. Lacking policy, mired in a disastrous situation, subject to a war of attrition, the leaders thanked the heavens for the unhoped-for assistance the diva was bringing them. Her concerts had become the only events capable of improving the country's morale. Her name and Nasser's would be linked forever. There were happy moments, and bitter moments, but it was the same adventure. She was carrying a legend on her shoulders, and wherever she went she was able to mobilize the people in a way no speech could ever do again. She was followed from one region to the next, and every railroad station rolled out the red carpet for her. Still, she refused receptions and honors; elegant evening gowns and jewelry were no longer appropriate. She was adamant. There could no longer be any question of musical ecstasy, at least officially. I was not fooled. Even if the music was full of pain there was, no less, the presence of pleasure. The sap rose, each time. Perhaps we had too much of this poisonous pleasure, but I didn't know any other. Her voice was made for it, there was no way round it. And our ears, our bodies, our soul. Patriotic words didn't change a thing, nor did the military music. She didn't want to know. It wouldn't have taken much to persuade her to wear a uniform. But even that would not have changed anything. The dizziness of sensuality which went through her before overwhelming the crowed was much more powerful than she was.

5

S HE PLACED HER HAND ON MINE, and smiled. She had just come back from Paris, where she sang at the Olympia. I should have been with her on that trip. But a pain in my left thigh had kept me bedridden. I had heard of sciatica but this was my first experience of it. She had gone there without me. During her absence I'd become acquainted with other words in the vocabulary that I'd never used. Illness, pain, time in bed, old age. I had been so looking forward to it. Paris, like a homecoming, but with her. Two lovers in their souls who had come all this way and were returning to the point of departure, having found peace, or almost.

She must have been moved when she saw me bedridden like that, I don't know, perhaps she imagined the day I would no longer be there.

"After the second concert I wanted to be in Cairo, the smells of home, the tastes . . . I told Saadiya to pack my bags. Poor woman, she's so old. She can't see well, can't hear well, but just knowing she was in Paris gave her a second youth. But she was glad to come home all the same. And there was this telegram from Nasser, too. He's giving me a diplomatic passport and the title of ambassador. I had to come back."

I didn't say anything, there was no need.

"And . . . I missed my friends too much."

I relaxed a bit, and she smiled.

"I'm singing at Aziza's tonight."

"And I won't be there. This has never happened."

"And it never will happen. Everything's arranged. My nephew and three of his friends will come to get you at eight o'clock. They'll take you there, on your back. Tonight, you're the lord."

I wanted to reply, but the words formed a knot in my throat. Fortunately, Hoda came in just at that moment. She placed the tray on the bed and drew up another chair. For a long moment, and with a feeling of serene equilibrium, I had before my eyes the only two women who had ever mattered. Then, as if she had merely wanted to offer me that spectacle, Hoda went out and left us alone again.

"Tell me about Paris," I said quietly, after a silence.

"I used all the French you taught me. My nephew never left me alone for a minute. At the hotel he had a room next to mine, I couldn't move. If you let him he would have slept in front of my door. For him this trip was like an operation in enemy territory. You remember, everyone said the trip was too risky, so soon after the defeat, the Zionists are powerful in France and they might trigger demonstrations. In fact a lot of the tickets were bought by Egyptian Jews, the head of the Olympia told me as much. On the first evening the orchestra was coming to the end of the instrumental introduction and I got up to sing *Amal Hayati*, and all of a sudden I saw a young man jump onto the stage and rush toward me. Nobody had the time to react, he threw himself at my feet. He wanted to kiss them! As he rushed toward me I lost my balance and fell flat out, just like that, on stage in front of everyone! In the meantime the security people had overwhelmed the young man. He was a young Tunisian living in the north of France. Poor boy, he'd used all his savings to pay for the trip and the ticket. I insisted that he be allowed to stay in the theater. And then, while I was singing, I couldn't stop looking at him out of the corner of my eye. If you could have seen how his eyes were shining! That's the greatest danger I escaped in Paris."

She was laughing and leaned with her palms against the edge of the bed. A little girl. Then she seemed to make a decision.

"I came to tell you . . ."

"What?"

"I have to go away again. In three days. I'm taking my diplomatic passport and I'm going away."

"Where?"

"I want to repeat my Egyptian tour all through the Arab world. I'll fly to Khartoum to start with and from there go directly to Fez, Rabat, Tunis, and so on. I wanted to let you know. I won't be stopping in Cairo between concerts. I'll be gone . . . a long time."

"You're leaving and you won't come back, is that it . . ."

"Yes. I'm leaving and I'm not coming back."

She too was suddenly serious. Then, laughing again:

"That's not even true. Of course I'll come back, you're silly. Once I've reunited the Arab world. But when will that be? God is wisest."

6

THE TELEVISION HAD JOINED IN. They were broadcasting her concerts two or three days after she gave them. I saw her on stage at the Olympia, while the radio was broadcasting, live this time, her recital in Khartoum, and the press announced her imminent departure for Tripoli, in Libya. Everywhere she went she was greeted like a head of state, like the last lifeline. The names of the places she went were not important, this airport could have been anywhere. She seemed to be forever coming down the steps from the plane, reviewing an unreal honor guard, shaking the hands of ministers with perfectly invisible faces; her feet no longer touched the ground. She had earned ubiquity.

If I wanted to see her, all I had to do was turn the knob at any time of day or night, move the needle and there she was, always, in her true home. Held captive by the three square meters of my bed, I lay there resonating to the sound of that immaterial voice wafting over the Arab world. She entered through my pores, singing inside me, murmuring in my chest. The days were all alike, and even resembled the night. I inhaled her voice with the air I breathed; I was filled with her to the brink, incapable of overflowing, all I could do was roll my head on the pillow like a dervish.

The experience of being transported to Aziza's left me with no desire to try again. They had almost dropped me in the stairwell, and my sciatica came back to life. All evening long her singing seemed to be a part of my physical pain, taking it to its height. Now I had to stay flat on my back no matter what happened.

Tarek came to see me every day after school, as my house was on his way home. He wore a beige overall with two pockets in front, his schoolbag on his back. Breathless from running, he would come in and sit down on my bed. He didn't say anything, nor did I. He stared at me, his eyes wide open. Together we listened to the voice.

Khartoum was not only an imaginary place. The evening of her arrival there she had taken part in the Night of Henna, having her palms painted with fine arabesques, a ritual which made her part of the tribe like a married woman. "The Sudanese and Egyptians are one and the same people," she cried, holding up her hands, "one people within the great Arab nation." The applause died down only to allow an official voice to announce that one of the schools in the capital would be named Star of the Orient, our sister. A few months earlier, in this same town, Arab kings and heads of state had gathered to say no to the recognition of Israel, no to direct negotiations, no to concessions on the rights of the Palestine people. Saying no, three times no, had become our only line of defense while we waited for our army to be rebuilt. In the meantime, she sang.

In Libya, one of her concerts was performed in front of an all-female audience. "Unveil yourselves, sisters, we are the force of production of our societies, we can keep our heads high, and bare." During the same tour through the country she reiterated her appeal for Arab unity: this caused a monarchy whose days seemed numbered to feel extremely uncomfortable.

In Rabat, I don't know what happened. My sciatica had improved, and it was my first time out in two months. Muhammad had invited me to listen to the concert at his place, we were sitting by the radio. As she had often done since the beginning of the tour, she started with *Al Atlal,* Bayram's song, and it could still be taken as a call to arms. The ovation of the Moroccan audience showed that they understood the language and belonged to a same family. But after the intermission, she launched into *It's True That Love Is the Winner*, a sentimental, joyful song, a hit that dated from the early sixties, long before the defeat, a time when hopefulness was still within view. Perhaps it was because Morocco was so far from the battle-fields, or maybe it was some miraculous conjunction, the vibration in her voice betrayed her, and she wanted to escape for the night, play hooky, go back to the original intoxication. A parenthesis, but imperious, a nocturnal leave that she offered unwillingly to herself, trailing in her wake an Arab world that had suffered too much.

"Just a wink . . . a wink I took for a greeting." Her voice, challenged by the cheering and applause and proving itself capable, this evening in particular, of responding, gradually filled with emotion to the point of breaking. Muhammad and I looked at each other.

"She seems to be in top form," he murmured.

That was an understatement. Her vocal cords lingered over the same phrase, repeating it relentlessly, but never twice in the same way, stopping on one word alone, *narza*, "a wink," and putting it through all its paces. All she had to do was let it out. Her mastery was so sovereign that she could ignore the rules. She wasn't singing as a virtuoso but as someone freely in love, flinging herself into the void. *"Just a wink . . . a wink I took for a greeting / Did it contain / Commitment and promises and suffering."* On the second syllable of the word *salaam,* "greeting", she went off into incredible variations which moved further and further away from the core, she didn't care, she was creating autonomous arabesques, perfectly circular and improbable little units, an entire vocal architecture. I suddenly felt that something unique was taking place. The orchestra was following, like a ship turning on its stem, watching for a changing wind.

And she suddenly drew her players with her, first in one direction and then in another, multiplying the associations, pushing them to the limit. The audience acknowledged what she was doing with fervor, shouting whenever she paused then immediately dropping into a hush to allow her to continue. With a crowd of such precision, she gave a sudden little contented laugh which she then tried, unsuccessfully, to repress. She had to sing, "*And which passes so quickly / Did it contain . . .*" with laughter in her voice. For once, this woman who was renowned for her self-control on stage was giving way, in public, to her pleasure. I was one of her oldest listeners, and Muhammad a fine connoisseur, and neither of us had ever seen her sing with such happiness. For me this recital was one of her crowning achievements, a farewell.

She left Morocco laden with medals. When she arrived in Tunis, she learned that a major avenue was now named after her. The Rabat concert had not gone unnoticed. A variety of political leaders were falling over each other to pay homage to her. And they weren't the only ones. When the collapse had been at its worst, she had managed to touch people, by the millions, those who'd been forgotten; she'd managed to stir them, to give them a reason, perhaps the only one, to feel proud.

It may have been that the voyage was taking too long, or that the explosion had been too strong. Suddenly the papers announced that she was postponing the following concerts for health reasons. Dr. Hifnawi left his practice to go to her side. The very next day he sent us a reassuring telegram. She was overworked, that was all. A few days' rest on the Tunisian coast and she would be fine. The journalists filed more and more reports about the beach resort of Hammamet where she had found refuge. Then, gradually, as they saw that she was prolonging her stay, they went back to Egypt or to their respective countries.

To be sure, the radio continued to play her songs, but these were only recordings. As a personality, a whirlwind one could follow from town to town, she was slowly fading. That is when I began to realize how much space she had occupied. Thanks to her, to the cascade of her voice—but not only—and thanks to the ascendancy of her soul, things existed, made slightly incandescent by an inner light. She went away and reality suddenly became lackluster, overwhelming, inspiring no more desires.

As I no longer knew what to do with myself, I decided to devote two afternoons a week at the National Library to reading poetry to students, both mine and other poets'. I told myself that I wanted to keep busy. But from the very first meeting, without even thinking, I chose verses by Shawqi, in particular those that she had sung. *Ask My Heart; Ask the Glasses of Beauty; By My Father and My Soul; The Nile; Sudan.* As I recited them, I could hear her voice accompanying mine. Very soon that was no longer enough. I started speaking of her directly, recommending this or that song to the students; they could find them, quite affordably, on a new medium, magnetic cassette tapes. To my utter surprise, I discovered that they were only mildly interested in her. For them, the Star of the Orient was the singer of their parents' generation, or even of their grandparents'. They had been born into her presence, and her voice was one of the everyday odors of the streets of Cairo. They took her for granted, she was the very nature of those things they took for granted.

I was stupefied. Perhaps she had enraptured only one or two generations, had sung only for us. I refused to believe it. I understood that she could not really be appreciated by eighteen-year-olds. You had to get the initial shock, swallow the first sharp bone. It was only afterwards, once you had the knowledge of love's pain in your throat, that you were ready, that you were hooked forever.

7

I WAS NOT HOOKED, I'D BEEN EATEN ALIVE. The few days of rest she was meant to take had become three weeks: I couldn't bear it anymore. The moment I believed it was no longer possible, she came out of her semi-retirement to announce she was resuming her tour.

Before leaving Tunis she sang at a *zikr* ceremony, the ritual celebration of a saint, an obsessive repetition of eulogies. She brought us back into the womb, into chanting. She did not face the audience, in any case it was not an audience, but concentric circles of the faithful sitting cross-legged around her and entering the same trance. The dizziness which took hold of her during the incantation was transferred to their bodies, and spread all through the Arab world.

She flew to Amman. King Hussein received her, the people greeted her like a prodigal child come back to life. This was the first time since the defeat that she had returned to the Middle East, to one of the countries most severely affected, and which had paid a very heavy price. The television showed her live, self-confident, almost cheerful. Clearly the rest had done her good. I waited impatiently for evening to come, for the streets to empty and for people to gather and hear her inject her new-found strength into the battle.

"*We are fedayeen / We die rather than submit / No truce in combat / No more oil, no more canal / My enemy, you will not see the sea / Nor my land, nor my sky / We are fedayeen.*" For her return she had chosen the anthem she had sung just before the war, when nothing had yet been decided. In the meantime the meaning of the words had changed. *Fedayeen*, those who are prepared to die, was the name that the Palestinians had adopted as, en masse, they joined the Fatah and other movements which emerged immediately after the defeat. Since the conventional Arab armies had been crushed and had no hope of rising again for a long time, Nasser had decided to encourage these small organizations which, at least, had the merit of combatting despair. Just as she did.

Her voice carried the words like a shout, a cry, only a few kilometers from the Israeli lines, and provoked a shock wave, in particular in the refugee camps surrounding Amman. Palestinians who had just fled the West Bank now joined those who'd been clustered there since 1948. The day after the recital, sporadic demonstrations spread through the camps, to the cry of "We are fedayeen!" The Bedouin army of the Kingdom was visibly nervous. But it was too late, the initial impulse had already been given. The Palestinians who, up to that point, had counted on their Arab brothers, now knew they could count on no one but themselves. They reclaimed their independence and rose up with one of her songs on their lips. In a way, she had passed on the torch.

From Jordan she flew to Lebanon. Never had there been such a contrast. She sang at the international festival in Baalbek, in the ruins of a city which had been Roman, Greek, and Phoenician, set in the middle of a fertile plain far from the capital. Suddenly she was on another planet, on a stage where the art of the real world continued to exist and move forward without us. Béjart was performing, and Jean Vilar, and Miles Davis and the Berlin Philharmonic. And Lebanon itself was like an other-worldly enclave which had mysteriously sprung up in this region of the world.

Another sort of festival was being held a little farther away. To get there, one had to follow the black cables winding their way outside the ruins. The inhabitants of the small town of Baalbek—shopkeepers, hash growers—were normally rather indifferent to the yearly festival. But when they heard that she was coming, they demanded to attend the concert. If they couldn't, they would block the roads. She asked for loud-speakers to be set up in the streets and squares of the town to broadcast her voice live. By nightfall every house was deserted and the entire town was out under the open sky. The squares and narrow streets of Baalbek lived through a night of collective intoxication, to their heart's content. The Palestinians from the neighboring camps came timidly to the gates of the town so that they, too, might listen.

Then she went to Kuwait, a strange closing journey, one of utter contrasts. The wealthy oil emirate gave her a stiff, starchy welcome, one prince on the heels of another, through gilded salons lush with vivid sprays of flowers. Yet in the evening the sizeable Palestinian community, who virtually administered the country, filled the concert halls and became hopelessly drunk on her lips. This stop raised more money than anywhere else on the tour. It was time for a reckoning, and the press published some figures. The trip had earned almost four million dollars for "the war effort to remove the after-effects of aggression." Yet when the real need was examined, this amount remained almost insignificant. Still, by helping to foster solidarity for Egypt in the Arab world around Egypt itself, my peasant girl had contributed a much greater amount. And an infinitely greater amount to the frozen heart of each individual.

The tour was over. Almost a year had gone by since she left. Kuwait was only a four-hour flight. Suddenly I was frightened. I had grown used to her absence, or rather to the situation, characterized by the feeling that *she existed elsewhere.*

I hadn't looked at myself in a long time. My features seemed to have slowly melted into their own caricature. I had lost a lot of hair, my nose had gotten disastrously flat, my ears stuck out, thousands of tiny wrinkles underlined every yielding of my skin. And in my eyes was the insane anxiety that she would see me like this. Tomorrow, or even today.

She announced that before coming home she would spend two or three weeks in Austria to get some rest, in the region of Salzburg. Hifnawi left to join her. This trip gave me some respite. I had no hope of growing younger, but at least I would have time to get used to my face, and to the idea.

I went to see old Saadiya. She was indignant, and said as much. She doesn't think about anything else anymore, not even me, it's a betrayal, that's what she's done to me, after all these years, the apple of my eye, I rocked her in my own arms, God forgive her, He alone knows if I'll still be on this earth when she has the decency to come back here but never mind, she'll cry and it'll be too late. Saadiya had been talking about dying for so long that no one took her seriously anymore. I was in such a good mood, I spent more than an hour with her. I managed to cheer her up and even to make her laugh. In the end we just looked at each other without speaking. We shared the same love.

8

SHE WAS MAKING AN EFFORT; the tension on her face against the pillow betrayed her. I spoke very quietly. "When we celebrated Cairo's millennium, you chose my poem, *Ya Msaharni*, 'You Make Me Grow Old.' That's the last one you sang. I always wondered about it, but basically it's true. That really is what you've done—make me grow old, all my life."

She tried to smile, but was in too much pain. Her feverish hand clung to mine.

"Resign yourself to your fate, give yourself up to God. A nephritis may be painful but it's not serious. That's what your husband is always saying."

"Don't talk to me about that. Tell me again . . ."

"You kept people from sleeping."

"You say that . . . to make fun . . . or to . . . make me happy?"

"It's not such a bad thing, keeping people from their sleep. You obliged them to keep their bodies awake, and their minds. That's how you supported the people after the defeat, through insomnia. You stopped them from breaking down when everything got so difficult."

She was hardly listening, and was squeezing her eyelids. The main thing was to keep talking, not to stop, to keep my breath against her ear. I felt her hand relax gradually.

Ever since she became bedridden, six months ago, I'd been coming every day. My wife watched me leave and said nothing. Appearances were no longer kept up; we'd done enough hiding. Both of us were over seventy years old. Hifnawi himself had encouraged me. He had welcomed me like a member of the family. We were the oldest ones, now; of the old guard, he was the last one. I didn't know anyone at the villa now. The new servants and cooks were kind but they knew nothing, had known nothing. In a way I was as much at home here as Hifnawi was. He was in a real house, and I was in this other, imaginary domain, where I had lived with her.

The door of her room closed behind me. We knew how to play together, she and I, we always had. I would recite the poems, speak to her of the past, of Sheik Abu al-Ela, Sabri, Mounira al-Mahdia the Sultana. I reminded her of the jokes she played on Qsabji; we talked about the cinema, her rivalry with Muhammad, the fits Sheik Zakariya would throw. She listened like a little child who knew the story already, but for whom that was precisely the pleasure of it.

I would tell her random incidents, jumping through time, backtracking. I avoided the present day, too many people had died. Nasser to begin with, five years ago, and then Saadiya. Saadiya who had been so afraid of suffering, afraid of flying, afraid of not being up to something, afraid of the devil and of nightfall: one morning she did not wake up. They'd found her like that, smiling, in her bed, departed for the beyond almost inadvertently. That day my peasant girl ranted against death; the last obstacle which had separated her from the end had brutally disappeared, and there was nothing to hold her back now.

The war in October, 1973, had set her back on her feet. The Egyptian troops had crossed the canal and planted their flag on the other side. She got her color back, got dressed, wanted to give a concert. The nephritis stopped her in her tracks. In the meanwhile, her mourning for Saadiya had passed.

"You've stopped talking . . ."

Her eyes were half open, two split almonds looking at the ceiling.

"I thought you were asleep. What can I tell you? Today was Tarek's birthday. His parents decided to celebrate it at our place and the house was invaded by children. He was blowing out his eleven candles when Hifnawi called to ask what time I'd come over. When I put the phone down, I began hurrying through the ceremony, I didn't even realize. I gave Tarek my present, a Meccano game, and I helped him to cut the ribbon and tear off the paper. I was already putting on my raincoat when he told me he had a present, too. He stood there right in the middle of the living room. He'd learned a poem by heart, for me. He didn't know it very well. He was nearly at the end and then he broke off, unhappy, and started all over. He could tell I was in a hurry, he wanted to go quickly, so he made a mistake again, and stopped, on the verge of tears. I was ashamed. I took him in my arms and slowly recited the poem together with him. You'll never guess which one it was. *If I Forgive*— you sang it forty years ago."

Her breathing was calmer, her hand rested in mine. She remained pensive, she was feeling better. Just exhausted by the pain in her kidneys. Her complexion somewhat pale, perhaps, and shadows beneath her eyes . . . she'd lost weight.

She dug her nails into my hand. Her face twisted again.

"It's nothing," she whispered, "it's nothing, just a sharp pain . . . it's already gone."

Her breathing grew calm again. She gave me a humble smile. I whispered:

"'*Just a wink, a wink I took for a greeting / And it's already gone . . .*'"

"That's wrong, it's '*And which went by so quickly.*' Rabat, six years ago already. You remember?"

"I remember everything."

"That night, there was a sort of exultation . . . I can't even describe it . . . it was stronger than me, as if I had finally reached the finish line, something coming from my own body."

"Everything has come from your body, always."

She gave a silent little laugh. I believe she was even flattered.

"I didn't even expect that much," she murmured. "I sang my best, that's all I wanted, to be allowed to sing. I discovered that right at the beginning, the first day. I spent my life pacing up and down the same stage, a long wooden stage, endless, getting longer from one country to the next. I've always been on the same side, standing with the spotlight in my eyes, singing one and the same song. As if I'd lived only one instant, but an eternal instant, a single note held forever, right to the end."

She fell silent, and I didn't know what to say. Her hand had relaxed in mine. I looked at her, she looked back, silently. Our eyes reflected our thoughts, without shame. We had frequently been having this wordless dialogue, for some time now. Not moving, just staying there at her bedside without talking. The last barrier had fallen, at last. The accomplishment of love, at last.

"At the celebration for my fifty years on stage I was very pleased with that song, '*The heart is in love with what's beautiful . . .*'"

"Go on."

"I've forgotten it. '*God, you did not ask but I gave to you / Let me be led to Your door, the door of Your house / To Mecca where there's the mountain of light . . .*'"

"Yes, that's it. Grace to God. The heart is in love with beauty, is fascinated by it, and by it alone. That's a message I can live with. A good way to end."

"Who's talking about a way to end?"

"You think I don't realize what's going on? Already Sunbati was stretching out the instrumental sections to give me time to rest between couplets. I wore myself out running from London to Boston for treatment. And my last recital was over two years ago."

"It wasn't cancelled, it was postponed. When they announced that people could get their money back, not one single spectator went to the box office for a refund, not one. People have kept their tickets. They're waiting for you."

"And you think that maybe the curtain will rise again, and the applause and everything?"

"Absolutely."

We laughed together, and then the pain returned. She tensed her body and made a terrible effort to resist, didn't manage, cried out. In that instant Hifnawi burst in the room and I realized he'd been waiting all this time outside the door. Instead of looking after her, he took me by the shoulders, scrutinized my pale face, told me it would be better if I left. In the corridor there were visitors, men in white. An odor of ether. I could not stand all those expressionless gazes, those women with their silent tears. I would have liked to stay, but after a short moment my head began to spin, it hurt too much.

9

WHO WERE THESE PEOPLE? Old men dressed in black, too well dressed, ties and serious expressions, smelling of eau de cologne, too clean for me, I didn't know any of them, they were shaking my hand, endlessly, murmuring inaudible words, pebbles in their mouth, some of them embraced me like old friends, white hair, gray hair, tortoiseshell glasses, I got the impression they went around the rows of chairs lined back to back only to return to me, the procession was endless, what did they want with me, they weren't even trying to make themselves known, not a smile or a sign of friendship, the sun outside coming in to strike the reddish-orange canvas transformed them into interchangeable figures, a procession of penitents performing a meaningless ritual. Better to raise my head, the ceiling of blue fabric was obscured by lights, so numerous that they helped me not to see all those people. Why had they brought me here? I'd been parked at the entrance to the huge tent, the men's entrance, my right arm was beginning to ache and my legs were trembling with fatigue. But I couldn't sit down, because of him, Hifnawi, standing to my right, doing the same thing I was doing, shaking hands with strangers, and I could not leave him alone.

The tent went into the street, the carpets half-covering traffic signs on the ground, we were right at the edge. A black limousine pulled up, a limousine with a flag, preceded by three motorcycles, a young soldier climbed out as it was still moving, not quite stopped, the last few meters, he was trained to do that, to jump into the cloud of dust and open the rear door. An old man in a black tie stepped out, unfolded his legs and stood up, a mummy. The hush of voices announced the arrival of the representative of His Excellency President Sadat, and I didn't know him any better than the other ones. Was Sadat too busy, his presence too important, did he have something better to do? I had to shake the hand of this anonymous stranger. If Nasser were still alive, he would have taken the trouble, but then, that was Nasser. He'd been sent off from this very same place, this red tent erected at the entrance to the Umar Makram mosque. The people had come to see him off, the streets of Cairo had disappeared beneath their mass.

When they came to get me this morning, we sped through deserted streets, not a single tram, not a passerby. Every two meters a policeman was standing guard, like a tin soldier replicated to infinity, a stroboscopic army of robots in uniform staked out along the empty avenues. It was only when we went onto the interchange that I discovered, behind the soldiers and firmly restrained on the sidewalks, a crowd spreading as far as the eye could see, clustered together in silence, a terrifying silence.

Someone was taking me by the shoulders, he looked like Muhammad, it was Muhammad, his hands were firm and warm, he put his head to my neck and held me against his chest, the first human face! In a broken voice he said,

"*And even if you separate the drop of water from the sea . . .*"

"*. . . The vastness of the ocean will be its final destiny,*" I replied, automatically adding Omar Khayyam's response.

These few words were my undoing. I had been on my feet for too long, no doubt, but now my legs gave way and Muhammad had to hold me up. He put his arm around my waist and led me into the tent. I tried desperately to put one foot before the other. People made way for us and then closed again behind us, just long enough for us to see their expres-

sions full of pity, indignant, the kind of miserable stare
reserved for drunkards who misbehave and have to be led
away, faces of old age, severity forever written in stone in their
wrinkles. We had gone into the mosque itself, I realized
because it was suddenly like an echo chamber around me. I
saw a hand place before me a wooden chair with an arched
back. I preferred to slide down onto the carpet, with my back
against the wall. Muhammad sat down next to me.

The solitary space worked on my soul. The perfect emptiness, filled only by chanting from the Koran, the endless melodious breathing of the muezzin rebroadcast by the loudspeakers, with long silences between the phrases. *"My God, You
know what we are hiding, and what we want to reveal / Nothing
can be hidden from You on earth as in heaven . . ."* The sound
lingered, hung suspended for several seconds before dissolv-
ing. *"Grace be given to You, You know how to receive requests
as well as laments."* So much gentleness. I held my palms open
before me and my lips silently followed the prayer.

At the foot of the minbar was a coffin, facing south, covered
in a ruffled silk fabric of cream and light green, with ribbons
and a sort of small incorporated stele which showed where the
head and the feet were. Its position and orientation seemed to
confer a particular significance, its density a counterpart to the
emptiness of the space. All I wanted was to be forgotten there.

The men in black I had fled from were invading the mosque,
lining up in narrow rows opposite the minbar. They sat on
their heels and their seams stretched to cracking. They held
themselves shoulder to shoulder but their humility was false;
they leaned toward each other, exchanging signs. Their sidelong smiles revealed gold teeth at the back of their mouths. I
recognized them, they were the pure products of Sadat's so-
called "opening," their fortunes amassed in a space of a few
years: Nasser was well and truly gone. That is who they were:
the new era.

I ran a finger under my collar, I was beginning to suffocate again, Muhammad understood. He got up and helped me as far as the exit, I didn't really need his help, or perhaps it was just to prevent me from walking on those other mourners.

We put on our shoes and took a few steps in the sun, breathing. In the middle of the street there was a sort of demonstration, while waiting for the procession to move off: military musicians, brass to the fore, drums behind. Some of the men were chatting quietly with uniformed motorcyclists, at a loose end. There were also the bearers of giant wreaths, and policemen appeared incongruously amidst the flowers and branches. Utterly calm, Muhammad pulled me along. The heat was gentle, we moved up the column. A little group of women of all ages were holding a banner on which was written: "Workers of the recording company *The Voice of Cairo*." They wore black, of course, and they may not have worn stylish clothes, but their sorrow was genuine. They let the banner flow like a collective skirt. Their agitation seemed genuine.

Suddenly the flaps of the tent opened wide, lips of the red wound. The coffin emerged, like a battering ram carried at arm's length, amidst a whirlwind of buzzing insects.

Muhammad was holding me by the arm, I was part of the chain, I was having trouble keeping pace, the entire row had fallen out of step, perhaps it was my fault, the drums were beating too loudly and my feet always landed out of synch. I would have liked to escape, but it was impossible, I had to go on, stumbling, picking myself up, persisting in spite of common sense. I kept my eyes riveted to the coffin wavering above people's heads. Long wooden slats allowed it to rest on the shoulders of several dozen firemen, a compact group, a tapestry of black outfits and berets, the coffin seemed about to tip over with their every movement. It would steady only to tip to the other side, buffeted in pursuit of a military music that was too slow to follow. It hardly mattered; it was this vision which pulled me forward, the coffin, making me seasick as I struggled for air, but Muhammad's grasp on my arm remained firm, and even if I had wanted to break the chain and escape I couldn't have, how could I manage, nobody would listen.

People were crowded onto balconies, black clusters hanging to the facades, to the buildings. The procession came out into the free air of Liberation Square, the largest and most central square in Cairo. It wound its way across the deserted space, a human caterpillar drunk on funereal hymns and exhausted with solemnity, stumbling its way under the sky. And I stumbled along with it, incapable of freeing my arm to raise it to the sky and ask for help. On the horizon of the square, far far away, I saw the cordon break like a necklace of pearls, I saw it distinctly. Truncheons were raised, caps were flying, I could hear whistles blown, it was too late, the dyke had broken for good, in several places, and people were spilling, rushing, hundreds of thousands, a million of them, darkening the entire square like a cloud, shouting as they ran, waving their arms, and their shadow ran before them. As they drew near, the policemen escorting us linked arms and readied to parry the shock. I felt a wild joy rise inside me. The flower bearers wanted to precipitate the movement, their feet were caught in the frame of the wreath, the procession seemed to be filled with panic. People were no longer holding each others' elbows, they had broken ranks to run away, every man for himself. The human tide crashed against the uniforms, Liberation Square had disappeared beneath the mass of shouting mourners, tens of thousands of close faces. The massive crowd behind the first arrivals swarmed to occupy the enormous empty square, drove the flow into every street, tides pushing against each other, the blood circulation of one same body.

The last police cordon broke. The pressure from behind was so great that a giant human wave invaded the street and caused the procession to swell. I felt the flow reaching me, it tore me from the chain and dragged me away. I turned around and saw Muhammad carried away in turn, as he raised his arm toward me. Above all I must not fall over, that was the only thing. How could I fall, the density of people was keeping me standing, crushing me, twisting my limbs. And yet I felt happy, strangely happy, and the crowd propelled me forward in spite of myself. I could see that the distance separating me from the coffin was shrinking. I raised my arm in the direction of the elongated arch, I desperately wanted to place my hand on it, too.

The coffin was shaking as if it were caught in rapids, a torrent carrying it away. The crowd's embrace caused the entire group of bearers to drift across the width of the street, and they knocked and bounced against the facades. The squadron of firemen clung on. All of a sudden they lost control of the situation. The wooden slats disappeared, the coffin began to float freely above people's heads. It moved alone from one raised arm to another, from hand to hand. I watched as it zigzagged through space as if it did not know which way to go, every avenue was blocked. Finally Kasr el-Nil was chosen, the widest street, which led in the direction of the large mosques of Al-Azhar and Al-Hussein. I saw it move further and further away above the motionless human flood, bobbing like a drunken vessel, only to vanish into the tide of noise, levitate above it, and disappear on the horizon. It sailed for a long time across the crowd to whom it belonged, growing worn under the callous hands and the oft-repeated gestures, until finally it dissolved in the body and the soul of everyone, its true eternity.

December 29, 1981

Tarek,

You've just left, and I didn't tell you. You were so excited, you're in your last year of high school, with your final exams. You kept saying, Can you imagine, can you imagine, poor words, I love the way you are.

You left me the package. You left, and I opened it. I saw the seven little boxes, with the portrait on each of them; it left me breathless. Her face, when she was a young girl, you have no idea the effect it has on me. And the inscription, "Anthology of Arabic Music," *with the participation of UNESCO, I had the feeling she was suddenly taking her place in the heritage of humanity. I went through the titles. All the seventy-eights from the early years, or most of them in any case, nine or ten on each disc, over sixty in all. Her hits from the 1920s and 1930s, the forgotten ones, the ones no one knows anymore because the old gramophones are just a memory.* "Passion Is Betrayed Through the Eyes," *is missing; my very first one,* "If I Forgive," *is missing too. But* "You Share Your Charms With Others Than Me," *is there, and so is* "My Beloved Has Come . . ."

The discs are tiny, all smooth, I didn't know how to play them. I called your grandmother, she came in with the player, it was your father's.

I took the first disc and the machine swallowed it. You have no idea. Music by Sheik Abu al-Ela, by Da'ud Husni, Qsabji's first compositions, others by Sheik Zakariya. It's been forty years since I last heard them. And suddenly there was her voice, like a fist in my gut, her youthful voice from the very first day. I was breathless. "My paradise is in your love / I've loved nothing but you on this earth." *It's not just the fact that I know the song; I can see her singing, I can see the stage, the concert hall, the color of her dress, I can see the era, the moment. It all entered the room on this compact disc, and everything came back.*

I too have a gift for you. I've been preparing it for a long time, almost three months. She's singing. Her voice holds me in her hand, my pen rushing across the paper, I get the impression she's talking to you at the same time as I am.

She disappeared six years ago. The suffering—I can't begin to tell you, it made me lose consciousness, years. Not to have died before her annihilated me. Not a depression, not at all the same thing, just a limitless anger. I became indifferent even to my anger. Eating, sleeping, waiting . . . for what? Death didn't want any part of me.

Nothing affected me. When Sadat was assassinated, I didn't care, it was like everything else. That the Islamists had gunned down the President in the middle of the official reviewing stand, in the middle of the parade: news that meant nothing to me.

But you were there. You asked me if I'd seen the images on television, you told me how the truck full of soldiers had pulled up opposite the tribune, they thought it had broken down, how the men jumped out of it, and ran up shooting with all their weapons, throwing whatever they could, grenades, fire, all the country's leaders gathered in a space of twenty square meters. The survivors were even more impressive than the dead, climbing over the bodies amidst the overturned seats, Mubarak came forward covered in blood, you told me that. Why did this happen, why did this happen?

I didn't know how to explain it to you, and yet I tried. In this country, the black thread and the white thread are woven togeth-

er, we have one foot in the past and the other one elsewhere. Our hopes were dashed during the Six-Day War. Six years later, the war in 1973 was not a military victory, far from it. But it represented a symbolic revenge which put us back on earth and allowed us to negotiate without shame. It was less flamboyant than in Nasser's days, but this modesty opened a path for us. A winding path. And this is as far as we've gotten, this wobbly Egypt between two chairs, that's all we've got.

It was already too much for the Islamists. They wanted to eradicate the sin all at once, no one left alive, just bodies laid out, radical suppression, therapy through the void. They are the past, seeking to wipe the slate clean. Compared to them the Muslim Brotherhood in the old days were choirboys, so to speak. They belonged to our generation after all, for them too it was the beginning, they were trying, we could discuss, at least a bit. Whereas this lot, nowadays, their descendants, there's no more hope, they are the end, divorced from the world.

I saw your disappointment, your reproach even. You didn't answer, but I felt it. You were horrified by the country which awaited you, your country, the catastrophe we were leaving to you.

I roused myself from my torpor. I wondered how we had really come to such a pass, one thing leading to another, what chain of events. I took up a sheet of paper and began to write. After a few pages had gone by I realized I was telling my love story, right from the start. As if I had to understand that first in order to understand the rest; as if it were the essential thread.

But the thread did not hold. Very quickly I no longer wanted to prove anything, to illustrate anything, I let myself be consumed by history alone, so that it might, at last, go out of me. How the feeling I had for this woman became the climate in which Egypt and the Arab world were living. I was writing and could no longer stop. Eighty years old. A new strength was driving me, a need to expel or give back, which is not exactly the same thing. I hid my ink-filled sheets of paper.

Now it's done. It's all here. I would never have believed it would fill three hundred pages, the size of a book.

I am leaving it to you. It is my gift.

Om *means mother, everyone knows that. In the literal sense, as in* Om *Mohammed, the mother of Mohammed, or in the figurative sense as in* Om *Kalthoum, the mother with rounded cheeks, the full-faced woman. But not many people know that its actual origin,* Amma, *is from the Aramaic, meaning the act of arising, beginning, leading. An entire family of words is derived from it:* Umma *(community, nation),* Imam *(the sheik who leads the faithful),* Ima *(the venal woman from the time of the Abbassides, the Arabic equivalent of a geisha), and others. For me, the word designates the atavistic feeling which dominated us throughout the century, that of belonging to a same belly which we could not leave.*

"The night grew longer / The night grew longer / And the hurt found its place . . ." *She wasn't yet twenty-five when she sang that song, already the night, the hurt. But how she was reaching for the future! You could hear it in her voice, you can still hear it, a fresh young voice she was trying out with wonder, that too you can hear, distinctly, her sense of wonder.*

This isn't nostalgia, nothing is more boring than the past. On the contrary, it is the present, the present in her voice, so fresh: "I myself am a mystery in his love," *that's what she says in this forgotten song, accompanied by the lute and cithara and violin alone, an instrumental simplicity, myself in his love, a mystery. You cannot imagine what a gift you have given me. You have brought her back to me, and left me alone with her.*

Next year you'll be at the university, studying architecture, that's what you want, a lot of people might envy you. But you won't have that voice in your life, no. You won't go learning Persian in Paris to translate a poem, you won't see one evening on stage a young Bedouin boy to whom you'll tie your fate. We were full of hope, this country was as young as we were and about to break its chains. There were only fourteen million of us back then; over fifty million now.

I'm not writing this to clear my name, don't think that. We are not innocent of the present situation, it's not like we had nothing to do with it.

She died without leaving any children, that's the thing. I'm not thinking of actual children, I had them myself, but that didn't change anything. What I mean is that what we experienced has left no children. My friend Muhammad comes to see me every day, I love him tenderly, he tried to save us by rushing to embrace the West, a futile effort. He too is the last of the Mohicans. And what of her? No other voice has been born of hers, she has no daughter, she is too great even to be imitated. Hamuli, Osman, Manyalawi were the trunk of the tree, Sheik Abu el-Ela told me as much, she would be the heiress to an entire art, and she was. But she would be the last heir, the fruit, the last fruit, and what a fruit! Only one such fruit could ever exist, dazzling. And after her, nothing.

The renewal of ideas, of Islam, of literature and politics: nothing. The renaissance that was to shake our culture, to beat it like an ancient carpet in order to revive its incomparable colors, came to a sudden end, that's the truth. We burned with such intensity and gave birth to nothing. Those soldiers who opened fire with their shouts of "God is great!" are, in the end, the children of our failure, our only children.

My eyelids are closing, I have no tears, my heart is so tight it is aching. What did we do, where did we go wrong, where did we lose? I keep my eyes closed, her voice envelops me. "To my beloved's country, take me there . . ." *Where is my friend's house? There will be no eastern modernism, there simply won't be any.*

"Oh voyager on the Nile, take me there . . ." *The disk is playing as I write. A traveling song, a Bedouin song, keep my eyes closed, no bitterness, no rancor, she's taking me with her. In ten years, in twenty, all one will have to do is switch on the radio at any time, any station, from Baghdad to Casablanca, the Arab world will continue to live under her empire. They will say it is a beautiful voice, nothing else; they will fall beneath the charm without understanding why. I know why. That palace of dreams which we built with our own hands was where we lived; it was our era, the very mood of our world. And we know what it was made out of, of such genuine love. They'll switch on their radios and they'll think they're just hearing a song.*

What happened will not be lost. Maybe that's something one always says in one's final hour, so what, I'll say it too. What you like will be your heritage. Despite everything, we too were carried by the wind. She was carried, and Muhammad, and Sheik Zakariya, Taha Hussein, all through that time when we wanted so passionately to become engaged to the rest of the world, and it all stayed in the secret of the air, books, songs. If they were powerful enough, and God knows they were powerful, our dreams could slip into the folds and travel for a long time, surviving like seeds which know how to resist the winter.

But maybe I'm wrong, what do I know anymore. Perhaps nothing really happened, just pollen carried by the wind, an illusion. I open my eyes, there's too much light, it's a bit cold. I try to write a little more. Close my eyes again, and she's still singing in my ear, I no longer recognized the song, her voice is making me dizzy, slightly nauseous. I open my eyes again just as I am falling, I open them wide, I realize a cold sweat has broken out on my brow. Nothing has happened, I'm still alone, lying in bed, the room has not changed. I try to get my breath back. She is singing Yom al-Hina, *"The Day of Tenderness," it's a joyful song, a woman in love who is reunited with her lover, all I have to do is hold onto the air and follow, I'm in no danger if I am with her. I feel it, something has loosened, there, in my throat. I feel like all I have to do is shut my eyes one more time to extinguish everything. God knows we tried to make it shine, this world of ours, to bring it out into the sun. And now, it's darkness. All I have to do is lower my eyelids. Open them. Close them again.*

The poet Ahmad Rami died in 1981. He wrote 137 of the 283 songs performed by Om Kalthoum in her lifetime. His story inspired this book. But the memoir published here is strictly imaginary.

Sélim Nassib is also the author of *A Lover in Palestine*, about the secret and startling relationship between Lebanese-Palestinian banker Albert Pharaon and Golda Meir. Nassib is well known for his journalism, particularly that for French newspaper *Libération*, and for his work as a foreign correspondent. He has lived and worked in Paris since 1969.

AVAILABLE NOW from EUROPA EDITIONS

The Days of Abandonment
by Elena Ferrante
translated by Ann Goldstein

"Stunning . . . The raging, torrential voice of the author is something rare." —Janet Maslin, *The New York Times*

"I could not put this novel down. Elena Ferrante will blow you away." Alice Sebold, author of *The Lovely Bones*

AVAILABLE NOW from EUROPA EDITIONS

Minotaur

by Benjamin Tammuz

translated by Kim Parfitt and Mildred Budny

An Israeli secret agent falls hopelessly in love with
a young English girl. Using his network of shady contacts
and his professional expertise, he takes control of her life without
ever revealing his identity. *Minotaur*, named "Book of the Year"
by Graham Greene, is a complex and utterly original story about
a solitary man driven from one side of Europe to the other
by his obsession. "A novel about the expectations and compromises
that humans create for themselves . . . Very much in the manner
of William Faulkner and Lawrence Durrell." —*The New York Times*

AVAILABLE NOW from EUROPA EDITIONS

The Big Question
by Wolf Erlbruch
translated by Michael Reynolds

Best Book at the 2004 Children's Book Fair in Bologna.

A stunningly beautiful and poetic illustrated book for children
that poses the biggest of all big questions: why am I here?
A chorus of voices—including the cat's, the baker's, the pilot's
and the soldier's—offers us some answers. But nothing is certain,
except that as we grow each one of us will pose the question
differently and be privy to different answers.

Total Chaos

by Jean-Claude Izzo

translated by Howard Curtis

"Jean-Claude Izzo's [...] growing literary renown and huge sales
are leading to a recognizable new trend in continental fiction:
the rise of the sophisticated Mediterranean thriller . . .
Caught between pride and crime, racism and fraternity,
tragedy and light, messy urbanization and generous beauty,
the city for [detective Fabio Montale] is a Utopia, an ultimate port
of call for exiles. There, he is torn between fatalism
and revolt, despair and sensualism." —*The Economist*

This first installment in the legendary Marseilles Trilogy
sees Fabio Montale turning his back on a police force
marred by corruption and racism and taking
the fight against the mafia into his own hands.

AVAILABLE NOW from EUROPA EDITIONS

The Goodbye Kiss

by Massimo Carlotto

translated by Lawrence Venuti

Giorgio Pellegrini is wanted in Italy for a series of crimes linked
to political extremism. He has been hiding out in Central America,
half-heartedly lending a hand to a group of leftwing militants
engaged in a bloody civil war. After the Comandante orders
the assassination of Pellegrini's companion and conational,
he decides it might just be time to head back home. As devoid
of morals now as he once was full of idealistic fervor, an inveterate
womanizer and a seasoned opportunist, Giorgio seems willing
to do almost anything to avoid prison, from selling out his old pals
in The Movement to cutting deals with crooked cops.

Master of Mediterranean noir, hardboiled crime novels in which
seductive cities like Marseilles and Naples become principle
protagonists, Massimo Carlotto is arguably "the best living
Italian crime writer" (*Il Manifesto*). At once a harsh criticism
of Italy's social malaise and a scathing indictment of its political
elite, *The Goodbye Kiss* tells the gripping story of a solitary man
with nothing left to lose.

FORTHCOMING FICTION from EUROPA EDITIONS

Love Burns

by Edna Mazya

translated by Dalya Bilu

Ilan, a middle-aged professor of astrophysics, discovers
that his young wife is having an affair. Terrified of losing her,
he decides to confront her lover instead. Their meeting ends
in the latter's murder—the unlikely murder weapon being
Ilan's pipe—and in desperation, Ilan disposes of the body
in the fresh grave of his kindergarten teacher.
But when the body is discovered… "Starts out
as a psychological drama and becomes a strange, funny,
unexpected hybrid: a farce thriller. A great book." —*Ma'ariv*

Release date: March, 2006

FORTHCOMING FICTION from EUROPA EDITIONS

Departure Lounge
by Chad Taylor

Two young women mysteriously disappear. The lives of those they have left behind—lovers, acquaintances, and strangers intrigued by their disappearance—intersect to form a captivating latticework of odd coincidences and surprising twists of fate. Urban noir at its stylish and intelligent best. "Entropy noir . . . The hypnotic pull lies in the zigzag dance of its forlorn characters, casting a murky, uneasy sense of doom." —*The Guardian*

Release date: April, 2006

FORTHCOMING FICTION from EUROPA EDITIONS

The Jasmine Isle

by Ioanna Karystiani

translated by Michael Eleftheriou

A modern love story with the force of an ancient Greek tragedy.
Set on the spectacular Cycladic island of Andros, *The Jasmine Isle*,
one of the finest literary achievements in contemporary
Greek literature, recounts the story of the old sea wolf,
Spyros Maltambès, and the beautiful Orsa Saltaferos,
sentenced to marry a man she doesn't love and to watch
while the man she does love is wed to another.

Release date: April, 2006